The Air-Born Series

Air-Born
Earth-Bound
Sea-Drawn
Fire-Forged

FIRE-FORGED

LAURA POWER

Winter Goose
PUBLISHING

For Graham, who championed these books from the beginning.
Every time I write I will remember you,
and I will never stop writing.

Winter Goose Publishing
45 Lafayette Road #114
North Hampton, NH 03862

wintergoosepublishing.com
Contact Information: info@wintergoosepublishing.com

Fire-Forged

COPYRIGHT © 2024 by Laura Power

Cover Picture by Winter Goose Publishing

Cover Design and Formatting by Winter Goose Publishing

ISBN: 978-1-952909-30-6

Published in the United States of America

Night of Omens

Watched by a heat-fractious moon, the salt-crust earth cursed and creaked, the surrounding empty sands bereft and eerie amidst a feverish night. Beneath this waning protection, the serpent twisted and coiled in her sleep. Many more nights, and the water would be lost—and with it, more than her skin.

It had been months since greens had crisped into greys, and now words had begun to filter through the dark, becoming compressed through the layers of the earth into ideas and intentions, into sharp and spiteful things that could pierce the hide of one long hidden.

A serpent shall spill forth and bring the end of days. When the serpent emerges, the end is nigh.

So, the serpent had twisted on herself and coiled in anguish, attempting to retreat from the words even if she couldn't retreat from the future they foretold. But as the words faded, so did her hope, for the whisperers had retreated with the water, and the pan lay near-dry. The earth had been heaving and breaking for weeks now, amidst the insufferable swelter, and the inevitable felt imminent.

A crackling succession like the breaking of bones and promises erupted around her, and all at once the sanctuary that had sheltered her, and that she had sustained herself for aeons, collapsed. The remaining water drained away with shocking suddenness, the sucking sound of it as desperately empty as the desert.

Moonlight lanced, its touch intrusive and not nearly cool enough to balm the hurt of the night's hot-as-a-held-grudge air which was as painful to the serpent's slickened scales as the just-as-sudden realisation: the skin of the Realm had split. There was no longer space or safety for her anywhere. Braving the moon's dispassionate eye, she squeezed herself out between the drying cracks, not birthed with hope and help but vomited, ejected, by a Realm that could no longer sustain her.

She lay exhausted with the trauma of it, sensations sticking to her now that the amniotic pool had drained. Once she had sung songs of wetness and life; hummed rivers into movement and lakes into fullness, while the Realm was still forming itself into being. Like the rains, that power had long since slipped out of her reach. She could barely hold on to the memory of it, let alone the ability itself. Now the insufferable heat held in the scorching sand engulfed her, threatened to overwhelm and consume her. Perhaps she should sprawl here, like an empty skin, and let the wilds do their work.

Yet from far away, beyond the point where sand gave way to shale and tunnels twisted as the serpent had once into the very depths of the Realm, a summons sounded, shattering the miles of disconnect between them. It vibrated through the very being of the serpent, whose entire body was attuned to such sensations. Momentarily, the depth of another's suffering eclipsed the magnitude of her own. A breeze lifted, older and more everlasting than the suffering that had begun to seize the Realm, promising not just to outlast this sorrow, but overturn it. Something ungraspable flared in the serpent's mind, and a membrane as cloudy as distant galaxies slipped back across the creature's eyes as she readied herself for action. Her time stretched thin—but the other's stretched thinner. And so, the serpent, who had not cried for centuries, thrashed in her urgency, and surged from her collapsed restraints to spill racing across the sands like ink, trying to redraw the line between what was impossible and improbable, determined to help the Realm one last time.

***

"I thought I heard something." The lanterns of the Great Hall flared like greetings from old friends as Amber stumbled in blearily, her pixie-short hair as scruffy as ever but her eyes bright with the resolve of one determined to elevate the discomfort of recent times into the easier-to-endure hardships of adventure.

"Hallucinations are common after traumatic events," Jasper dismissed mildly, his green eyes piercing, and his dark hair smooth and annoyingly well-groomed considering he must have been here for hours, seated as though seeking reassurance at the oaken table that had withstood many a longer night than this. "It's not that long since you were dicing with hypothermia on the icefields and reducing a forest tyrant to rags in the Wildwood Labyrinth. Give yourself time. Go back to bed."

"Says the man who couldn't sleep either?" Amber retorted, slumping down companionably beside him. Drought or no drought, her glance rested on her Prince and the others with the kind of easy comfort which meant that, here amongst her friends, she found herself lacking for nothing.

"Strange dreams disturbed me, and my waking thoughts couldn't chase them," the Prince admitted, dishevelling his hair by running a tired hand through it. "I thought I heard something, too. I would offer you a drink, but our rations run low."

"It's a sensible precaution, not your own personal miserliness," Amber reassured equably. "We're used to it by now. Still, it's the kind of night that makes you wish things were as they used to be."

"It's the kind of night that makes you rise and check on your pack," Yenna agreed, her wolf-gold eyes watchful, her veils wrapping her like shadows, and her olive skin aglow as she stalked the flickering edges of the flamelight. "Strange scents are on the air."

"Trodden into the ground, too," Racxen added, padding in from tracking. "I couldn't identify one spoor out of the rest. It's as though the earth itself is under attack." As he crossed the threshold into torchlight, the tell-tale glint of night vision flared in his eyes and lent urgency to his words. His brown skin gleamed sweat, almost Kelpie-feverish, and his black hair was tangle-wild, but the kiss he greeted Amber with was as certain as ever.

"The brine is a-shiver wi' something, as weell," Hydd confirmed in his shingle-soft voice. His seal-stout frame was solid with the sense of someone securely inhabiting their skin once again, and the pelt which draped across his shoulder like a heraldic sash shimmered with the ethereal calm of a moon-touched sea. But the paleness of his face betrayed something of the shifting undercurrent of anxiety that had begun to ensnare the Realm.

"The bubbles in the fountain chamber grow milky and hard tae read." The Selkie rubbed the whiskers of his beard thoughtfully. "The Nymph is a' peace, an' her training o' me continues apace, but she has nae lang left. An' she's as preoccupied as anyone about the dryin' o' t' waters an' the absence o' rain. She hears whispers frae the desert that the auld oases are dryin.' This could prove a catastrophe worse than any monster."

"Although, that noise could have been from a monster," Jasper pointed out.

"Not your serpent, again," Amber dismissed firmly. "I thought you were past scaremongering by now."

"I have to remain vigilant to any possible threat not only to the Kingdom in particular but also to the Realm as a whole," Jasper reminded stiffly. "A serpent shall break apart the Realm, and herald the end of days," he added in an obstinate tone.

"Where did that story even come from?" Amber challenged. "For years we'd forgotten the legend about the Realm's core being inhabited by a giant snake who warmed the Realm and turned the ice at the core to water, and now you're claiming it will be the one to destroy us. If that's not paranoia closing in with the drought, I don't know what is. Plus, the noise didn't sound like a monster," she insisted before the Prince could contradict her. "More likely a summons in response to one. So, *we* have to respond. If only we could hear it again. In this wind, I've no idea where it's coming from."

"It's no signal I've ever heard," the Prince countered, worried. "It's not from the Selkies, Arraheng, or Wolfren. Or Han. But it's probably miles away, anyway," he added guiltily. "We stay put."

"You've come here drawn to action, like the rest of us," Amber shushed.

Jasper grimaced. "But we don't yet know to what action—or against which adversary."

Ruby wandered in, twirling her long red hair into far more glamorous an arrangement than the dire hour deserved. "We've proved stronger together than any adversary before, though," she reminded brightly. "And we've enjoyed a lot together since, too."

"True, hen. Yet it isnae always together tha' we are fated tae fight," Hydd warned gently with a whiskery kiss, as she slipped an arm around his stout frame.

The noise that rang out next sang a clearer summons on a turned wind: one that chilled the listeners to the bone. The ring of a shell bugle.

"The Water Nymph." Jasper's voice bled as cold as the icefields. "We must to the cavern chamber."

The others surged to their feet in response and rushed to the threshold of the hall, but Hydd seemed drawn into a void unseen, so still he held.

"You can pay tribute after, if it is too painful to bear witness now," reminded Jasper in an awkward but earnest attempt at understanding. The set of Ruby's stance told that she would not leave either, if the Selkie were to stay. She had spent increasing amounts of time with both Hydd and Zaralathaar after the Selkie's initiation.

"Nae the Fountain nor the Realm depend upon me tending her now, but ye an' she may depend upon it still," the Selkie promised with great solemnity. "An' dinnae let me slow ye down. Whoever gets there first must get there fastest. Ah jes' want her tae be comforted now. It disnae have tae be by me."

The friends nodded their respect and locked eyes, filled with the magnitude of the moment, before parting ways in haste. Yenna stalked outside, flinging aside her veils, and tumbling into wolf form, rising snarling to snatch the bundle up in her jaws and speed away in a tawny blur. Jasper's wings sprang proudly, and he leapt into the sky, as the Zyfang call spilled from Racxen's lips.

"It'd slow Orbitor down, carrying two of us," Amber insisted when Racxen turned back to her as the chiropteran bulk of the Zyfang blotted the moon. "You heard what Hydd said. I'll meet you there."

The look that passed between them swelled with understanding, and Amber watched him swoop away with a soaring heart. She set to her own path with equal alacrity, racing the well-trodden route across the meadows.

Her head pounded from dehydration, but it was a relief to have something practical to pour herself into. Since the drought, a restless boredom had filled her, so pervasively that she had begun to worry she would always feel like this. Realising this, Racxen would wrap her in his arms, his words as soft as water, as he spoke promises he believed in about the rain's return—promising that he didn't know when, but he knew that it would—to the extent that she half believed this too. After all, Racxen was from Arraterr's marshlands; water was a deeper part of his Realm than hers. But the longer it went on the clearer it became to both of them that without action, the issue would only worsen—and yet what action could be taken? How could they reanimate the earth? How could they bring back the rain?

As she wrestled with the insurmountable again, fear reached out for her like icy fingers—but the Nymph had always held dominion over ice, so she refused to let it seize her now. Instead, she let the night fill her with its strength as she ran. The Realm was changing, surely—diminishing even, some would say. But dawn had risen before she'd finished running, and all around her clung examples of resilience and resolve. The drying flowers of the meadows seemed to lift their tired heads as she raced past. The shades of sunrise that rippled through the grasses spoke as much of glory as of pain, and if they rustled a little more dryly than usual, she could almost convince herself it was just an early turn of season.

Beyond Fairymead, however, she could no longer lie to herself. The once arterial river had reduced to a turgid ooze of mud, and the Great Lake had shrunk until it barely covered Finsbury. Accordingly, the great Karp had buried himself determinedly and formed a cocoon of slime, but nothing could be done to mitigate the horrific effect the uncanny drought was inflicting upon neighbouring Arraterr. As Amber skirted the marshlands once thriving with verdance, she was confronted with a truth worse than she'd dared anticipate.

Arraterr had always been a place of wildness and wetness and wonder: a mist-clung swathe of marshland, concealing the cave haunts of the Arraheng. A trespasser should not be able to tell which of its labyrinthine waterways tangled into deadends or sank away into nothingness, and which held unseen underwater entrances, while the thick beds of rushes flanking the channels whispered their distractions and protected the secrets within. To some it would appear a sodden wasteland into which one would fear to stumble, and indeed the tribe's survival had relied upon the safety afforded by that impression. But Amber counted herself lucky that she had been granted access, and the swollen shift of silken mud had always proven more inviting to her than crystalline waters.

So it was with real pain that she bore witness to its current diminishment. The swirling waterways had slowed and sunk, lowered so much as to be pathologically congested with silt, and the usual viridescence of vegetation was reduced to rotten reed-remnants clotting in perpetual decline, leaving a stagnating travesty of what had once been one of the Realms most diverse and lush environments. Here amidst the stinking sludge, she still considered herself to be standing on the most hallowed ground in all the Realm, but she could no more conjure water to save it than she could to save herself.

Racxen had stayed with her so long he hadn't visited for a while, and Amber wished suddenly for his sake he had stayed away instead, had soaked up a few more moments of the marshes as they used to be: saturated and sumptuous. But they were a landscape bereft now. The once-rich mud was crusting dryly along the banks and congealing like an untended wound. Fairy culture didn't pay as much heed to water as it deserved. Their paths were not marked by it, their home was not awash with it. But without the mud, the Arraheng had almost lost a language; without the water, their homes lay bare. Racxen would be feeling even more vulnerable than her, and she needed to remember it.

Still, painful as it was, she couldn't stop and afford Arraterr due reverence. Her priority had to remain getting to the Fountain basin, which would have taken days to reach but for the Way of Ice and Fire which lay open still, unobtrusive and for a large part ignored. Amber took its dark passages gladly now; it had been a long time since that season she had first needed to take it in its full ice-and-fire fury, and familiarity had flushed out the fear that had once coursed its passages. She found herself, guiltily, almost wishing for those times again. It had seemed easier, somehow, fighting monsters—easier, at least, than battling the elements themselves.

But, as she darted along tunnels forged by ancient lava flow, the walls pressed closer as though to shore up her defences, and she let her thoughts fly back to the lessons learnt and courage gained along the way. The Realm had withstood all kinds of calamitous events in the past. It stood yet and spun still.

She let the knowledge saturate her skin as she clambered the foreboding slabs spiralling upwards that urged she was nearing the Water Nymph's chamber. Yet, as ice seeped beneath stone and the cavern overlooking the Fountain loomed, the echoes sounded lonelier than they used to and the expanses felt emptier. In any other circumstance, it would have been a relief to feel the chill lifting from the formations like otherworldly breath. But she didn't want to see the ice crystals risen in their towering columns or folded into frozen falls, their mere existence a promise that neither magic nor water nor hope had drained away entirely. She just wanted to see Zaralathaar, and the Water Nymph was nowhere to be found.

The Nymph and the Serpent

Amidst a sinuous darkness, exhausted by the effort of sounding the shell bugle, Zaralathaar sank back against the steadying embrace of the rock and drew what sustenance she could from the solidarity of its chill touch. She might not be able to summon water, but she could evoke it at least. Without the melt-rivers that used to course through the subterranean tunnel network, she wasn't sure how she would achieve the release she could find only in the arms of the sea, which, having been born from so many years ago, she now so ardently wished to return to. Perhaps, as so many things, it was not to be, for loneliness engulfed her as the echoes of her efforts died away. She had spent so much of her life in solitude, and in darkness.

And yet she called out, because she had people to call upon, so the silence did not strangle her.

Moments later, she found herself wishing that silence would shield her a little longer, for the first footsteps she heard were not welcome. Of course there would come a Goblin skulking, Zaralathaar acknowledged coldly. They congregated like spores of mould whenever hardship reared its head.

"Your kind have always liked bargains," the Nymph pre-empted in disdainful warning. "But you shall not hear mine. The ear-less one approaches, and it is to her alone I shall speak."

Shadows splashed, turning everything slippery and uncertain. "You would lay yer final words upon the tongue of a serpent?" the Goblin mocked. "You think she'll change her course of her own free will, when we have harried her all this time?"

"You might harass her from afar, but you wouldn't dare confront her at such close quarters," the Nymph rejoined acidly. "Leave me to my presumptions and leave me to my end, coward. I am not afraid of dying. Not on my terms, in my element, and in service to my friends. Go now, or fear my retribution from beyond."

"Women have always been of the serpent," the Goblin hissed. "I leave you to her." His echoes scurried away like frightened rats, but Zaralathaar awaited the inevitable undaunted.

"No," Zaralathaar murmured, keeping her voice light, as though beckoning a friend. "You leave her to me."

She didn't have to wait long before a sigh of scales like the drag of a merfolk's tail slithered forth. The temperature seemed to drop in accommodation; the implacable rocks seemed to shrink back to make space.

Zaralathaar exhaled. Settling into the presence of the other felt like sinking appreciatively into a depth as encompassing as the seas still far off, which were brought now closer in her mind. Muscle, encased in jewelled scales shimmering like the surface of a stream, rippled in a wave along the edge of the cavern as a serpent, like the soul of a river made solid, shifted her length into the light.

"You risk much, in coming here," Zaralathaar whispered, in a voice that sent shivelights through the shadows. Her breath rasped, but her heart felt eased. Still, the jewel-scaled bulk stuck to the shadows. A strange stare glittered, as though guarding a secret she dared not share.

"You guard your tears from spilling from your eyes as though they were venom from your teeth," the old princess murmured. "Save your effort for something better worth your energy. I do not fear you. Come closer, child, and do not fear me. I know you torment yourself that you are unworthy of a gift, but there is something I must share with willing audience, in order for it to be manifested . . ."

At her words, the serpent finally turned her head, fixing Zaralathaar with her gaze. An ageless understanding flowed between the two of them. Of this other being the serpent had no memory, although she had raced to her aid regardless—but recognition now flickered of a space shared between separate aeons. If footsteps could echo through the ages, Zaralathaar's would have traced the serpent's own tracks. They had shared something, once. A guardianship of water. A Realm full of wonder.

The possibility shook the serpent's own aims too sharply. "I came as quickly as I could, my lady." If she kept her talking, the Nymph wouldn't guess.

"I am sorry to have unearthed you," Zaralathaar offered opaquely.

"It was the state of the Realm that unearthed me," the snake dismissed sibilantly. "Do not concern yourself. What is it that you wish for?"

"What I wish for, is a little more time," the Nymph whispered, "but that is not in your power to grant."

The great serpent coiled around her, gently, while a flame of memory flickered briefly and protectively, like a nictitating membrane across her mind instead of her eye. Diberkati had warmed the core of the Realm once, and embracing the Water Nymph felt not so different. "You are held in many hearts, and spoken of in many voices," she hissed, finding her own burden eased a little. "I will stay, until after the end."

"But you are being chased by many."

"True. The Goblins hound me." The serpent's voice seemed to hold all the sorrow in the Realm for a moment. "They would burst my skin for a final drink before the endless dry." She dulled her voice protectively, as though in doing so she could shield the Nymph if not herself.

"They might wish it, but they won't manage it," bristled the Nymph, her words more biting than the remaining ice as the fierceness of life flared within her even now. "There are friends of mine, who will be here soon, and they will protect you. They have their own fight—for it is as you say: we have not seen rain for many months, and none know why—but they will aid you when they should think of themselves, as they have ever aided me."

The Nymph smiled; a smile filled with all the power she still possessed, the smile of one divulging a secret. "It was not in fear that I called out. With one's dying words, one can send forth life. Their aid is my gift to you yourself—but my gift to you all is this: I can alter a curse but a little, yet a little I shall alter it. How, you must unearth for yourselves, for I have not time to tell you . . ."

The words the Nymph spoke crowded into the serpent's psyche with such urgency that the deep emptiness she'd felt destined to be filled with forever was squashed to one side for now. No matter how still Diberkati held herself, she could not stall what was happening. The Water Nymph was being pulled by a tide stronger than the ocean, and towards a shore none living could reach.

It was only a few breaths later that the words became only an echo, unable to sustain themselves without the spirit who had brought them life. Diberkati barely dared breathe herself. The moments she had just shared felt fragile, turning brittle on the air like a snowflake that must dissolve at any moment. Before she could catch hold of them properly they sank into the great unquenchable silence the serpent could not enter, and she feared that without she who had spoken them, the words themselves held no power. With great care and infinite gentleness, she unwound herself from around the body of she who no longer needed protecting or comforting.

Diberkati let the deep sadness of the Nymph's passing permeate and fill her. But once she had, there was no need to stay any longer. Those the Nymph had spoken of would come and attend her body as they should.

The serpent wouldn't trouble them by remaining here. Better that they have the chance to save themselves, than be burdened by an unsaveable serpent. She knew she should have felt hope, at Zaralathaar's speaking of a gift, but such emotions reserved themselves for those who belonged in the Realm. She herself, by contrast, shouldn't even be here. And so the serpent took refuge in a morose night, and left only a drying trail.

A New Path

"She's passed," Racxen warned gently, hearing the pounding of Amber's footsteps behind him as he knelt in vigil beside the still form of the Water Nymph who had watched them all from the Fountain so many times before.

Skidding to a halt as she abandoned all her urgency in a flung heap on the floor, heart punching painfully against the run, Amber gulped down air and leaned against the stone strength of the cavern wall in despair, staring at the ground as she tried to steady herself. She daren't look to Zaralathaar yet, daren't see her lying dead. Instead, she kept her eyes on the rock paths that had been trodden by her times innumerable. Slight traces of wetness glimmered across the harsh stone, leading into the distance: already fading, but still just visible.

"Zaralathar wasn't alone at the end!" The knowledge surged like a beacon as Amber's words startled through the solemn silence. "Look." Then she grimaced in confusion. "The trail winds like a snake—I don't understand—"

"So, I was right about the serpent." Jasper's smugness pierced his sadness for a moment.

The rest of the Realm faded for Racxen as he studied the tracks intently. His eyes gleamed appreciatively as he smiled his verdict. "But an amphibious serpent. There is more wonder than water left in the Realm."

"Your version of wonder and my own are somewhat different," Jasper interjected stiffly.

The Arraheng ignored him. "A female—and her scales are drying rapidly, slowing her progress. She needs to return to her element, fast."

"Then she'll be heading for one of the oases in the desert," Yenna predicted confidently.

Racxen nodded. "And in her weakening state, we've a good chance of catching up if we follow the trail now, if you want to."

His eyes were on another Fairy, of course, and Jasper sighed, all too knowingly. "Have you not had enough adventures to last a lifetime?" he asked Amber pointedly.

"No, because I want a whole lifetime of adventure," she promised firmly, a spark of glee still glimmering amidst the gloom.

Jasper raised his brows. "Amber, we don't need to escort home a monster large enough to devour the banquet hall. Have you learnt nothing these past seasons?" he protested tiredly. We can't just run off after a serpent. We should make the necessary arrangements for Zaralathaar's funeral."

"I shall," Hydd promised, the sadness of an apprentice becoming master too early shimmering behind the dignity of a Selkie lord. "But she would ask ye tae do this, ye ken."

Jasper pulled a hand through his hair. "Might it not prove folly, to set out on so frivolous a mission at a time when water is so scarce?"

Yenna eyed him steadily. "Would it not mark the beginning of the end, were we to in the face of danger abandon all decency? This being has done the Nymph a great service, and we owe her our thanks."

"And you told me we have mere weeks of water," Amber pointed out, staring at the rapidly diminishing trail as though it were an omen. "This might be all the time we have. And this was the last creature to trade words with our princess," she added pointedly. "Do you really not want to find out what was said?"

Jasper sighed in resignation. "When you put it like that—we can check on the oases while we're at it. Not all water sources will still be viable, but I want to start mapping those remaining; it will help ensure access for everyone. This will not be brief: we need to gather sufficient supplies."

Racxen nodded thoughtfully, tracing the trail gently with the back of a claw. "She is slowing," he conceded. "We can afford to wait."

"Whereas we cannot afford to rush preparations," the Prince reminded resolutely in acknowledgement, more relieved than he wished to express at the support. "Meet back at the castle."

The company parted at once, united in purpose. Amber sped away on flying feet. For now, preparations could crowd out thought, so she set to them fervently, and if she couldn't organise her mind, she could at least sort her packing. Her waterskin, her sleeping mat, her pack: they were as dear friends to her as any, and a frisson of excitement shimmered as she gathered them. Amidst waning resources, she could still remind herself she had enough for now. And going into the wilds might yet prove a tonic in the absence of other refreshments.

Now that her pack was full of kit and supplies, she felt herself suitably bolstered too. And she knew she'd been quicker at it than Jasper, so she detoured slightly: to the Fairy Ring.

The soothing mist of the site enveloped her in its timeless dusk as readily as it had when she'd been only a winglet. So many years later the monumental toadstools still towered over her, shimmering in the vaporous air, their spores offering a soporific affect even now. She breathed their earthy scent, let their peace envelop her, and remembered that not all had been lost. At the edge of vision, a Bicorn lingered; more angular, yes, and ribs more noticeable, but still here. Gaunt, but not grisly. Cautious, but not panicked. Enduring, if not overcoming. Still, as Amber leant against the stalk and felt it wobble spongily with lack of water, she felt her tears begin to well.

"Zaralathaar's passing is a sadness, but it is not a tragedy," the King offered gently, emerging from the haze. The embellishments of his ceremonial robes glinted in the preternatural twilight as he paused beside her. Amber smiled despite herself. Of course he came here still, on occasion, just as the Queen went to the desert sometimes. His grizzled beard might now hold more white than grey, but his eyes shone with as sense and shrewdness as ever. Being in his presence still gave her hope, still filled her with a sense of what once was and could be again. King Morgan had led the Kingdom through crises past with a cool head and an even hand. With him at the helm, they could not be fated to succeed, but she could at least trust that all would not descend into anarchy and accusations. Or could she? Rumours were floating over the Realm, already. Of course, everyone was blaming everyone else: it was always some other corner of the Realm that had begun mining too deeply or farming too heavily. Amber couldn't say she'd seen any of it happening, and it would be easy to claim defensively that Fairymead mined their gems sustainably and ethically and had never overused their water. But could she really claim that, when Arkh Loban had always had to make less last longer? Also, while she would never dream of hurling accusations, she was looking to run off into the desert after a snake amongst all this, so perhaps she wasn't one to talk.

Those worries were too big to voice yet, so she grappled them into a smaller version, although she still hesitated, because it almost seemed sacrilegious to ask. "It can't have been the Water Nymph's death which caused the droughts somehow, can it?" She chewed her lip. "It's not Zaralathaar's fault her time ran out. She even trained Hydd to be her successor. And I could never think ill of her. I'm just trying to understand."

Morgan laid a comforting hand on her shoulder. "Our energy, like the remaining water, is limited," the King advised, his gravelled voice both holding his own pain and cutting through the tangle of her thoughts to ease hers. "Were that I could find out what caused this, and put it right," he admitted honestly. "But sometimes moving forward is more about tolerating uncertainty than it is about finding answers. Instead of wasting our energy arguing over what might have caused the droughts, let us instead use it in pursuit of the actions we can all take to mitigate their effects."

Amber sniffed industriously and nodded. The King was right, of course. Everyone now needed to focus on what they themselves could do to ease the water pressure—and look after each other in the process. Even if she didn't know how to manage the former, she had an example of the latter to attend to right away, and she voiced it to royal ears now.

Morgan nodded his approval. "That's the spirit, Amber." The King's grey-green eyes fixed on her, clear and knowing. "Proactivity and patience will get you most places. You can take positive action, even when you don't feel positive. I sanction Jasper to leave with you, to find this creature who came to Zaralathaar in her final hour. But I must remain here: I have negotiations to complete. You know that Hydd has overseen as many water deliveries as could be safely completed, but the changing climate has made crossing the vast expanses of the north too treacherous an enterprise to be maintained."

The King sighed gravely, staring into the distance across a fading Kingdom both his deepest pride and his greatest responsibility. "It is an ill wind brings a serpent when we are so fixed on survival that we have precious few resources left for protection."

"Perhaps it isn't the serpent we should be worried about," Amber suggested stoutly. "Perhaps she is as worried and in need of protection as the rest of us."

She hugged the King goodbye and strode out to rejoin the others with renewed determination. She might feel more alone than ever with her thoughts, but she was lucky to be joining her friends. Ruby and Hydd trod a lonelier path, accompanying the Water Nymph, although she couldn't think of a pair better suited for it. Still, she wished she could send them her own companionship by thinking of them, and wondered how they were faring.

***

"What's wrong?" Ruby blurted aghast, seeing tears brimming in her lover's eyes as he returned with an armful of kelp to re-enter the slippery darkness that cloaked the ice cave. She dropped the strands that had formed her initial attempt at weaving the stretcher aside and took his webbed hands in hers. "Tell me what I can do."

The Selkie's eyes filled like the ocean, threatening to overspill.

"Well, if that's too much," Ruby reminded gently, "tell me instead what's happened, and I'll tell you what I can do."

Hydd nodded gratefully and breathed himself closer to composure.

"I've checked the beginnin' o' the river route, but we cannae tak' it; there is nae fresh water left tae speak of. An' I'm afeared the ritual cannae work without it." He passed a webbed hand through sleek, greying hair. "It seems a cruelty to not allow the Water Nymph a final touch of tha' which she loved best."

"If it was in our power, we would provide it instead of just permitting it," Ruby promised. "But the sea she loved most of all, and we will take her there even if every course we meet upon has dried."

Her own tears lent her eyes a brightness. "Your sea magic might not be able to help us now, and I have no jurisdiction over water, but perhaps I can weave a magic of my own."

And so, as Hydd at her urging returned to weaving the stretcher, his lilting voice rising and falling like the tides in a timeless ode to the Nymph and her home, Ruby delved into the prettiest pockets patched across her skirt and produced just the assortment of supplies she needed. Lending her own lullaby-like humming to the Selkie's song, she sat with the Water Nymph equably, daubing just a touch of powder here and a stroke of pigment there, to evoke the shimmering water they could not anoint her with.

Hydd beheld the result in awe, having finished his own work. Tendrils of weed and waves caressed the Nymph's hands, and her face was brushed with the sparkle of sunlight upon a stream's surface. "Yer touch gives more life than any river," Hydd breathed tenderly in thanks, his whiskers brushing Ruby's face as he pressed a grateful kiss against her cheek.

Ruby smiled, pleased and proud. The shimmering light of the ice cave washed aqueously across the scene in place of true water, and she felt refreshed. They could manage this together.

Steadily, reverently, together with Hydd she positioned the Nymph's body onto the stretcher. She thought she would never again feel anything so cold as the weight of Zaralathaar, but being in the presence of the Nymph could not scare her and would never sadden her. She would carry the memory of Zaralathaar with her, like a story there would always be space for in the back of her mind.

"We're ready to accompany you on your final journey, my lady," Ruby announced decisively, if self-consciously. She met Hydd's ocean-calm gaze and, counting together, they hefted the stretcher. Ruby set her sights on the far exit, following with her eyes the tenuous spool of winding light that threaded between the ice-glistened lavastone to flare boldly at the tunnel mouth, out into the space that shone blindingly and beckoningly beyond. The Realm was out there, bigger than each of them, and it encompassed so much more than death.

Ruby adjusted her grip in readiness and nodded to Hydd.

"We'll tak' a smoother route than to the shore," Hydd promised, his smile both assured and anxious as they took their first faltering steps with the stretcher. "Th' drop in water through the tunnels has opened new passages—we kin gang across the salt flats."

Ruby grimaced in remembrance. The evaporation of a salt lake and the subsequent revelation of the flats might not have been the most uncanny occurrence in the recent times of strangeness, but it had been strange enough for her. Still, it would be a shortcut to the sea. One unmapped and as yet unencountered, but the dubious distractions afforded by the anticipation gave Ruby something else to focus on as she and Hydd made as stately a way as they could amidst both the solemnity of the situation and the almost sacrilegious reality of melting ice that skittered beneath their feet as they bore the most sacred of shared burdens, wending through passages carved so long ago that the Realm had been awash with rivers not only of water but even of lava. Ruby took strength from the strange, gnarled formations that loomed around corners of the tunnels. They stood as proof that the Realm had withstood even more tumultuous times than these.

Even so, she almost laughed in relief as they stepped free from the clutching claustrophobia of the ice-gleamed tunnels and streaming sunlight spilled over them congratulatorily. Warmth salved her skin while there was no rain to do so, and she felt her spirits lift out here in the open.

The same sun could not dissipate the fear that crept towards Hydd as he blinked across a landscape rendered unfamiliar by the absence of the element most dear to him. Salt stretched like sand, here, in a cracked-skin crust. Sand, he would have been able to read. Sand would have made sense, here beneath the searing sun. Of course everything was different now, he tried to remind himself. But he'd thought, as a Selkie, he could have found them a quick way to the sea. And they were still a long way even from the shore.

"Not all ends need meet upon the shore, though." Ruby's hazel eyes glittered. The creaking earth and piling salt defied conceptualisation, but she knew that, while it would be too saline to drink, the pans must retain pools of water. Mustn't they? She glanced to Hydd, unsure.

The Selkie returned her gaze unerringly. Everything else in his vision shivered in the heat and became less certain, but not her.

In response, Ruby's expression shifted protectively, and she scanned the salt flats in readiness. A decision tensed within her as she glimpsed an anomaly amongst the vastness. "Wait here."

Settling the stretcher and the Nymph's body, Ruby let reach her wings and sprang to the sky. Reaching a vantage point where the Realm diminished into patchwork neatness and made sense again, her focus fixed itself in disbelief on the intruding aberration. But she had to be sure. The heat made short work of the flight's distance as she flew on ahead, and she arrowed down towards the broken stain she'd glimpsed from afar, now lying gaping beneath her. Landing beside it in cautious dismay, Ruby trod closer in confusion, noting the jagged, wound-gaped edges peeled back and the swirling thickness eddying beneath. Around it, the salt was clumped into strange crystalline structures, but it was the site itself that drew her eye.

She struggled to make sense of it. Of course she'd known on some level that the crust of the earth was thinnest, here; that was why they had come: in the hope that they could access here some small part of the ancient reservoir of water hidden in the mantle of the Realm according to Hydd, and thus reunite Zaralathaar with her most beloved element. Ruby had also quietly hoped that even if the salinity of the pools here proved unhelpful, they might out here still find a route to the sea. She had expected to find a fissure, a crack: a suitable place for the reunification ritual. What she hadn't expected was to find evidence of something having exited where they'd hoped Zaralathaar could enter—and to Ruby, it looked awfully like something had broken out from beneath the crust of the Realm itself.

She breathed shallowly against the knowledge, as though that could keep it secret. Hydd had enough to deal with. They were supposed to be focussing on the Water Nymph, it was the others who were supposed to be tracking the serpent. Still, her friends were trying to predict where the snake would go. Ruby, on the other hand, was beginning to understand where she'd come from.

Across the lifeline cracks of the pan, she looked back to the Selkie, as though in doing so she could realign reality. "Hydd?"

The Selkie set up at a stalwart jog. She'd flown further than she'd realised. The fissure drew her eyes again while she waited, and time seemed soaked up by the salt as Ruby stared with mind suspended. It felt as though the rest of the Realm were an age away. The more she stared at the site, the more she felt unsettled. This wasn't an opening. It wasn't an opportunity. It was a fracture, a rupture. It didn't put her in mind of a birth, so much as of a breach. She wrinkled her nose in distaste. Something about the site bothered her. She didn't know the sea, like Hydd. But she knew her own soul, and what it was telling her.

"If it's a birthing site, it's a traumatic one," Ruby insisted firmly, as Hydd approached. "I don't think we should use it."

"Fair enaw, lass. We'll find another site," the Selkie promised, touching the salt around the gape as though to sooth it, almost unable to believe that something of the sea could be involved in such suffering. "Ah've niver seen aught like it." He slipped a comforting arm around Ruby's shoulders, sweating beneath the heavy pelt that was more suited to the frozen reaches of the icefields but that he wore now always, having once been parted cruelly from it.

Ruby nestled beneath it now, too. She took comfort from the fact that Hydd didn't rush her on from the site. She remembered he'd told her it was important for Selkies to bear witness, and she found his webbed hand and squeezed it. "Maybe we were meant to see this," she suggested quietly. "For the serpent's sake, if not the Water Nymph's."

In the silence, she had space to look further, and she tried to unpick what it might have been like for the serpent. During utter emptiness, a soul had found herself bereft. It was a discomfiting thought, and it led Ruby to a devastating conclusion. "I'm not sure she's heading to an oasis, after all," Ruby murmured, as though by gentling the words she could remove some of their pain. "I'm not sure she wants to be found."

Hydd's liquid eyes filled, as her words settled in his soul with the solemnity they deserved. "This changes everythin', lass. We main help her."

"Exactly. Whatever has dried the Realm has disgorged her—and the violence of that will have more repercussions than we can yet guess at."

"The sort that will shake the Realm." Hydd shivered with the heat haze lifting tremulous from the pan. "It's important th' others ken," he managed. "Ah kin finish th' ritual alone, if ye wish."

Ruby smiled her answer and shifted her sleeve a little. An impossibly delicate, feather-antennaed face peeked out. "I brought my Dartwing in case I needed to convey a message. I have no intention of abandoning you, or Zaralathaar. Or the serpent." Ruby felt a sudden flush of kinship with their quarry. She might never have tracked across the sands like Racxen, but she had trailed in her own way. She had been there for Amber when her parents had died, when she had lost her wings and her flight—she had loved her through it all. Tracking was the piecing together of a story; even the pieces that couldn't be spoken, Racxen had told her one evening when she'd gone out with him and Amber and followed the toeprints of frogs by torchlight until they'd heard the marshes spill with song.

As Racxen had scanned across the wetlands then with his nocturnal sight, Ruby felt across the salt-encrusted stretches with her mind now. As he had taught her, she opened herself to the signs.

A rush of feelings tumbled, rearing and subsiding as she made sense of them. A depth of loneliness, an extent of otherness and disconnect, enveloped her.

"Ye ken whair the serpent's headed, lass?" There was wonder but not surprise in Hydd's voice, Ruby realised with a flush of gratitude as his voice anchored her again, his presence her safe mooring even upon this lonely shore.

"I fear so," Ruby began, trying to think how to explain. "She won't veer towards Arkh Loban, nor stay on the outskirts where the Wolfren keep watch," the Fairy warned. "She's never had the experience of being cared for or tended to—and to seek it, she would need first to expect it, when in truth she dares not even hope for it. So, instead, she'll head further and further into the desert, where she won't have to experience anything else dying. And there she can't seek help and be turned away, because there will be no-one to turn to."

"Her direction makes sense, when ye realise she has ne'er received support when she needed it," Hydd agreed soberly. "An' with the desert encroaching since the drought, the journey to reach her will be a fair auld way." Then, with Selkie stoicism, he smiled thoughtfully. "But we kin mak' sure she gets her first act o' care."

Ruby nodded decisively. "As we will provide Zaralathaar's last, now."

She blew encouragingly at the Dartwing, which fluttered away like a strand of gossamer carrying a wish beneath the baking sun.

A Shift in the Sands

As Jasper was taking a certain grim delight in reminding them, the others had known the trail to the desert oases would not prove a short one. Still, it managed to prove an enthralling one, Amber admitted privately. Sunbaked dwellings the colour of red clay crept into vision to squat like lizards basking at midday as the companions cut through the frontier town of Arkh Loban, the air clouding with the scent of woodsmoke and horses along the wending dust-strewn roads. Then, chewing dried supplies they picked up at a market beyond even the long-fingered reach of the Goblins, the friends continued into the clean-burning air of the open desert: that endless expanse of rippling dunes and shimmering heat-haze.

Insects buzzed like the echoes of sound a mind conjures in a certain quality of silence; a delicious drone that thrummed with spacious possibilities. Sand soothed the rough edges of Amber's soul, and her vision delighted in all it absorbed. All sensation settled into the strange, somnolent otherness that belonged to the Realm's oldest and most sprawling of places, as time rolled with the dunes, merging and melding amidst the scape of sand and sun and shifting shapes.

It had felt searingly hot even in town, but now that they were far beyond Travellers' Pass and truly into the desert, the real heat beyond stung Amber like a wave that caught her entire body—caught her and lifted her in spirit, sweeping her along gasping. Unfettered by the constraints and contaminants of the hectic-hummed town, the desert stretched so far, her vision struggled to contain it. So much space awaited them it made Amber's eyes water. Out here lay Wolfren territory: the sun blazing fierce and free from an endless sky, scorching fit to melt the dunes into shimmering mirages. And beyond could not be guessed at, for it felt as though here, instead of the icefields, lay the end of the known Realm. But the strengthening certainty was this: the desert had never had more water than it was experiencing right now—and it had never required it. Just because it was empty, didn't mean it had nothing to offer. Seek to conquer it, and it would consume you, but empty yourself into it, and you might return fuller. Out here there was no such lack as seized the rest of the Realm. It could just be, and so could the companions.

Amber let herself relax into the journey, and the heat embraced her tightly. *Welcome back to the wilds.*

Being out in the wilderness both quenched a thirst and reignited a hunger in Amber. The heat and sand and burning sun melded to forge their own kind of bliss, and she readily let it fill her, for it had been a while since they had last set out like this. Life had spread to fill the spaces again after the hardships of the icefields and, while she had of course made sure to consciously appreciate the warmth, and safety, and ease of living experienced after the fulfilment of that quest, she of course also had soon needed to return to the world of work.

So, she had taken shifts here and there to try out different apprenticeships and had saved the money carefully in defence of not having a clue about the future. Everyone else's lives had seemed to move on, while hers had remained stuck, Aunt Sapphire had insisted on reminding her at regular intervals. So, in truth, it was a relief to be out here again, with a shorter-term focus. Hard as tracking a serpent would surely prove, she could at least align her whole being with that aim so soulheartedly that she knew in her heart she had a chance of finding the snake—a chance which, however slim, was already seeming far more likely than the prospect of discovering an apprenticeship that didn't fill her with dread.

Far more likely so far, she corrected herself. Far more had already been found than would stay missing, she was reminded with a flush of recognition as she watched her companions: Yenna and Racxen striding out in front—Yenna reading scents and Racxen reading spoor—and Jasper trudging behind steadily. Plus, Ruby and Hydd would already be tending the Water Nymph. So, while the Realm might not yet be cured, it was still being cared for.

And it was also still caring for her, even now. Her soul sang to be amongst the numinous out here, and in a location she had not spent much time before exploring into the bargain. As though amplified by the constant heat, the silence of the desert roared around her, got inside her; poured into her ears like so much sand. And yet, it seemed to make her feel more solid, not less. She felt as though she was becoming a sand-being too: full, yet fluid, flexible, and able to meet what might come next. Time passed immeasurably.

"The longer we are out here, the more care we must take," Yenna warned, suddenly beside her, her voice an urgency not to be ignored and her scarves an indelible outline that the blistering heat of the desert could neither capture nor waver. "The silence of the desert can shore up one's defences—or it can strip them down. The ennui creeps stealthily, steadily. We must not let our purpose drain away like so much sand."

Amber nodded decisively, grateful. She resolved anew to keep her eagerness, awareness, and attention in balance through these shifting dunes.

She thought, half wistfully, of the icefields she had so recently traversed. Back then she had felt as though those lands had scoured her out and remade her in their image so that no other environment could contend or intrude. Yet the wilderness of the icefields had seemed a presence in itself: brutal, but vital and vigorous. It had been a wild creature, constantly in contact with her; testing her boundaries and asserting its own. The blizzard, the bluster, the bleakness, all had had claws and teeth, and in affirming their otherness they had helped her establish her own self. Here, in contrast, the landscape felt empty. There was no angular wind or jagged cold, there were no sharp edges for her boundaries to steel themselves against. Here, the heat bled inwards and outwards, too insidious to resist, like the subtle rub of sand that would scrape her skin raw before she noticed. Its otherness would demand differently of her, and equally earn her new lessons. But she couldn't deny that, just as the Wolf Sister had warned, the heat was beginning to slow her. Everything took longer, and it didn't matter. It was too much effort.

"Here." Yenna sounded sandpaper-insistent as she passed over her waterskin.

The word loosened Amber's mind like liquid. She had to drink—and it had taken a wolf's voice to remind her. "Sorry. Thanks."

Yenna smiled knowingly, her lupine eyes shining between her scarves.

"You don't have to become the desert to survive it," she promised in solidarity. "Let it develop you. Don't let it dissolve you."

Amber nodded gratefully. That was the endless search: to find a way of becoming part of something greater, while remaining one's own self.

She shook out her thoughts determinedly as Yenna strode on ahead once more, and caught up to walk alongside Racxen, aware that the stark silence of the desert might be encroaching upon his mind in unnerving opposition to the reassuringly constant hum of life that used to enfold the marshlands of Arraterr. She thought of a rumour to mention, to engage his mind and lift his spirits. "Sarin used to speak of a Harpy desert community, when I was working with her," she disclosed with a hopeful grin. "Yenna says they're closer to the town now, being needed more with how things are. Do you think we might encounter them?"

Racxen's dark skin shone with sweat, but his stride was loose with the comfort of being in his element: tracking, if not through known territory. His brown eyes lifted in relief at her welcome interruption and darted in enjoyment of a secret shared. "Very likely. Don't tell Jasper."

Amber grinned back. "Of vulture-descended women who guide the dying and guard the dead? Wouldn't dream of it."

Racxen's chuckle was low and just between them, and Amber kissed him appreciatively as they settled into pace together. Amidst the hypnotic quietude and surrounded by her friends, she let herself relax into the journey. Before her stretched hardships, yes; but they were the kind she thrived on, not shrank from. The incomparable heat seared strongly enough to burn away all past and future, letting her fall with relish into the rhythm of the present as they followed Yenna.

Amber trained her eyes admiringly on their leader. Even after hours of trekking, the Wolf Sister was bristling with confidence.

Until, suddenly, she wasn't.

"You think the serpent has outpaced us?" Amber murmured in solidarity as she caught up to offer her water skin in return.

"Never." Yenna flashed a quick smile with canine confidence. "Yet I have not walked these unseen paths for many moons," the Wolf Sister admitted quietly. "I did not expect to see them so barren. The creatures I heard stories of are no longer here."

"Tell me of some of those creatures?" Amber asked eagerly, hoping to distract Yenna from the pain catching in her voice. She felt the lack in her own knowledge, that she'd assumed the desert had escaped the problems of drought.

"Sand Giants, for a start," Yenna divulged conspiratorially, delight upon her tongue and peace spilling across her fierce features. "When there were thunderstorms in the desert and we were camping out as whelps, we'd tell each other it was Sand Giants mock-charging. Huge, near prehistoric creatures, so large the only armour they needed was their fingerprint-folded skin, cracked like the dry-baked earth. The only thing more incredible than their size was their prehensile, trunk-like snout they used to snuffle beneath the sand and draw out insects and other delicacies. To defend themselves, they bore a horn beneath their brow, of a similar substance to our hair but infinitely hardened. They look like creatures from myth, and that is what they will become, if the rains don't return."

Yenna sighed softly. "Perhaps we have less rain today because there are fewer of them around," she mused. "In times long faded, the Sand Giants would furrow the sand into water with the depth of their tread and the regularity of their footprints." The Wolf Sister's brow furrowed instead now. "Yet they have been driven away."

"By the Goblins?" Jasper checked, catching up as the pair slowed.

"It would be easy to blame them," Yenna grunted. "Yet I cannot. They live as we all must. I have lived in these deserts without paying overmuch heed to their encroachment. Lack of water turns predator into prey, and prey back into predator. We must all keep our guard, instead of blaming others."

"Talking of keeping our guard, the section of desert we're entering extends beyond all known haunts—even yours," the Prince cautioned with a tight smile, rolling his map up resignedly and burying it in his pack. "Its shifting paths may be stalked by stranger beings than Wolfren. Dragons, Harpies . . ."

Yenna slipped her hand calmly into Jasper's. "Stranger, my love, but no more to be feared. The desert is my home. I would introduce you to its wonders. We cannot cease to live, simply because the Realm is ending. We must simply live with more courage—and with more care."

Out of respect for the unchartered nature of the territory stretching before them, the companions held a hasty council and agreed amongst themselves an organised formation. Yenna and Racxen would lead, marking signs for the others, who would follow forming a wider flank, and whomsoever found the next track would assume the lead. Then Jasper— who volunteered himself with solemn dignity for this awkwardly perilous task—would remain at the rear, stationing himself at the last known track until the next was found.

As Yenna led them on once more, everyone settled into their positions and a reverent silence spread through the company as they continued through a landscape barren but unblemished.

Amber relaxed into the steady hypnosis of scanning the shifting swathes of sand, while the desert reached out before her expectantly as though encouraging her to expand herself accordingly. And was it the sand singing? Or the desert itself? Thrumming chthonic harmonies she could hear almost in her blood rather than through her ears reconnected her with something primal and wondrous in the Realm. The hum of the desert filled her, left her too full to be fearful of the vast emptiness, and she let the heat of the desert swell around her, holding her as though she would never feel cold, never feel alone, again. Warmth held such hope, and she found herself feeling more and more sure that they would find the serpent before nightfall.

She walked like that for miles, buoyed by the journey itself as well as the company. The sand scoured away the rough edges of the past and kept at bay the encroachment of the future, while the heat baked solid the present, and so time passed as unperturbingly as the subtly shifting dunes. Far above whirled the only other occasional life: the birds, like stitches in the fabric of the Realm, holding everything together above her.

Yet as noon rose and fastened its grasp, hope shrank with the retreating shadows, and the blazing sun offered neither comfort nor courage. Amber suddenly felt the need to keep everyone in her vision for, all at once, there seemed to have been reached an impasse.

"The signs grow scanter," Racxen admitted.

"And the scents more fleeting," Yenna agreed. "The wind is restless."

In silent unison they all stopped, and returned to Jasper at the last track. The Prince was sweating fit to believe he'd managed to lose that which he had guarded so fervently, but between his boots it remained unmarred. Proximity proffered reassurance, and the friends fanned out again to search with renewed care from the axis Jasper provided.

Flooded with an irrational conviction that she'd somehow misinterpret the tracks they were after, Amber started looking for any sign at all. As she did so, her eyes were drawn to an arrow-like print sunk into the sand: birdlike, three-toed, barely there—and almost human-sized. Amber stared, entranced, as more of the tracks revealed themselves as though her gaze itself was summoning them, calling forth a being to walk through the sands of time out of a barely remembered myth now rendered real. The two-dimensional impressions granted Amber such imaginings that she was almost disappointed not to see corresponding figures shimmering in the haze of distance. Still, sensations of both kinship and contrast twined enticingly at the sight and, feeling flushed with the discovery, she signalled Racxen, not wanting to disturb the others. "Just there," she murmured.

"Are those—?"

"Vultures," Racxen declared with eager delight. "Auspicious company. There's life out here."

"Massive for vultures," Amber pointed out suspiciously, forgetting to be quiet.

"The softer the sand, the more the size of a track gets distorted," Racxen mused. But he sounded less sure, now.

Rumours rustled through Amber's memory like the wind beginning to gust across the dunes. "They congregate in the presence of Harpies, right?"

"They congregate in the presence of death," Jasper corrected severely, with the aggrieved air of one having been left out of the conversation too long. "Focus on the serpent tracks. We need to move on from here." He waved a demonstrative hand at Yenna, who was already striding on ahead again.

Racxen picked his pace up and Amber followed, her eyes darting between her friends and the new tracks, but Jasper remained planted astride their known track and stayed put resolutely, awaiting further instruction. He was the only one paying attention to the sky, and it was easier to watch it now that the sun's fierceness had lost some of its force. Weather changed strangely in the desert, he told himself in explanation, as a billowing, cloudlike haze that had moments ago been merely drifting into vision swept closer, filling the horizon. His vision shuddered as he struggled to comprehend what he was seeing.

"Stay together! Get down!" he managed to yell, fixing his eyes helplessly on Yenna far ahead, before the sandpaper wind smashed into him, turning the desert into a storm as vicious as any blizzard. His sight was torn away, but he felt a reassuring Wolfren bulk beside him, shielding a space for him to breathe. Hastily unravelling his sash and tying it about his face, he leaned on Yenna as much in gratitude as necessity, burying a hand in her coarse fur as he struggled to his feet and staggered blindly next to her, trusting her to both guide him and find the others.

Amber lunged desperately towards Racxen, but he was too far ahead. The winds were a wall between them; she would have howled if she'd had the breath. She felt Yenna's teeth grab the scruff of her cloak to drag her back, and reason bit as well. She needed to survive to save Racxen. Automatically, she scrabbled her cloak out of her rucksack, and drew it up as a shield even as Jasper did the same, Yenna using her body as a further barrier. As their Realm shrank into each other, the friends huddled together and hunkered down as the desert shrieked its protest outside.

The previous illusion of safety ruptured, Amber stared mutely through a gap in their cloaks as the dervish tore away the horizon, the wind screaming fit to drown any plan of escape out of their minds. Never had the desert felt so alien, so horrendous before—a hateful nothingness barring them from aid. And worse, barring them from Racxen. Struggling against her rising panic, she brought her attention back to her companions.

"We can't afford to wait it out," Jasper was arguing, his hoarse shout weak against the might that railed outside.

"That's a problem of ego, not of survival," Yenna growled. "We sit tight."

"Once upon a time, yes, but the weather is not as it was," the Prince insisted. "We have no way of knowing when this sandstorm will ease. We could wait until dusk only to die in the night."

"Fear is a liar; listen instead to me," Yenna reminded firmly. "We're not going to die in the night."

"No," Amber agreed. "But we're not waiting here either. We're finding Racxen."

"When it has eased." The touch on her arm might as well have been Yenna's teeth. "We're not losing anyone else."

"But it's easing already: I can hear you," Amber argued hastily, too elated to question the uncanny suddenness of the quell. "There are vultures again," she reasoned. "And I'm certainly not waiting for nightfall." Into the spears of the sun's sharp rays she ran.

Thrilled to have refound the serpent's tracks, Racxen gave himself over to the chase, bounding across the melting sands. The barren landscape burst with signs, and he drank them in, following them at reckless speed in his urgency—so fast that even as Yenna snarled a warning the desert was already swirling around him, obscuring his companions and stripping away his senses, until the Realm itself spun away from him and he was falling through sands that engulfed him like flames . . .

The dervish-winds rose like the mocking voices inside her head, but Diberkati couldn't bring herself to care. She was deep into the desert now; far enough away that what must happen to her wouldn't matter, for there was no-one here to witness it, no-one here to cast aspersions.

And so, the one who had struggled for so long ceased now to strive. As the sands railed and tore, her great head sank for one last time and she waited for the desert to cover her.

Racxen sprawled through the maelstrom of whipping sands, arms flailing as he struggled to keep his footing. In a wild attempt to slow his descent, his claws gouged through the sand as he fell—meeting something solid, muscular, and scaly.

The pain of their claws scraping her scales wasn't much, the serpent thought dully, but it served as a primal reminder of her aliveness, and adrenalin spurred through Diberkati's entire length to realise the Goblins must have found her. She realised with the sharpest clarity that she was not ready to die. Hissing her fury, she shook away the shackles of the crushing sand and rose freely to her full and terrible height, spitting wrath like venom.

A towering, serpentine shape reared through an explosion of sand and a fanged face soared above Racxen's own, hissing fit to shake the desert apart.

Instead of springing to his feet, Racxen knelt in prostration, the sands burning into his skin. "*Ek shenka Rashika:* My apologies, Queen," the Arraheng gasped. "I am Racxen, from the Arraheng tribe of the far marshlands, and I ask your forgiveness. I will ask my partner to tend your wound—she is trained better than I in these matters. My friends and I were caught in the storm and I flailed unseeingly in my fear. I never meant to hurt you and will make whatever amends I can now."

The sands stilled, and the desert held its breath as Racxen fought to regain his own. The quietude was eerie now, held like a half-taken inhalation. Had the serpent conjured the storm? The Arraheng found himself wondering. Had she stilled it?

He felt the shift of her inscrutable surveillance as she watched him unblinkingly, tasting the air in consideration. "I am Diberkati." Her voice was the effort of gravel dragged across sand at midday. "I have ignored deeper wounds than these mere scratches and lived."

In the potent, problematic silence left, Racxen assessed that her dismissal owed less to the slightness of her injuries and more to the heavier impact of a crushing weight of apathy. Despite her considerable bulk the serpent's manner haunted Racxen, and he wondered at the hurt she was hiding.

"Only those who come to die linger here," she warned roughly, and Racxen worried suddenly that she might have sensed his concern in the same manner a viper would scent weakness in their prey. But then amusement flickered with her tongue. "So, you cannot stay," she explained more softly.

Racxen grinned in relief and apology, and held out his waterskin to the serpent.

"Do not waste your water, or your time, on me," Diberkati hissed in response, and Racxen found he'd have preferred to find malice in her words, instead of the resignation that seeped from them. So, he spilled some water, and stayed.

The serpent's fathoms-deep gaze locked onto Racxen, holding the complexities of dying stars as she drank. She shivered with animation now, and a frisson of understanding sparked from her to the Arraheng. "I will take you back to your friends," she offered, her words more welcome even than water. "They lived, and I am glad. I can feel their heat, even amongst the blistering sands," she promised, her elliptical eyes hypnotic. "Follow."

She began to pour herself across the sand, and the Arraheng raced after her, exultant.

Amber's heart slammed in awe to see Racxen walking beside the colossal serpent they had been searching for. And what a serpent: her scales gleaming like ink spilling over jewels as she sinewed towards them, all soft-bodied steel, all slackness and strength in one. The colour of wet sand, she flowed like water—and she was just as welcome in these parched times. She was mesmerising.

Yet, as she slid closer, Amber tempered her elation. Yes, those sun-blotched scales were burnished like the sun-shone marshes, and that taut-muscled body rippled as proudly as a river coursing through the driest gullies—but the ophidian eyes that should surely, the Fairy assumed, be narrowed fit to guard the secrets of the Realm, containing as they did wisdom deeper than the fissures of the earth, now gaped, stress-widened and gleaming brokenly. She longed to embrace Racxen in relief, but it would have felt wrong in the presence of such a lonely creature.

"You have helped us so much. Is there some way we can assist you in return?" Amber asked courteously, unstoppering her waterskin. She realised instinctively that now was not the time to extend thanks or an excess of emotion.

"There is nothing you can offer me, although you have my gratitude for trying." The act of speaking suddenly seemed to either exhaust or terrify the serpent. "I return your companion to you and take my leave."

As she turned to slip away, Racxen crouched beside her, as though admiring her tracks and committing them to memory. "Diberkati?" he reminded quietly. "I remember what you said, about these reaches of the desert, and those who seek them. I would have you stay with us awhile." He put the kindest weight he could behind his words.

A tremble seemed to set through the serpent, as though the strength of her skin could barely contain the extent of her sorrow. "I would be an imposition," she hissed. "There is nothing you can do to make me feel better. There is no need to make yourself feel worse."

"At least let me tend your wounds first," Amber tried evenly.

"Your letting me practise would be a kindness. Sarin's always telling me I should improve."

"She's not wrong," put in Jasper dryly. "Might be best for Amber to practise on a less-than-fully-invested subject, no offence."

The serpent shifted listlessly, presenting her injuries, and the Fairy worked as quickly and adeptly as she could, cleaning with their precious water and applying appropriate herbs to aid healing. The cuts were barely scratches, but that wasn't the problem. She could feel despair leaking from the serpent: like blood, or pus, but worse. Finished, she nearly asked Diberkati if that felt better, but she realised early enough to stop herself. She wished miserably that there was something more she could do.

"Perhaps we cannot make you feel better, but we can keep you safe," Racxen suggested carefully. "I saw Goblin tracks, not far back. It's an ill time to be alone."

"It is an ill time to keep my company," Diberkati corrected. "They have been following me for days now." The great serpent's eyes filled with tears that she did not blink away. "They think I have caused the breaking of the Realm. Perhaps they are right. And if so, they are also right to hound me. After all, I am no use now. It would be better that they burst me, as they want to, and slake their thirst on me until I am dead."

The friends quietened at the voicing of such brutality.

"No-one wants to do that," Jasper protested in horror. "The heat and isolation have been affecting your mind. You can't breathe well without the water your kind needs, so you're not thinking healthily. Stop with us a while. Let us help."

The serpent grimaced frustratedly. "You can't help, princeling. Trying would just prove it and hurt me further. Just go. Please."

"Before we do go, your findings would be great help to my Pack," Yenna interjected coolheadedly. "If you can relay the Goblins' movements, I would be in your debt."

While the Wolf Sister exchanged news from the desert with the serpent to soothe her, the others held a rapid counsel.

"I know we all want to help her, but we're going round in circles, and rapidly losing time by delaying here," Jasper cautioned despairingly. "She has refused our help, so we must focus on our own safety now—and it is dangerous to linger longer in the desert than necessary. We should go on without her."

"No, we need to stick with her," Racxen retorted levelly. "I have been doing this for years, Prince—I do not fear the wilds. I do fear, though, for Diberkati's state of mind. We have to find her water, at least, before we leave her alone."

The Prince grimaced in exasperation. "But you can't scent out water, Racxen. *She* can. She can do this on her own."

"The danger is that she won't, though," Amber interrupted. "Not without support. And who are we to deny her that? We all need help right now."

Jasper didn't dispute her appraisal, so Amber continued. "Diberkati won't agree if she's made to feel like an imposition, but she might extend assistance when she won't ask for it. She guided Racxen, and she let me tend her wound. We could offer her protection from the Goblins, under the guise of asking her help with finding water."

Jasper sighed. "It would hardly be a guise," he conceded grumpily.

Without hesitation, Racxen approached Diberkati. But the Arraheng didn't speak straight away. The Realm had begun to fracture, and into a breaking Realm the serpent had come. Amidst all the chaos and crumbling, here was the chance to construct a coherent narrative around events and move the story forward—for their new companion, if not for themselves. Understanding her better would be the first step to achieving this.

So, Racxen watched Diberkati intently. "Someone offered you help before," he suggested, his voice as full of compassion as his eyes. "An offer that you couldn't accept, because it didn't make sense?"

The moment hovered, approaching truth. Diberkati's stillness bunched, like something afraid. She curled like a river, like a symbol of all that stood to be lost.

"Please," Amber begged simply. "You have shown us a great kindness by returning Racxen to us. If it would lighten your burden, tell us what happened."

The great serpent's eyes filled with tears, until it seemed like her very body were about to burst with them. "I do not deserve my burden to be lightened. I was not deserving of what she gave me, either." The rest of her words dissolved into sobs.

The friends exchanged charged glances. They knew whom she meant.

"She told me she had a gift," the serpent quavered. "She told me she could change a curse."

"So you saw Zaralathaar?" Jasper prompted gently, to encourage her to continue. He dared not reveal they'd been scouring the desert for the creature for this very reason, of course, for fear it might entirely overwhelm her.

"The Water Nymph? I didn't kill her," she protested, eyes entirely of tears.

"We know," Jasper gentled. "My Dartwing brought word of her peaceful passing." He congratulated himself on the kindness of this small lie. "We think you spoke to her, that's all."

"Except it wasn't just 'all'," Racxen promised. "It was everything."

The serpent's tears fell freely now. "Speaking to her, and surrounding her, was the only thing I could do. I couldn't save her. But she altered a curse, and in doing so gave me a blessing which I am unworthy of."

"Perhaps you should trust her wisdom, when you dare not trust your own," Racxen suggested kindly. "The blessing is her gift to you, and we will not intrude upon it—but could you share with us how she changed the curse?"

Diberkati shook her head wretchedly, as though she could wring reason from her rememberings. "She told me: 'I can alter a curse but a little—yet a little I shall alter it.' She assumed I'd know what she meant, but I didn't, because nothing has made sense in my head for a long time now."

Amber's heart seized with compassion to watch the great serpent wrestle with so much pain. "Please don't let our questions distress you. We didn't come here to ask anything of you. We came here to thank you. Zaralathaar gave you her last words. You were the right one to give them to."

"And having thanked you, we can move on. Together," Jasper concluded, with a brisk attempt at jollity.

Diberkati's elliptical eyes refilled. "But I told you: I am not deserving."

"Deserving is a relative term, and not one to concern oneself with. I am a fool, any of these will tell you," Jasper divulged lightly, "and yet these three have saved me more times than they know."

"And it's not like you're delaying us on some vital quest—we're only heading to an oasis," Amber interjected quickly, as though it had been their plan all along.

"Indeed we are, to collect our allocated rations," The Prince affirmed, brandishing the waterskins smugly. "So, it is settled. We will travel with you. You must have been seeking the oases as well, to have ventured so far into the desert," he surmised quickly before Diberkati could conjure a reason for refusal. "And, while we have two of the Realm's finest trackers with us, we are hopelessly lost," he added conspiratorially. "So, we will keep you safe from the Goblins, if you will be so kind as to accompany us to our destination."

"I will accompany you," the serpent acquiesced. "But I must also warn you: the Goblins hound me still. We may not reach water, before they reach us."

"In that case, let us commit to taking precautions, instead of making promises," Jasper amended smartly. "But let us still commit."

"And if they reach us, it will give us an opportunity to return your courage tenfold in your service," Yenna added in pledge, her ember-glow eyes afire. "We *will* keep back the Goblins. And you will give yourself the chance to write your own end. Come with us to the water, before you decide what that will be."

Diberkati's eyes began to gleam once more, like sunken coals reigniting. "Careful, Wolf Sister," she hissed, her voice a thousand stones across sand. "The promises made to a serpent are advisable to keep."

Yenna raised an eyebrow and reshouldered her pack, gesturing with flowing sleeves for the serpent to lead on. "Means you have to stick around long enough to check that I do," she challenged.

Diberkati replied to her wolfish grin with the wink of a serpentine eye. Wordlessly she began to carve across the distance, her great length tying the company together as securely as the most trusted rope.

"Bet you wish we'd found the Harpies instead, now." Amber grinned at Jasper as she overtook him. The others had settled comfortably into following the serpent, but the Prince was still regarding her prodigious length with a dubious eye.

"I'm not sure I would prefer the company of human vultures to that of a talking snake," came his prim retort. "But it's nearing nightfall, and I'd rather not consider that they're still out there."

"And yet so are we." Amber couldn't help smiling expansively as she considered the prospect, her eyes dancing into the distance. The possibility that the vulture people she had only read about might still be out here anchored and elevated her in equal measure.

Jasper sniffed guardedly, knowing too well the look in her eyes. "Well, I couldn't stay behind: someone has to keep you lot safe. Even from Harpies."

Yenna drew a comfortable breath. "Safe from Harpies?" She laughed. "Those women know the desert like no-one else." The Wolf Sister looked wistful. "I grew up on tales of them. I wanted to be one when I was a whelp."

Jasper raised his eyebrows. "I'm not sure that makes them sound less dangerous. They live among the dead," he reminded her nervously. "They are not to be trusted."

"Would you rather that the dead were feared or, worse, left lonely?" Yenna countered. "The Harpies took their vows years ago and built camps of refuge amidst the mosaic of scrubland fringing the desert. If you're going to fear them for their dark cowls and darker wings, you're a fool I did not take you for. The Harpy Order will be out there, and we shall leave them be. They are as likely escorting us, as stalking us, and we've a long way to water yet." Her penetrating stare was full of knowing.

"And for tonight, a serpent will stave back the shadow," Diberkati promised, slithering back towards them. She lifted her great head to check the air. "We shall stop here tonight, and no-one will stalk you."

Jasper slung down his pack and raised his waterskin in relief. "Then let us put talk of Harpies and death out of our mind—let us make a fire and toast the life and memory of Zaralathaar."

Racxen prepared the roots, Yenna the dried meat, and Amber shared the biscuits she had made with Ruby. After a shared meal and similarly shared tales of the Water Nymph, both lingered over with equal reverence and relish, the friends bedded down around the fire. Diberkati stretched luxuriously and encircled them all to stare into the dancing flames.

Deeply moved by the gesture, Amber tried to find words to thank her.

"A serpent was once trusted to protect the centre of the Realm." Diberkati hissed softly in explanation, like shifting sands settling at last.

"You trusted me again."

Amber drank the sight of her in awed appreciation, watching the firelight play across the snake's body like a flickering tongue as the night worked its magic.

"And you claimed *we* would protect *her*," Jasper griped mildly, unlacing his boots.

"Shut up," Amber grinned, flicking stones out from underneath her sleeping mat and rolling triumphantly onto it with a sigh of relief. Racxen's shadow was next to her, and the stars were above her, and everything felt as it should. The sky began to growl with the storms that came every night. Usually they sounded dry, complaining voices venting the increasing frustration of a desiccating Realm, but tonight it was easier to let their sounds roll over her without letting those messages into her mind. Tonight, they just sounded like a far-off storm, and the storm didn't sound scary. One day a storm would come again, and they would dance beneath it with the abandon it would deserve.

She didn't know when, but she knew they would, and that was what mattered. And until then she would remember when they had before. So, Amber sighed contentedly. The night billowed out like a blanket shaken before sleep, and the stars shone so brightly she might never sleep, and not mind. The feeling danced across her skin and through her mind. It felt right to be back in the wilds, with her friends, and with the stars so close she could have snatched one for herself.

"We will leave before first light, before the heat gets too much," Yenna reminded, padding over. Her veils crumpled to reveal her Wolf form, and Amber watched her thread herself in prowling protection between each of her companions before stretching out alongside Jasper. On her other side Racxen reached out a hand, letting his claws twine with her fingers as they touched in silent, sacred language. The smoke drifted lingeringly over the camp, extending the spell of intimacy cast around the fire.

"I'll take first watch," Racxen promised comfortably, as silence settled.

"No need." Life glowed like coals in Diberkati's eyes again. "I will wake you later if you wish, but for now, sleep soundly together. A serpent watches over you."

Filled with drowsy gratitude, the companions found themselves encircled by a hum of contentment deeper even than that mystical drone of the desert, and it swelled Amber's heart to feel Diberkati's happiness.

She felt Racxen's gaze on her in the darkness, and she kissed him softly. With the others so close, they would lie together simply as friends, but that would make it no less special. In truth, being next to him like this felt as intimate as any feastnight dance, and with the close-slumped silhouettes of Yenna and Jasper just as comforting, Amber almost didn't want to sleep. She felt time slow into an ancient rhythm as night tucked in around the company, soothing their souls and salving their spirits. She lay there, drinking it all in, the night draped over her closely, shielding her from whatever tomorrow might bring. Insects trilled, their vibrations so slight in a silence so thick that she couldn't pick out where they were: they could have been miles away or in the now-cool log pile not far from her feet. The wind set up a companionable calling, adding layer upon layer of experience to ensure she didn't feel like she would float away in this spilling darkness. She was anchored. She was home. She'd never lain so exposed, nor felt so safe.

Diberkati hissed slumberously, in counterpoint to the growing buzzing of the sand grains across the dunes as the night cooled steadily. The quiet sound, not much louder than Amber's own breathing, soothed the Fairy more than she'd expected. It spoke of companionship: a continuous presence to stave off even the encroaching vastness of the desert, as reassuring as a hand to hold.

Amber lay there and listened and thought how much the serpent's breathing sounded like rain. She felt her pulse slow and slept.

Beneath Unseen Eyes

Settling into the heightened trance that was nightwatch, Racxen found his eyes drawn by Diberkati, still circled around them. She slept now, coiled— but not like a spring: like a neat, relaxed muscle, all tension gone.

A lid flickered, and she saw him watching.

"Never take your eye off a serpent," Racxen joked amiably, his voice quieter than the night breeze. "First rule of survival."

Diberkati stretched, at first cautiously and then luxuriously. It had been a long time without the sun, but she felt warmer now this night than she had in the morning. "You think I am to be trusted in any matter of survival?"

Racxen smiled. "The dunes have rearranged while we were sleeping. Don't think I haven't noticed."

A membrane flicked unreadably across her eyes. "Your senses, tracker, are not those of a serpent."

But she uncurled just a little, for him to investigate.

Amber woke into a silence so solid she wasn't sure she was truly awake. Nighttime in the icefields had been saturated with experience: it had been bitingly cold, floodingly wet, awash with hallucinatory light and dark. Here, in contrast, she felt caught in a kind of half-suspended animation, as though she were floating amidst a darkness so expansive it might preclude the Realm's unravelling into a soft, dreamlike oblivion.

To combat this unsettling sensation Amber rolled over, and with a deliberate effort pushed herself into crouching. It would be all too easy to succumb to inertia here. But the vision of her companions, anchored still in slumber, roused as well as anchored her. And Yenna was on watch.

Tawny fur aflame with the hues of a newly-smouldering fire, the Wolf Sister opened her throat in a howl. The tentative, ululating call, rippling in exploration before rising and rounding to a guttural and triumphant finish, shivered through Amber's whole body. The haunting sound seemed the exact timbre to melt into dreams and not wake a sleeper. Amber listened as the sky began almost imperceptibly to lighten, and she started to realise why the Wolfren howled.

"When we are out of range of our Pack, we howl to reconnect with our own souls," the Wolf Sister murmured in explanation as she changed form again, the low growl of her warm voice barely louder than the companionable crackle sparked amidst the fire she roused from the night's embers. "Sometimes the only meaning of a howl is to tell the Realm you still stand. That the sands haven't subsumed you yet."

Amber nodded supportively, keeping her gaze on her emerging surroundings while Yenna robed herself. But, even accounting for the fickle crepusculine light of a rising dawn, the Fairy hadn't expected her vision to feel this confused. Amidst the muted, softly luminous hues of the sands, the dunes definitely seemed changed—rearranged even. Amber stared into the yearning reaches of the desert. What had she slept through?

Yenna picked up on her thoughts as easily as she could catch a scent.

"Racxen told me of the shift, when we exchanged watches," she admitted, her fire-flecked eyes agleam with a mystery to seize on. "He took a quick scan but didn't want to stray too far and leave us alone in the dark."

Amber grinned fondly. "Well, that's very noble—but now it's virtually daylight."

"Exactly. We'll scale the dune and take the lie of the land."

"Should've known you'd have it covered," Racxen grinned, padding over to them.

Amber hugged him warmly. "You took a longer watch than the rest of us. I wanted you to rest."

"Whereas you'd happily start without me," Jasper griped mildly, shuffling towards them half asleep.

Amber turned to the Prince with a playful bow. "Fine, then, your highness. Lead on and give us your report."

Jasper sniffed in acquiescence, swept his cloak around himself in a pleased sort of way, and advanced solidly up the dune. "I can see a stream from here!" he called back, in his astonishment only just remembering that the serpent was still sleeping. He lowered his voice self-consciously.

"Diberkati did it! She reconjured water!"

Yenna took the dune at a run, her scarves rippling as she drank in the sight before her, exultant. "I knew our serpentine friend controlled more than she let on," she confirmed, overjoyed. "That river goes on for miles."

Racxen joined them, more cautiously. The tracker knew the signs that accompanied a watercourse. "That's not . . . real." His voice wasn't judgemental, just startled.

Amber stumbled catching up with the others, and was about to protest, but Racxen's words had drawn back a veil. There *was* no water. The oasis was a shimmering, carven emptiness, glittering with a wish that could not be fulfilled. It was a phantom, and far more haunting.

Jasper stared, aghast. "She's led us astray."

Yenna snarled, conflicted and wary. "I don't understand. There must be another explanation."

Amber felt as though the sand were slipping away beneath her feet. "It won't have been intentional," she insisted. "She wouldn't be the first to have hallucinated water in the desert."

Yenna grimaced, her veils wrapping around her like thoughts. Unspokenly, the company descended the dune and returned to the remnants of their camp. No-one wanted to look again at the barren lugga or confront what it might mean.

Around the ashes of the fire, the friends convened hastily. More shaken than any of them wanted to admit, they kept their voices quiet.

As she beheld the still-sleeping serpent, Amber struggled to make sense of what they had seen. She couldn't forget the intensity of Diberkati's sorrow when they had first met her. "So, you think her despair is what made it stop raining?" she suggested quietly. "Or, at least, is what is preventing it from raining now?" She didn't want to voice it, didn't want to risk making it real. But how could they help if they couldn't first recognise what was happening?

"I'm inclined to believe it." Jasper's lips thinned as he thought. "But it doesn't exactly help us."

"She's not obliged to help us, Jasper! I'm saying that we should help her."

Jasper frowned. "It might not be safe to do so. After all, it's her behaviour that is hurting us. She might not have come here to cause the Realm's ending, but it'll end at this rate none the less." His voice flattened despairingly.

Amber chewed at her lip. "You can't hold Diberkati's emotions against her, when her behaviour to us has been beyond reproach," she insisted. "She's in so much pain, Jasper. We can't just be kind to her for a day and expect that to heal. However worried we are about the water, and the Realm, we can't minimise the magnitude of her own suffering."

"We all suspect Diberkati can influence the weather, and maybe the landscape—perhaps last night she was trying to conjure the water," Yenna interjected in mediation. "She fell asleep peacefully; she seemed truly calm around the fire with us. And she wanted us to sleep, while she kept watch.

She may have had every conviction that when we woke, we would find water."

"So, you're saying during the night somehow her hope evaporated, and so did the water?" Jasper's face blanched. "I'm already partially responsible for the wellbeing of an entire kingdom," he pointed out queasily. "I can't be held culpable of a serpent's erratic thoughts as well."

"I'm saying," the Wolf Sister corrected, stern and soothing at once, "that she must have felt so renewed at her first sliver of hope, that she simply overstretched herself. She thought it would be able to reconjure water, but it has been beyond her reach for a long time now."

Amber swallowed, letting the words and their truth sink in. She watched the serpent with sympathy. "She spent the little energy she'd regained in trying to help us," she murmured contritely. "All the goodwill and positive thinking in the Realm can only go so far. She needs real, extensive help. And it is not fair of us to expect it from her until she receives it herself."

"Exactly."

Amber sighed, and her gaze sought refuge upon Racxen. While the rest of them had been talking, he had simply settled down beside the serpent, murmuring memories of caves and water while she slept. Amber's heart swelled, and her spirit lightened. She might have known.

The sand, and its serpent, stirred. Amber watched a great shiver set up through Diberkati's length as she dreamily began to shift, as though hoping to warm her companions as they woke. But then she woke herself, saw the friends already up and gathered, and seemed to sink a little into the sand. "It didn't work?"

"You showed your gratitude by attempting a great kindness," Yenna promised quickly. "Which of itself worked very well indeed." Her fierce glance to the others reflected her sheer determination to protect the serpent in any way she could, but it also betrayed the Wolf Sister's uncertainty about how to practically assist Diberkati right now. It wasn't often Yenna looked helpless.

Amber wasn't sure how to help either. But, while they might not be able to guarantee the serpent safe passage into the future, they could at least be an audience for her story, and help her speak about and make sense of her past.

There are any number of ways out of the desert, Yenna had told her earlier, against the ennui. *And you can't wait for certainty if you need to escape.*

Amber took heed of those words now as she spoke. "You began a story earlier," she suggested gently to Diberkati, her voice flickering like campfire flames as she settled down next to Racxen, who was still crouched companionably next to the serpent. "About curling at the centre of the Realm and being trusted to keep it safe for us. Would you trust us to keep that story safe for you?"

Something akin to pride, although she could not yet feel pleasure, lit an ember in Diberkati's eyes. "It was as though there was a womb, at the centre of the world. I was held there, but I was far from trapped: I belonged in the subterranean." Time slowed, as the serpent's voice swirled, and she took ownership of the words once more. "My movements lifted mountains, my shudders set free earthquakes, and my moods stoked the seasons. I moulded the Realm into being."

Her voice softened with remembrance. "I warmed the core of the earth, like an egg," the serpent mused wonderingly, as though she couldn't believe she had done it. "I was never supposed to breach the surface," she susurrated. "So, I don't know how the story ends." But, in truth, having voiced the beginning she felt a little less worried about the ending.

"You don't need to know how it ends. You just need to decide it's worth continuing," Amber urged. "You looked after the Realm for so long. But it doesn't mean you must be bound to that duty forever."

Diberkati rippled; a sinuous motion that could have indicated assent or agitation. "That duty may no longer be open to me, any more than the subterranean sanctuary I slipped from. The crust of the Realm—the edge of the only world I had known—became so wounded it could no longer protect me, nor I it. The Realm's skin split, and out I was forced like pus from a wound."

"A graphic image." Yet the Prince's voice spoke more of sadness than disgust.

"It sounds as though you blame yourself, for something that is far from your fault." Yenna couldn't keep the growl of concern out of her voice.

Diberkati's own voice was as gravel once more. "Perhaps I am right to. I was at the centre of the Realm, and I cannot return. Both the Realm and myself are too scarred. We fit together no longer."

"That was not in your power to control—and I am certain you might fit together differently, still," the Wolf Sister asserted more gently.

Diberkati rippled slightly, as though uncomfortable with letting her kindness stick. "I wish their words hadn't got to me," she admitted. "But I had to form my own skin to survive, and while it has hardened many times over now, pain permeated freely in the beginning. Voices pierced me when my scales were new: saying I had been cast out, saying I had to pay penance."

The friends listened soberly, giving the serpent's words the space they deserved.

Recognition reanimated Diberkati's eyes in response. "The hour is late for the Realm, and I cannot fix what I cannot understand," she admitted. "Had I done wrong, I would make amends. But I will not take punishment for what I have not caused."

Jasper frowned in approval. "It's a relief of sorts to hear you speak thus," he conceded. "But it means you do not know what has stopped the rain, either?"

"No," Diberkati shivered. "Only the same thing that has broken the Realm and disgorged me."

Jasper nodded. "We feared as much. And the hour grows late for us, as well," he admitted awkwardly. "We really had hoped to find you water, by now."

He stared dejectedly at the riverbed, and Diberkati followed his gaze miserably. The emptiness of it gaped like a wound, and the serpent seemed to sink further into the sand, as though the effort of keeping her body together was too much.

"You can leave me here with a clear conscience," she promised sadly. "The land I once looked after has forsaken me."

"Well, we haven't," Racxen interjected suddenly. "We might not be able to fix what we can't understand," he agreed. "But there is something about dried riverbeds that I long ago learnt."

The serpent's eyes swelled fit to burst with tears. "But there is no water. And I am bereft of hope."

"Let us bear the burden of hope, for a moment," Amber insisted, gesturing for her to watch as Racxen padded the course of the lugga and abruptly knelt to touch the seemingly scorched ground with the back of his hand before scooping his claws into the crust of the earth.

"You can't always control what happens," Racxen murmured, dark eyes glowing confidently. "But you can always make a plan." He dug and dug, and at first the only moisture was the sweat of his endeavour. His claws rasped against grit and stone, but he kept digging, his movements deft and sure. Yenna joined him in Wolf form, her paws overtaking his effort. Amber found stones to shore up the sides and Jasper jammed them in.

Finally, their combined shouts of exaltation brought the serpent spilling forward in relief. Droplets of dark, precious water oozed forth from the sand as if by magic, and the friends urged them out with whoops and yells and howls. As the water swelled into a rich pool, the Arraheng lifted his clawed hands high in joyous celebration, letting the fierce sun gleam on the droplets trickling from his grasp. It felt a little like home. It was shallow, but it was water, and it was a wonder.

"One should always do a little digging, before one resigns hope to be lost," the Arraheng promised with a grin, thanking the others with back claps, hugs and, in Yenna's case, ear rubs, as Diberkati sank gratefully into the embrace of the impromptu waterhole.

"Thank you," whispered the serpent. "I can't believe I didn't think of that."

"Do you think a beleaguered mind should be left abandoned, to make such a leap alone?" Racxen pressed gently. Was it his imagination that as her happiness swelled, the pool grew too?

"Zaralathaar said you would help me. I don't think she realised how much." A smile flickered with Diberkati's tongue. Round and round in the muddy water she coiled, and her parched skin grew smooth and slick, and she closed her eyes in happiness.

"She knew more than all of us combined," Racxen grinned in reverent memory as he let some water sieve through Amber's sash into the waterskins and dropped purifying herbs in. "And she would know that, although we take our leave from you now, this is not goodbye. We are not turning our backs on you, Diberkati."

The serpent rippled happily. "It is more than I deserve for you to leave me safely here, before moving on to help others. I can breathe, again. I can sleep. Both are enough reason to live." Thick, sludgy water coated her scales like armour, and she bunched and stretched luxuriously.

Racxen's voice softened encouragingly around her like the sediment. "Do you really think you're unsaveable, when you can turn this small help into surviving the whole Realm?"

One reptilian eye opened and gleamed ambiguously. "I will make no promises. But I am too content, at this moment, to argue with you, Arraheng."

"That's good enough for now," Jasper confided briskly. "We shall think of you happily as we journey on. And we trust you will be safe here, however long it takes us to find drinkable water." His regal features almost relaxed.

"I will last a good while, here," Diberkati agreed languorously. "Go on in good heart."

"We'll find you a bigger expanse," Amber urged. The serpent's words were full of hope, her skin secure and her spirit filled again, but the Fairy knew this fledgling confidence might prove fragile once Diberkati was alone. "We're not asking you to hold out forever: only a little longer. We will be back before this pool dries."

"We hope," Jasper tempered soberly, under his breath. The Prince stepped back, looked to the sun anxiously, soaked his sash and wrung it out into the waterskin, and tried to not focus on how long the whole enterprise had taken.

But it was Yenna's turn at the serpent's side. "We cannot promise when, but we promise we will. In the meantime: feeling better is not a betrayal of how difficult things were, it is a testament to how resilient you always will be. Like the sands, our internal landscapes shift and reshape. Sometimes that shift requires half the Realm—but other times it needs only the words of a friend. The latter might be rarer—"

"But rare still exists," the serpent concluded, tentatively and tenderly. "I accept your offering, when I could not accept Zaralathaar's." Diberkati lifted her great head decisively from the water, splaying her hood and scattering sundrops from her dragonscaled snout. "I will not forget this. I will not forget any of you."

Then she sank, like a thought into the subconscious, or sunlight under one's skin, and as the friends moved off Amber felt lighter. As minutes lengthened into hours, though, she fell into step with Jasper. The Prince seemed even more pensive than usual.

"Are you worried about the oases?" Amber checked in solidarity. "I know initially we just wanted to find Diberkati and thank her, but you did want to map the waterholes after all."

"I am worried about the oases, but even more so about the serpent who slumbers within one," the Prince confessed with a wry grimace. "I am ashamed to say her tentative joy somewhat curtails the possibility of my own, for she is happy again, and the sky remains unchanged. I had dared entertain the notion that, should she feel better, she could somehow return the rains to the Realm."

"I think we all hoped that, to an extent," Amber admitted. "But you know it's too much to put on her, Jasper."

The Prince had the grace to look contrite. "I do, truly. I just hoped it might be enough for her to lift herself out of it."

Amber managed to not roll her eyes. "If effort were enough, few things would be a problem."

"Sorry." The word slipped more quickly from the Prince's lips than it once would have. "I know it's rarely that simple." They walked in silence for a moment.

"I know you want to right the wrong," Amber assured forgivingly, hoping he knew she did admire him for it. "But some things cut into you. Even if you manage to get them out, the fight leaves its own scars."

"Hm," the Prince agreed sadly. There was nothing more to be said. It was as indelible as it was unjust.

"I do have to admit, though," Jasper offered, switching tack accommodatingly, "that strange things happen around this serpent. Sandstorms do not just still like that."

"So, you're an expert on the wilds, suddenly?" Amber grinned easily. "We're all under pressure, so our minds are making connections where there are none to be found. Once we get to the water, we'll feel better. We'll think better. And we'll think of a solution—one which doesn't intrude upon the serpent."

But Jasper stopped suddenly, his attention on his companion no longer. "Speaking of the water, we've been walking for hours. Should we not have found it by now? Are we certain of our direction? Are we sure we are not straying aimlessly?"

Amber couldn't answer. Normally, she would follow Racxen or Yenna to the ends of the Realm unquestioningly and fear nothing. But normally, the Realm itself—its signs and tracks—could be trusted. Now, the alternative crowded terrifyingly, so intrusive and overwhelming that even the vast expanse of the desert was unable to contain it.

To regain her focus, Amber switched between walking along first Racxen's tracks and then Yenna's, following their ephemeral, unmistakeable trails as though by treading inside another's footprints she could indent proof into the sands that they were all still alive and still together, against the rising panic that she might slip beneath the sand like so many grains, and be lost forever amongst the vastness.

As though sensing her spiralling thoughts, Racxen dropped back from leading, and took Amber's hand. She slipped her fingers between his claws in a silent, oft-repeated promise: *We are stronger, too, than this. And, even if we are not, I would keep you by my side, and be glad.* Jasper and Yenna closed in likewise, and all found comfort in the closeness of the others.

By these acts the once-feared-inevitable was squashed beneath so many footfalls and dared not loom nearer for now. Still, it could not be staved back forever.

"This is taking longer than we bargained for," Jasper minimised lightly to break the silence. His speech reclaimed a space for the living, and his companions loved him for it, but they couldn't refute his words.

To Yenna alone, in a whisper, he voiced his true thoughts as he tilted his near-spent waterskin in despair. "Soon, we really will be in trouble. This heat is a killer."

Yenna didn't need to answer. The tightness of her brow spoke of her agreement, and her dread.

But in the next moment a darkness deeper than that dread descended, snuffing the sun's glare, and extinguishing the blistering lash of its heat. A cooling shadow swooped upon the company, as swiftly and completely as an eclipse.

In its suddenness, the companions could neither see nor make sense of it. "Diberkati?" Jasper crowed in relief, casting around to his companions. "So, she can change the weather! Took her a while, but she really chooses her moments, doesn't she?"

"Not this time." Racxen's voice was full of wonder, his eyes having adjusted before the others.' "Look—and look properly."

The friends found themselves squinting, disorientated, into a circle of living darkness, as sand and shafted light swirled amidst the distorted desert. An impression of feather and shadow shifted with the approach of bone-thin, birdlike women wreathed in dust-hued hooded robes.

Harpies. The instinctive knowledge arrived with utter clarity, at the meeting between the once-read and finally-realised. Amber knew these figures, as one would know a dragon even having gone a lifetime without smelling breath-scented smoke on a dream-still night.

Weak and grateful of the relief afforded by the supernatural shade they had been granted, Amber stared in awe at their rescuers. Up close their wings, even folded, were phenomenal: vulture-mottled and griffin-strong, protruding proudly from incisions in their austere attire. Completely different to her own wings, they were folded in the manner of a raptor's, held part-raised, dripping with weight and majesty. Their feathers spread like fingers lifted in worship, as though specialised more for shade-giving than soaring. Talons jutted like terminal phalanges from each joint, emphasising the Harpies' protection and polarity—they clearly thrived out here, in defiance of the desert's unending, bleak sameness.

In unison, the figures lowered their cowls, revealing more clearly their proudly aquiline features and piercingly keen eyes. Like vultures, their feather-cover stopped at their collarbones. And their skin was as beautiful as their feathers. Yenna's skin in woman form kept something of the tawny tone of her desert-wolf coat, and Racxen's was the rich brown of rainsoaked earth, while the Harpies' was deeper still: dark as the burnished seed pods of the desert trees were the hands that reached out to Amber and her companions.

Bone adornments clacked dryly from wizened wrists as the Harpies conducted a practised visual examination of the newcomers. Amber had the feeling each charm signified triumph over a trial, and now formed a talisman. These women wore hardships as enhancements, and Amber felt safe beneath their searching eyes.

"You've always been rather too apt to hero-worship," Jasper admonished dryly, as he stepped smoothly in front of Amber to intercept any attempt she might make at introducing the group. "I'll handle this."

"Not even we can foresee everything that happens in this desert." The beautiful harshness of the Harpy leader's voice broke the deathly grip that silence had seized over the sands: a silence that Jasper's own voice had held no power over, and the Prince wished suddenly he hadn't presumed he was permitted to speak, let alone able to take charge.

The speaker smiled, however, with the grace of one bearing enough authority to afford not to rise to such transgressions. "We witnessed your earlier act of kindness," she explained, looking over each of the companions as though searching for something. "Whether it will prove in our interest to repay it cannot yet be seen, but it is in our power to do so, and that is enough of an answer to satisfy my soul. First: rest."

"We have trespassed upon your lands and your kindness too long already," Yenna protested in apology. "We are sorry for having intruded upon you and have no wish to add to your work."

"Rest is the work of recovery," corrected Inqe smoothly. "It is the single most important gift you can give yourselves right now." Dark eyes twinkled good-humouredly as she added, "And us, for we have no wish to rescue you later."

And so Yenna submitted gratefully with the others, and Jasper held hasty council with the Harpy leader, while her associates stretched forth sheltering wings to shade his companions.

Amber watched the Harpies and, in the presence of such wondrously unusual people, lightheadedly found herself wondering. It had been a while since she'd considered the differences between herself and Racxen. Settling next to the Arraheng, she slipped her hand into his, watched sun and shade shimmer over the claws that were no more frightening than the gentlest fingers. If the Arraheng had evolved to live in the swamps, they would have webbed hands like Hydd. But Racxen had claws. So, the Arraheng hadn't evolved for life in the swamps, they had had to learn to live there. Of course, it wouldn't be as simple as that, but the indisputable fact of it spoke of displacement, and injustice. And she wasn't sure they'd yet really spoken enough about that, together. The realisation swirled and congealed like a still-healing wound. Of course, she had asked him about the past, in the quiet reaches of the night, here and there, when such things could be spoken, and held, and even healed a little. But it saddened her to realise she had misjudged the extent of its reach, and the depth of its hurt. She was going to say something, when she realised he had slipped into an easeful slumber. So, she sighed her pledge, to ask more and ask better, to the oven-hot winds, before she did the same.

Jasper stalked quietly back towards the others, unable to find similar comfort beneath the sheltering wings of the Harpies after his discussion with them. A self-inflicted wound prickled and would not let him settle.

He couldn't deny that the similarity in skin tone between the Harpies and the Arraheng had reminded him unsettlingly of his former prejudices against the latter. He had not looked down on the Selkies, for their webbed fingers. He had certainly not looked down on the Wolfren, for their lupine features. He could hardly even claim to view the Goblins as subhuman when their cruel intelligence proved them smarter than most people. Why, then, had he so long ago dismissed the Arraheng, singularly because of their claws?

As though reading the content of these morose thoughts, a Harpy who had previously remained at the matriarch's side now approached to question the Prince. In response, with the guileless directness of a young woman whose education had skirted the Fairy culture and focused on those far closer and more relevant to her own, she revealed in whispers an aproximate history of the Arraheng Jasper was ashamed to admit he had never before considered, and that he should have earlier realised. After all, the Arraheng had retreated far enough from the Realm's other peoples to develop a second language. And he'd never bothered to consider the reason.

"I tell you this not to encourage guilt, but to offer guidance," reminded the Harpy, and Jasper nodded resolutely.

Seeing his companions still sprawled in slumber, he resolved that self-improvement was more helpful than self-punishment. "Changed behaviour is the best apology," he agreed, sincerely if stiffly, before succumbing, despite his best intentions, to the soporific shade.

The Harpies woke them with a rustling of wings like the shiver of rain across a dying land. Having rarely found herself so refreshed on rising, Amber was almost surprised to find her surroundings as unchangingly empty and expansive as before. But the Harpies inhabited these reaches of the Realm so effortlessly that to find herself amidst them felt intoxicating, instead of isolating. Plus, Amber could feel herself slipping under the thrall of these guides as well as their domain. Those hawklike eyes gleamed with undeniable intensity, but they shone proudly, not desperately: they reflected, instead of lack, the level of resourcefulness and resilience that rendered possible not only survival, but also contentment, in the harshest of habitats. And Amber couldn't look away, for within them gleamed the suggestion that anyone—even Amber—could learn a little of such ways too.

As most of the Harpies swept now into a practised formation that preceded the presence of these newcomers and precluded their involvement, a young woman mayhap a little older than Amber stepped forward to explain with unselfconscious delight. "We are reading the sands for the serpent and making preparations to guide you to our shelter." Her voiced surged with ease across the awed silence that surrounded the others, like a bubbling stream across the sands. Unlike the older women's tightly braided hair, she'd left hers unbound, in seedhead-soft curls, but there was no mistaking that she carried as much strength within her as the elders. "I am Nzizi—I am the herb-finder of our people, and Inqe is our matriarch: the leader of our Order. Follow us."

"I'm not sure we can afford to," the Prince warned, courteous but cautious. He didn't have to look at the others to know they would have followed without hesitation, but someone had to keep a level head, he reminded himself with a mixture of guilt and exasperation. "I thought you guided the dying?"

"And those who are perilously close to death," Nzizi reminded, in a warning both cutting and kind. Her darting eyes were as black as the space between stars, and it felt disconcertingly soothing when she looked at Jasper: as though a shadow fell upon him mercifully along with her gaze. But he could not afford to wait in such shadows now.

"You cannot afford to stay out in this heat," Nzizi retorted, the reproach in her voice soft but substantive. The herbfinder swept up her sheltering wings decisively, lifting shade onto the company once more and causing the friends to almost cry with the relief that came. "We need not see into the future to guess your fate if you stay here," she prompted, as the collective of Harpies assembled behind her in a rustling of feathers that sounded like the turning of fortune. "You must come."

While Jasper dithered, Amber nodded eagerly, passing the water Nzizi offered to Racxen and the others before taking a gulp herself. She really did feel less ill now. The shadows of the Harpies' wings seemed to extinguish fear, as well as quench thirst and cool overheated minds. Falling into step with her rescuers seemed suddenly accomplishable, and as easeful as her now-unlaboured breathing. So, Amber strode forwards and the others followed suite. Nzizi smiled her pleasure and didn't have to say anything.

"Where are you taking us? Why have we not seen you before?" the Prince asked as he caught up, in a last attempt at bluster as he addressed Inqe with something approaching awe.

The Harpy matriarch met his challenge with the grace easily afforded by those possessed of real power. "We are guiding you to our shelters, in the scrubland beyond the sand, so you can recover properly. As for having not seen us before, you have simply not noticed us. In the same way you have not noticed the encroaching drought until it was already upon you."

Jasper opened his mouth to protest, before being stopped by both shame and a sense that her words came from a place of compassion, not contempt.

Inqe's thin smile held its own warmth. "We have greater problems to concern ourselves with than your imprudence," she promised. "And we saw you with the serpent."

Jasper's eyes snapped wide in startled response, but bangles shook from Inqe's narrow wrist as she waved aside his fear. "You misunderstand. We saw your kindness and would offer you our own. We would share our hospitality, and have something more to give you, once you are quite restored, if you can stay a short while."

"Your kindness is great, Matriarch Inqe, but our urgency is greater still," apologised Racxen. "We cannot leave the serpent, Diberkati, for too long. She has borne deep hardship and feels incomparably vulnerable." He realised now that, in contrast to his original assessment, Inqe didn't look much older than the others—just carrying a heavier burden, which only seemed to lift when her sharp gaze settled on Nzizi. And Racxen remembered a time when he, too, had needed to shoulder a burden greater than his years. His heart went out to the Harpies.

"It is our job to accompany those who are dying, in whichever way they wish us to," Inqe agreed solemnly. "But it is a greater sadness to find one unconnected with their body in life, or who feels they wish to die. If your duty lies with her, we will not detain you."

Racxen nodded urgently. "We mean to take stock of the remaining waterholes, and escort her to the one she prefers. Her survival depends on it. She cannot afford for us to delay."

"Something tells me we shared the same land once, Arraheng. I do not doubt you can track as well as our best. You, we need not teach much—and it would hardly be honourable of us to keep you from such a quest." Inqe's smile was one of deep understanding. "In truth it would ease our burden a little as well as our honour to have you stay a while. Yet we were mistaken, and it is not the time to either offer or obtain what we wish."

"You need not offer, but is there something you can yet obtain from one of us, if not all?" As the Harpy matriarch settled her wings, the scent of a land not yet encountered tumbled out between her feathers towards Amber: rich, hot, and impossible to ignore. It lifted memories not yet made towards Amber—and an idea. Racxen and Yenna could help Diberkati better than anyone, and Jasper needed to head plans at home. But in what way was she needed, truly?

"You get the serpent to safety," she suggested to the others, impetuous and certain. "I will stay—if the Harpies will accept me." She looked to Inqe, shy but sure.

At the Fairy's words, the matriarch settled her hawklike eyes on Amber, appraisingly and approvingly. As one, the Harpies lifted their wings as wide as unfettered opportunity, and a breeze lifted across the sands as though whispering its own agreement. Inqe smiled a knowing smile. "You will be as suitable a recipient as any for our gift."

Amber's grin split her face.

A soft chuckle spilled with fondness. "And you may do more with it than most would. It is decided."

"I'm not sure it is. We don't even know your names," Jasper blustered belatedly.

The Harpy leader looked upon him with compassion, her feathers fluttering in the oven-hot air. "You know myself and Nzizi, and the others Amber may not have time to meet. I assure you it will be no imposition to have her with us. In these trying times, we are having to travel further to gather herbs. It will aid us greatly to be able to quickly train someone else to do this, so we can spend more time with our other duties. And before she leaves to rejoin you, we will gift Amber the offering you have kindly accepted."

Needing hear no more, Amber stepped back to steal a moment with Racxen.

"It won't be for long, and the quest for Diberkati doesn't need me," she reminded gently, taking his clawed hands in her own.

Racxen's dark eyes found their stillness in her gaze. "I will always need you, but I'll never stop you," he promised softly. "It's an amazing opportunity, and I am glad for you. But seeing the Harpies and hearing of their home has reminded me of something."

"Something important." Amber saw well-hidden pain in her lover's eyes and didn't step back. She closed the distance between them as though simply to murmur her goodbyes. "Tell me," she urged gently, while the others couldn't hear.

Racxen grimaced in recognition. "It has been a while since I've seen another tribe of similar skin to my own," he conceded. "And they are living out here in the open, rightly unchallenged, and unafraid. Because they have wings instead of claws. I know things are different now, but it brings back how it was. How my tribe had to leave the jungle surrounding the scrubland and go into hiding in the caves."

Amber kept still, her heart overflowing. "I should have known you grew up in the most animal-rich area of the Realm," she smiled sadly. "And that it was where you learnt to be the best tracker in the Realm."

"Being a tracker made more sense back then," Racxen acknowledged with a shaky grin. "I could interpret the movements of predators, keep the tribe out of harm's way. Still, in the marshes, I used those skills just as often: to trail; to make sure the youngsters didn't get lost and get into difficulty around the water." His grin grew broader. "Before they could swim as well as Mugkafb."

Amber pulled him into a hug. "I think you should stay with the Harpies, instead of me. Reclaim lost time." She kissed him encouragingly. "Yenna will be in charge of the rest of us. I'm sure we can manage with the Realm's second-best tracker."

"Undoubtably." Racxen huffed a chuckle and kissed her back softly to thank her. But something in his smile drifted as he sighed. "After all this time, I still feel safer around animals than around most people," he admitted.

Amber held him quietly, until he was ready to continue. "So, I will go with the serpent, and you will have the best time with the Harpies." His smile reached his eyes again and Amber knew he truly meant it. "Engo ro fash. Even Jasper knows they're good people," he reminded with a grin, his voice soft and secret. "And I shall approach them myself in a time far from now, when we have won back the water and there is time for such dreams again."

"I will hold you to that, and help in any way I can." Amber kissed him in confirmation and kept hold of his hand in tight solidarity as they rejoined the others. Elated and emotional as she felt, she knew she owed it to Diberkati to keep their goodbyes short.

The Prince cleared his throat awkwardly as he saw the truth in her eyes. "So, you're going to stay here?" Jasper blanched. "By yourself?"

"Of course not," Amber grinned. "With the vulture women."

Jasper gave that response the eye roll it deserved. "Well, I know you're sure. But do you others agree?"

Racxen fixed his eyes on Amber only. "Sen," he smiled, his eyes alight. "Not that you need my permission, but you have my encouragement always. And this might even become a new apprenticeship."

"Oh, you fools deserve each other," Jasper acquiesced in exasperation.

He gestured helplessly to Yenna. "I suppose you, too, are happy for her to do this?"

"The decision is Amber's, not mine," Yenna retorted, with the steely mildness of one who knows she is right. "But yes. I will entrust my death to the Harpies, one day. Until then, I would trust them with my life."

The Wolf Sister's blazing eyes were as calm as Amber's were eager, and Jasper felt himself relent. "Fine, Amber. Receive just as much hospitality as will assuage the Harpies' sense of honour, accept their gift with gratitude, and then rejoin us."

Nzizi beamed as she refilled the companions' water skins and handed them back to Jasper. "That will give us time to teach you much."

Amber grinned in delight, not entirely certain that the Harpy wasn't including the Prince in that statement.

"You have revived us expertly," Jasper admitted, strangely restored after his time in the life-giving shade of their wings. "Now, we must move on with our quest to find the serpent. The day is cooling, and we will find her water by morning, Racxen is convinced."

"With his eyes and the stars, you will not get lost," Inqe acknowledged with admiration. "Tonight, the moon will be full and the skies clear. I wish you well, until we next meet and after."

Amber's friends hugged her cheeringly, but she found it as hard as ever to let go of Racxen. "It won't be for long," she promised.

"It could be, if you need it to be," Racxen reminded supportively, wrapping his arms around her. "Enjoy it. You're not limited to one adventure, and we shall share another together again soon enough." He rested his forehead against hers, closed his eyes and breathed with her. "Engo ro fash," he promised. "However long it takes my shadow walks with yours, until we are reunited."

A final kiss, an untangling of limbs and fingers, and she was watching Racxen and her friends leave, small against the vastness of the desert.

The Harpies were a flurry of activity; a great sweep of purpose she suddenly felt apart from. Then Nzizi was at her shoulder silently, to assuage her sudden loneliness. "We will show you to our shelters," she offered friendlily. "They are not so far, when you know the way."

Nzizi was right. As the quiet cavalcade advanced, the landscape changed quickly, the yielding sand beneath Amber's feet packing down reassuringly atop a rocky underlay that grew scattered with ramshackle, resilient bushes and shrubs. This new environment punctuated the vast emptiness with the roughest of promises as a sparse and special patchwork of green sprang across the sand. Hopes of prosperity and protection pinned themselves into the unfamiliar prickles and pines, and the scrubland felt a welcome change from the endless vastness of the empty desert beyond.

Away from the exposure of the open plains, Amber felt her heartbeat slow in recognition of arriving at a phenomenal home she was privileged to share. Every wizened tree, every resolute thornbush, was a magnet for settlement and solidarity, acting as a buffer against the desert wind and a diminisher of the blazing sun. As the gathering dusk seemed suspended between day and night, so too seemed the land now suspended between desert and grassland. Bristling vegetation sprang everywhere, catching life amidst its branches and holding it safe. Amber saw proof of such an arrangement all around her now, for in a land that should by all accounts be too barren to sustain life, life still packed itself carefully around her. And as the twisting roots caught sand and bade it settle and turned it into soil, the stalwart silhouettes of the trees urged her likewise: be supported and stay.

Through her wandering reverie Amber realised they were approaching the Harpy settlement now. She was thrilled to witness the bushstrewn wilds converging into oft-walked tracks which reached surely and secretively towards woven-roofed baked-mud round-hut structures that blended expertly into the surrounding scrub. The site looked a hub of assimilation and accommodation: a place both sheltered from and supported by the wilderness.

Amber was entranced. Superficially, in the fierce heat the land flowed and shivered as though about to burst into flames at any minute, but subconsciously it inspired trust. Even this region bore the scars of rain-loss: patches of erosion had lain bare the rock beneath, leaving it protruding through the scant powder of earth like bone jutting through skin—but the Realm here lay restive: a land that could tolerate extremes and still renew itself perpetually. Hope thrived here, as did an astonishing array of animal life: Amber was so excited by her frequent glimpses of prong-point horns and watchful liquid eyes flickering behind the denser bushes, that she clutched Nzizi's arm happily.

"Antelope," Nzizi divulged softly. "They have not left us, yet. I love them, too. Especially the Snub-Horned species. They need to drink often, so they are the ones who best lead you to water."

"You will need to brief our newest assistant on safety when we arrive," Inqe reminded with an arch smile from up ahead. "For there are far more than antelope out here. You will encounter both prey and predator when searching for the herbs we will teach you to identify. But we will arrive at our settlement before darkfall, so there is no hurry for tonight."

The matriarch laughed softly, for instead of seeming shocked the Fairy looked as though she might burst with joy. Encouragingly, Inqe added, "First, I will explain what we do here."

She gestured towards the refuge coming into view through the trees, at the centre of the settlement through which they had strode. Here an organised arrangement of dwellings—some open-sided and scaffolded with iron-strong branches, some walled roundly with homely baked earth, and all crowned deftly with thatch from the leaves of neighbouring trees—stood tall in the clearing ahead, clustered around a stone-cool, dark hall which was protected by a half-wall of intricately piled rock fragments mortared with sand.

"We are a community of caring, not healing," Inqe reminded soberly, as Amber gazed in silent impressed astonishment. "Not all ills can be cured, but there is still much that can be done. As I mentioned earlier, your role here will be to gather herbs. There are plants, I am sure you know, that ease both pain and fear. We require a ready supply, and your efforts will free our time to provide what easement we can."

Amber nodded willingly. "Of course."

Inqe regarded her appraisingly. "Your acceptance is refreshing," she noted approvingly. "Some shun us because we live with the dying. But no-one should pass through the final gateway alone."

"Zaralathaar didn't," added Nzizi consolingly, remembering the Fairy's connection with the Water Nymph. "She came here, before the end. She wouldn't tell me why: I think she wanted to see the truth about the drought and the remaining water. She pored over every inch of our stores before she left. She was adamant that she need not stay; that another would come to her aid. I foresaw it on the winds, and I see today she was right." The Harpy's gaze rested softly on Amber. "The Water Nymph had many friends."

"Nzizi has some vision into the future," Inqe explained protectively to the Fairy. "Not every Harpy does. It is best for such an individual to be granted rest and distance, but not all accept such advice." The fondness in Inqe's eyes was palpable.

"I can hardly concern myself with the future, given the gravity of the present," Nzizi reminded in justification. "And, anyway, my visions have faded since then, overtaken by the urgency of our current situation. My focus is where it should be," she added loyally.

"As it ever has been. I have never doubted you," Inqe reassured. "But we can no longer rely on the winds to guide our steps, as we once did. The patterns of the Realm are changing. They grow ill."

"Exactly. I do not need to see the future through foresight," Nzizi added, furrowing her brow sadly. "I see it in the cracks splitting apart the Realm, and in the clouds that scud across our land laden with rain that never falls. But we still have some power," Nzizi pointed out cheerfully, determined to not worry their guest. "In our form, and in our feathers. It has been a long time since we've had anyone to teach. I'm nearly ready, Inqe. Can Amber be my student?"

"You mean: can teaching her be your initiation, as you saw tracking a Sand Giant was mine a few short years ago?" The matriarch's eyes gleamed presentiently. "Yes, Nzizi. I would trust no-one above you. You are no longer my apprentice. You are now Amber's mentor. Just—" She smiled as Nzizi's squeal of delight eclipsed all chance of words for a moment. "—please remember how hazardous a landscape this can be for one unused to it. Amber may be versed in the dangers of some of the wildest reaches of our Realm, but the deserts are as cavernously hungry as the northern icescapes and stoke a heat deadlier than their frozen reaches. Plus, she needs to learn to live safely in close proximity to our wildest animal neighbours—before you can even consider teaching her the complexities of herb identification."

Nzizi nodded readily. "We'll start tomorrow."

Inqe's eyes crinkled knowingly. "You started the moment she stepped in."

She turned to Amber, and her heart softened at the Fairy's eagerness. "But yes," she conceded. "Nzizi will show you around, and you will start in earnest tomorrow."

Her smiled widened, and she looked for a moment both younger and more carefree: a twin flame to Nzizi. "You cannot know what you have let yourself in for," she promised Amber. "But I hope you will enjoy finding out."

Amber grinned excitedly, and watched in awe as the other Harpies who had accompanied them bowed and took their leave, returning to practised duties. Moving like living wraiths, they shifted peaceably in shadowed symmetry; actions graceful and at ease, wings unfurled to cast life-giving shade upon long-parched ground. As their otherworldly voices lifted, Amber felt tears well behind her lids, clamouring to fall despite the dryness. In the midst of the wilderness, these voices were civilisation.

Inqe smiled, understanding. "Welcome to the Harpy shelters. You are home."

She enfolded Amber gently in her wings, before ushering her towards Nzizi encouragingly.

Amber took a deep breath, filled with the incomparable scent of the wild. "I can't thank you both enough."

Nzizi beamed triumphantly as Inqe swept away. "It is getting late. I will show you to our quarters." The swift-setting sun sank before them, and the darkness seemed to imbue the scene with even more magic as Nzizi linked arms companionably, and pointed out as many dusk-awakening things as she could to help the Fairy feel at ease.

Amber found herself grinning like a winglet as she felt a new Realm unfurl. Campfire flames danced in the distance, stretching out corners of safety far into the night, and the stone pathway she took with her companion shone amidst the dust and moonlight, while along the way gyptian eyes glinted like jewels in the darkness.

"Do not be alarmed by the vultures," Nzizi advised, her own eyes soft and unworried. "They are our oldest friends, and guardians of this land and its souls."

As Nzizi navigated expertly the paths Amber could not yet guess at, she continued her story as well. "Fairies are descended from Dartwings, so I hear. Well, our spirit animals are vultures, in the same way." Then the Harpy apprentice lowered her voice, as though she barely dared mention what she must speak of. "Sometimes Goblins come too close here, and try to kill the vultures, to make charms from their bones or feathers. As though a charm wrought from violence could ever bring anything other than suffering and shame! We take nothing from the vultures, we ask nothing of them. We simply revere them quietly and seek to emulate them in our ways. After all, vultures are vital," she promised. "They deal with the aftermath of death, without causing it. They do no harm to living creatures. They clear and clean—they even remove disease from the Realm, in their own small way." The Harpy regarded the nearest flames quietly. "Some say they see into the future. To harm one would bring destruction; could tear away the fabric of the future. And I cannot help but fear the present is doing a vigorous enough job of destroying itself. Still, there is space yet for love. We must not become so consumed by anger that it leaves no energy left for action."

Before Amber could form a suitably supportive and solemn response, it was as though a film had slid back from across Nzizi's eyes, and her voice lightened playfully again, as her gaze skipped softly across her surroundings once more. "Mind the spiders, snakes, and scorpions," she pointed out in delight. "They have wisdom too, but we must live carefully alongside them."

And indeed, their gait as erratic as the path's flickering torchlight, Amber glimpsed the button-black creatures scurrying hither thither near to their feet. The sheer amount of life astonished her. To think, that she would get to be part of this for a while!

She soon got a better look at the antelope, too. Swivel-eared faces turned to watch her every move, and she hoped dearly that they would soon be as unperturbed by her as they currently were by Nzizi.

"They tend not to stray too far from our last remaining waterhole." Nzizi pointed it out, through a tangle of vegetation. Like most things the Harpy had shown her, Amber found she could only see the pool, squatting as dark as any other shadow, once Nzizi had demystified it. "I hope your friends find one that lasts longer."

Amber grimaced sympathetically in agreement as she peered uncomfortably at the waterhole, such as it was: a mud pool whose darkened sides, even beneath the forgiving gaze of the moon, spoke longingly of the fullness it used to enjoy. Still, her gaze lingered there less in fear and more in amazement that the Harpies could continue so calmly, in the face of such hardship.

Nzizi smiled. "You see the antelope around us? They are closer to death than any of us, but do they stay shivering in the scrub? No: they lift up their hooves and advance into the Realm, living their fullest lives irrespective of the shadows that spill upon them. I might be closer to the vultures in descent, but I will always be closer to the antelope in spirit. Ah—" She refocussed immediately, changing the subject. "Mudwort."

She reached expertly through the cluster of protective thorns and plucked a sample, held it out to Amber and let the Fairy smell the fresh fragrance, feel the fleshy leaves, witness the latticed colouration clear even beneath the silvery moon. "It needs standing water to grow, of course," Nzizi explained, in her element. "One of our most prized plants. Inqe uses it in the most effective draughts to ease one's mind at the end. This is the most significant species you will ever need to identify—and the one we will most frequently ask you to gather. Our hall is far from here, in the heat, so we might need your assistance with it more than you think."

Amber nodded gravely and rolled the precious sample in her hands, trying to commit it fully to memory, promising herself that she would examine it every hour until she had locked it into her mind.

She was still fidgeting with it meditatively when they drew up at a round hut, crouched welcomingly amidst the tangle of thornbush on the outskirts of camp.

At the door, Nzizi froze, as though realising they had reached another threshold also. If she hadn't earlier intimated otherwise, Amber would have sworn a premonition had visited the Harpy, for her previously darting eyes grew distant, and she clutched Amber's hand suddenly with real insistence. "I will teach you navigation skills," she promised earnestly. "But if those flee your mind in times of trouble, remember this for now: There is a tree close by—beyond camp but close to our borders; the tallest one I know, crusted with thornlike bark. If a Harpy wishes to consider the future, they climb this tree. The climb and the view alike bring insight. This tree is visible from any horizon—head to it and you will return to us. One of us visits each day. Should we be parted, I promise I will go there every night, in case you need me."

The necessity of Nzizi's pledge made her shiver, but the commitment with which she offered it quashed Amber's fears. Infused with the solemnity of the situation, Amber nodded in earnest, and the weight in the air seemed to lift slightly as Nzizi returned the gesture, visibly relieved.

The Harpy laughed decisively, breaking the spell. "Recently I have spent many a night up that tree, but my vision remains the same," she admitted cheerfully. "Still, the deeper the night, the clearer the stars, and the strongest of allegiances are forged in fire. But for now, there is no fire to worry about—there is only the hearth of a home."

She creaked the door open with a flourish.

Blinking back sudden tears of emotion, Amber gasped appreciatively. The thatch had adorned itself with a variety of sticky-footed reptiles, and it was just as well that a long net draped atop the neat little beds.

Both beds. "Are you okay with me sharing?" Amber blurted, suddenly ashamed of intruding.

"Certainly." Nzizi beamed. "It has been a long time since I've been able to make friends with someone who will, at least most probably, live a while yet."

Her confession caught in Amber's chest.

"Also, there will be fewer predatory prints outside in the morning than if you were to spend the night alone."

Amber wasn't sure she was joking.

"You've had a lot to take in, today," Nzizi counselled, beckoning the Fairy inside and checking quickly underneath the beds with a practised eye. "Let your worries tangle into the thorns and leave them outside for tonight."

Amber beamed her thanks, swished aside the net, and threw herself happily onto the spare bed. Unexpectedly, considering the nature of the Harpies' sacred duties, Amber hadn't for a long time felt so alive.

She watched through drowsing lids as Nzizi pattered outside to tend the torches wending the long paths interlacing the shelters.

Amber saw her rejoin Inqe in the flamelight, bearing accidental witness while the two Harpies conversed, as the breeze lifted their voices like feathers.

"There are souls out here, Nzizi, so I must stay," Inqe murmured. "The night is long, and I would not have them be alone."

Nzizi nodded, with the lightness of one knowing love. "My night will feel longer without you next to me."

Amber watched Nzizi slip her hand into Inqe's, watched Inqe brush her temple with a kiss in response. She sighed deeply in satisfaction and rolled over to give them privacy.

Birdlike footsteps fluttered along the path and Nzizi darted in again, wreathed in smiles as she busied about, ushering out a few of the more suspect small cohabitants of the hut before shuttering the windows as best as she could with what she had.

Amber sat up companionably to greet her, the net barely a veil between them, and with a gentle smile Nzizi snuffed the lights so that only the soft glow of the night itself remained. Standing beside the bed as though in preparation for an intimate ritual, she unfolded her wings, and stretched them fully, luxuriously, before attending to each feather. Amber felt a sudden flush of awe. The Harpy was showing her her true self. She'd always assumed vultures were stooping, skulking—and yet she'd never seen someone hold themselves as proudly as Nzizi. Her wings held all the colours of the earth, and as much power. Even more so, for a few feathers seemed to be missing, but Nzizi was the picture of balance and wholeness. Amber swallowed. Had she ever felt about her own wings this way when she'd had them?

She watched, entranced, as a feather fluttered down, and imbued the dry ground with its vitality.

Nzizi caught her staring, and grinned. She picked the feather up and twirled it playfully. "My mother used to say, 'Be careful in whose company you show your feathers, let alone shed them.'"

She took Amber's hands, delighted to be able to explain. "Our wings are used more for sheltering than for soaring. They have lost some of their use, over the generations. But our feathers still mean everything. Different ones are said to manifest, or at least enhance, different abilities. You can read a wing as you might read a palm: a specific secondary is a wayfinder, a particular tertiary detects poison. There is even a pair of outermost primary feathers—the pinions—which if you gift to another, you can link your sight symbolically, to represent the joining of souls."

Amber squeezed her hand. "You're missing a pinion feather! You've linked your sight with someone?" She was so thrilled. She was beginning already to love Nzizi in the manner of Ruby, and wished desperately for her happiness. What she had seen on the pathway made sudden sense.

"Not yet." Nzizi preened self-consciously. "I merely have set the feather aside, to show it is not available, in case another should wish it. Our culture does not permit it to be spoken of openly, at first. There are too many shadows in the desert, too many hungry ghouls. One must be guarded."

She laughed at the excitement in Amber's face. "But there are ways of telling each other if you know how. Perhaps you have seen another, with a matching feather missing?"

An indelible memory flooded, of the arrangement of feathers when the Harpy leader had stretched her wing over her protectively in the desert. "Inqe!" Amber fair shrieked in her excitement. "When we were in the . . . Oh, Nzizi! She feels the same!"

Nzizi dabbed sudden tears. "Ah, in these times it must seem wasteful to cry. But we must live life even more fully, in case it ends, no?"

Amber found her own eyes watering.

"It feels good to tell someone," Nzizi confessed. "But look, the moon is watching. We must get some sleep."

"I can't keep you away from her!" Amber exclaimed, aghast. "Go!"

Nzizi's smile curled shyly. "But I have all my life to spend with her. When time is short, hospitality to guests is more important."

Amber's heart panged to remember the times she'd missed Racxen. "If you don't go, you and I are going to have a falling out, and I won't accept this gift you say is so important," Amber warned.

Nzizi's smile split her face, and she tucked the bed net reverently around Amber before slipping outside.

Amber lay there blissfully as the heat-thickened darkness wrapped around her like a cocoon. Noises filtered through, but she could listen forever to these sounds: the whistling coos of birds, the repetitive shrills of insects, even the improbable, porcelain-delicate tinklings of frogsong from the waterhole, were the nearest thing to silence she needed out here. Inhabiting the quietude without intruding upon it, they slipped inside her soul and ushered her towards sleep.

And she must have slept, for dawn spilled urgent light as Nzizi burst in, caked in dust and sweat, with wings heaving. "Sand Giant!"

"What?" Amber's mind conjured scorpions, Venom-Spitters, and predators beyond imagining all at once.

But Nzizi's face was flushed with excitement as much as urgency. "It's stuck in the waterhole. It needs our help. A Sand Giant, Amber! Think of it! Come on!"

As confused as she was excited, and just about remembering to shake out her boots before she squashed her feet back into them, Amber stumbled out of bed and after Nzizi, trying to conjure the memory of an image as well as a name.

An intoxicating scent, like dust mingled with herbivorous breath, bloomed in the heat of the air outside. It conjured ideas of hay and horses, and something far older—something that had roamed the Realm eons earlier. Snorts rang out, but Amber could see nothing yet. The air seemed to shake with the impossibility of containing something so wild.

She barraged after Nzizi to the waterhole, into a scene spun with splashes and shouts. It was hard to tell what was mud and what was creature, initially. A rumbling groan shook earth and ear equally, and a frightened eye as wise and wrinkled as the Song Weaver's gleamed fearfully from its state of entrapment in thickening mud.

"She's weakened by the drought, and in turn the drought has worsened the mud, as well as made the creature desperate," Nzizi warned in despair, amidst the dust-smell and sand-confusion. "And she's distressed and disorientated. She could be dangerous."

This, then, was a Sand Giant. Amber suddenly felt like Mugkafb reading about Gorfang. She had loved these creatures for years from afar— from books – with a love that was no less real for it. And she was seeing one now, in reality.

The creature managed to shake free her head, and the image seared Amber like a brand: a moon-curved horn arching above a trunklike fleshy proboscis, the mud caking her skin so solidly it blurred her outline between the realms of real and mythic. The wholeness of the creature arrived in Amber's soul as though bypassing all logical perception, and she knew the vision would stay bright in her mind through any number of ages. She felt like she was witnessing a mirage. The creature lived, and so hope remained. But the dragging mud that clung to the Sand Giant seemed more solid by the moment.

"She has been driven to exhaustion," Inqe warned. "We have to get her out before her strength fails entirely." Her bangles, her cowl, everything non-essential was off, and the churnings of the waterhole coated her feathers like oil. But the land itself seemed to come alive at her efforts, and as the strugglings of the Sand Giant increased, as though infused with the collective strength of the Harpies, with a sudden squelching heave the Giant shook free with a great effort.

Inqe fell back in relief. "Sand Giants used to furrow water with their feet—long ago when the Realm was green and growing," she managed, in teaching mode even now. "But they cannot stamp water from lifeless sands. At least this one will live, for now. She will move off into the wilderness, and we will likely not see her again."

But the struggle wasn't over, for a squeal at odds with the bulk of the creature sounded, and then she trumpeted pleadingly.

Inqe's face hardened in despair. "She wasn't just trapped—she's hurt—we have to get her back," the matriarch hissed in frustrated alarm, noting the Sand Giant's agitation despite being freed. "Her wounds will kill her if they are not cleaned. Our work here is not done. We need to subdue her enough to tend to her. Get a cloth over her eyes and she will calm enough."

Amber seriously doubted the Harpy's version of *enough*, but she nodded quickly. "What do we need to do first? Surround her?"

"Exactly. I will flush her this way, and you will hold her here." It didn't sound like Inqe doubted their success for a moment.

Amber saw the worry in Nzizi's eyes as her matriarch rushed forwards, and she reached out her hand in solidarity.

Nzizi clasped it tightly. "Stand with us."

It was a suggestion, not a command—but it intimated so much trust and conviction in her abilities that Amber found herself saying yes with equal confidence.

The ground trembled with the Sand Giant's approach, but their resolve didn't.

The surrounding bush splintered into the sight thundering towards them, and time seemed to slow. Taking her lead from the Harpies Amber froze, not in fear, but to sustain the gossamer spell that had woven this truth: that they were against all odds sharing space together.

In response the Sand Giant, however she might have interpreted the actions and intentions of creatures so different from herself, saw the reality before her: the line would not be broken. She skidded, dust billowing, and huffed her indecision, as primal as the earth itself.

Amber felt caught in this moment, knowing somehow it would prove one of those searing keystones that, however fleeting, becomes enough, stretched full by the strength of experience it contains. The fly buzzing at her ear, the dull ache of the sun on her neck—everything was both heightened and eclipsed in the presence of such an animal.

The essence of the Sand Giant filled the air, filled her senses, filled her soul. She heard her own soft breathing continue: instead of being shocked into arrest, her whole body had exhaled, learnt to be truly still, and had quietly continued.

Time shifted now, and distorted into a different space as each side tested each other. A rumbling snort rolled from the animal: a plea as much as a warning. The ground shook with her stampings, but Amber clutched the sweat-slicked hands either side of her and felt safe.

"Hold the line!" Inqe's voice cut cleanly through the confusion of the suffocating air. The sun pressed down like a headache, and they all held firm.

The situation stretched interminably: it felt so real it might not only overwhelm her, but also outlast her. And Amber, hand in hand with Harpies either side, and with the Sand Giant snorting before them, knew suddenly that here was exactly where she belonged; precisely where she wanted to be. With heart-thudding clarity she felt the repeated thunder of ancient feet pummelling the arid ground. And yet, as the Sand Giant's mock charges gathered pace, standing her ground felt the most natural thing in the Realm.

But she couldn't afford to get complacent. She rehearsed the plan against the beats of her heart: *Cover her eyes, clean her wounds, apply mineral clay.* As a briefing it had indeed been brief but, fired with urgency, Amber awaited the signal with the others with eager readiness.

The Sand Giant's next charge must have held some different quality Amber hadn't recognised, for now Inqe's clear voice carved the chaos into commands, and as the Harpies took position Amber swiftly draped her sash across the wrinkle-sunken eyes and struggled to knot it securely as the creature was guided to the ground by Inqe, her wings full-stretched and fearsome. Sprawling onto her knees Amber held on to the sash and managed to wrap it twice more round the great head, murmuring explanations and apologies in equal measure into the great swivelling mud-caked ears as the Sand Giant puffed and blew and finally settled, sightless and hopefully soothed, as her companions worked swiftly.

Nzizi rocked back onto her heels in triumph as she finished deftly applying the mineral-rich healing clay to the creature's wounds, while the other Harpies mantled the creature protectively for a moment longer, shielding her from the savage sun while Inqe orchestrated their extraction.

"I hope the Sand Giant stays safe once she leaves here," Nzizi admitted, breathlessly tired. "People think that by killing such creatures, they can encroach on the land. But the one cannot live without the other, and neither can we."

Amber shivered. "People eat them?"

Nzizi grimaced sadly. "My ancestors are vultures—I wouldn't lose sleep over anyone eating enough to survive. What motivates these killings is greed, and lusts as warped and irrational as they are revolting. There has developed a false conviction that a Sand Giant's skin bestows all manner of blessings and excuses all kinds of iniquities."

Amber shuddered, and stroked the creature's roughened, mud-crusted cheek protectively. It felt as though she were caressing the earth itself.

Nzizi swallowed. "There are those who think that in a time of water scarcity, anything can be justified. But we know that when the Sand Giants are plentiful, they improve access to water: they dig for it with their horns and hooves, and with their great bulks on their wanderings they open passages through clogged reeds and stop old ways closing up."

She paused, reflecting. "I wish I could convince people that being in a Sand Giant's live presence is blessing enough, and that breathing the same air as them bestows a vitality impossible to quantify. To know a being so wild and rare has graced you with an acknowledgement devoid of fear must surely transcend any desire to claim a piece of it in conquest. But it's easier to think in such ways when one has the privilege of education. I am blessed to live in a society where I can make such assumptions."

Amber nodded slowly, full of thought. As she cradled the Sand Giant's blunt head, heavy as the land come alive, she knew she wanted to stay in such a society for as long as she could.

Inqe signalled and they all scrambled back. The Sand Giant lurched to her feet, the ground shuddering with the power of a future being remade, and then the bush reformed around the creature and reclaimed her. She was gone—but she had been. She was out there now: back where she belonged.

Amber stood in silent tribute, exchanging elated grins with the Harpies to seal the memory away safely. As the rest of them turned away, Amber stood in the space the Sand Giant had left behind, and she felt like she belonged as well.

The morning's adventure infused the whole day's learning, until Amber and Nzizi could return to their hut. They sat up late into the night, talking of all that had happened, and might happen. Thrilled that Amber was thinking of staying, the young Harpy was attempting to explain the more nuanced aspects of their role.

"We watch over," she summarised. "For however long is needed. We do not hasten, and we cannot slow. But we stay, and we ease. This is our most sacred duty. We do not intrude, and we do not abandon. We are not here to make those who come here better. We are not here to *make* them do or be anything. They come not because they are ill, but because they are dying—and not from something that can be reversed, but simply because their life is coming to an end. They need strive no longer; they know they can rest here in their own way. When one no longer needs to eat, one is not distressed by the urge to eat. When one no longer needs to breathe, one is not distressed by the urge to breathe." She paused. "We wish to facilitate the kind of death we would like to be granted. A death in the presence of a Harpy is an easeful relief."

Amber listened in silence, both harrowed and impressed.

Then Nzizi sighed deeply and smiled brightly. "It is an agreeable distraction to be able to focus on herbs and teaching you. Tomorrow, there will be more to learn. And the next day—and the one after!"

The next morning, Amber yawned and stretched luxuriously, awake before Nzizi. She lay there, enjoying the sensation of dawn unfurling its petals outside. For the first time in a long time, she felt entirely at home in the Realm. Exactly as it was. Exactly as she was. Peace settled over the hut like a sand lizard finding the most comfortable stone to bask on. Was it wrong to enjoy the heat when the long cold days of the icefields were behind her? It certainly felt unusual, to look forward utterly to something that she could very well utterly fail in. But she was grinning from ear to ear as Nzizi stirred and summoned her.

And so, Amber's days blurred pleasantly into simple rhythms: rising with the sun, accompanying Nzizi on her herb-finding (even though she could at first do little to help but carry the baskets), studying plant specimens and learning about their uses, and savouring the camaraderie that formed itself around campfires in the darkened wilderness every evening.

In between her studies she assisted Inqe by sitting with those who were dying: making sure they were never alone, and summoning a willing Harpy any time medication for pain or fear was needed. Mostly, she spent a lot of time holding hands and hearing about pasts, and in truth it didn't feel like much time at all.

When the Harpies had time, Amber made sure to learn as much as she could from both the herb-finder and the matriarch. Nzizi was a trickster—but not in a mean way: in a taking-her-out-of-herself and chasing-away-the-fear way. In a reminding-her-she-was-supposed-to-be-having-fun way. In a life-was-an-adventure-to-be-lived-not-a-problem-to-be-solved way. In complement, Inqe's breadth of knowledge was as prodigious as the depth of her integrity. She even, as an aid to finding mudwort, taught Amber how to identify Sand Giant tracks. Once she'd learnt them Amber began seeing them everywhere; they were old partial prints but she grew to recognise them gratefully: every time she saw them they were a relief, pressed into the sand like fingers rubbed against a headache.

Even the environment became her teacher. The buzzing of insects became a kind of clock: the time could be told simply by the content of their chorus. Similarly, while the constant gossip of the birds was at first an enjoyable embarrassment of otherness and a reminder of a language she liked listening to, but had not yet managed to learn, it gradually began to become understandable—no, *she* grew into understanding—until it became her most constant companion, her dearest delight. Specific calls, that had at first seemed only a background distraction, she learnt now to listen to for reassurance or warnings.

The hum of life all around her became as much a part of her as the sound of her own breath, or the sense of her own pulse. The night felt like night, the day felt like day. Everything felt securely real, and that was deeply reassuring, despite and due to the differences this landscape held from every other in the Realm. The desert had felt empty—expansively, invitingly so—but here, life crowded in at every crack and corner. Spiders dripped from webs at every beam, scorpions pressed into every corner, lizards slipped under every door, and snakes spilled irreverently from gaps in the walls.

The plant life demanded respect, too. One day Nzizi noticed Amber staring curiously at an unusual specimen, entangled in a thicket near to where they were gathering herbs. "We call that one 'fire apple'," the Harpy warned. Her usually darting eyes were still and serious.

Amber grimaced. "It blooms after fire?"

"No, after rain—but inhaling its scent at the wrong time is like breathing flames. Now *this* tree is not one you want to be sitting under, when the rains come back. In a deluge it releases a sap so potent that even breathing the air around it is dangerous. The larger groves of this species are far away, in the wildest stretches of the scrubland. Still, you must promise me, Amber. If a single raindrop ever falls from the sky again, you stay away from this tree."

Amber nodded quickly and consigned the warning to memory, alongside the memory of rain itself. Out here, she had more to think on than drought and dangers.

For the first time in a very long time, everything felt clear—including her role. With that clarity came calm. In the past, every new job and even the training for it had felt like a nonstop confusion of questioning herself, doubting her capabilities, and being unsure of her direction. Here, though, she picked skills up more naturally. She was new and awkwardly unknowing, but she found she could be herself, and it was enough. Out here, amidst the scurry-scattered silence and the reassurance of the sun, she could give her all without it being too much.

And on the days she struggled, Nzizi would be there, softening her beaming smile and throwing her arms around Amber, until she felt steady again. Similarly, on the nights when Nzizi's duties had been long and the end had been no less saddening for its inevitability, Amber would find her, and bring her water, and ask for just one more look at a certain new-growing shoot, pushing its tendrils of hope up through the ground despite all the dryness and drought. And Nzizi would say in her soft voice: 'I know why you brought me out here, and I am glad.'

Amber wanted to reply, *I may not know why you brought me out here in the first place, but I am glad, too.* She didn't quite manage to voice all that, but on one such night, when they had found something else awe-inspiring to investigate—a track, or a twig, it never seemed to matter to Amber, she drank them in equally—Nzizi, watching the Fairy walk around in wonder, admitted: "I used to think the only way to realise how big the Realm is was when it rained, and I could hear the droplets fall on all the places I couldn't see. But the moonlight will suffice." And Amber realised what she might be saying, and her heart filled with hope.

Still, she stored up all the memories, in case she'd need them later. Because she knew that currently it was a half-realised dream: she was only here at the hospitality of the Harpies instead of really helping them. She needed to prove herself if she wanted to stay.

In this matter, the Sand Giant came to her rescue a few days later quite unexpectedly. As Amber headed towards the welcome shade of camp after collecting the samples from her day's training list, she felt instinctively that the usually unbreachable calm of the site had been punctured.

Nzizi was at the largest shelter tent, checking a supply cabinet with the practised ease of one determined to not show anything was wrong.

Amber hastened to her side as though merely in greeting and started to fold sheets so as not to cause alarm. "What is it?" she breathed to the herb finder in an undertone.

"A Dartwing brought a message from your friends: they have found a waterhole for the serpent—which is well for them, and I am so glad for you." Nzizi meant it, but she wrung her hands. "Yet we have an ulterior motive for wishing your journey there, for the Sand Giant came back here overnight, and she has torn through every scrap of mudwort." The Harpy was full of concern instead of condemnation. "Poor soul. She must have needed it badly, to have eaten that much."

Inqe appeared, as though only to receive the sheets from Amber. She flashed a worried glance. "It means our supplies are now dangerously low. I hope it does not sound a discourtesy to admit I would rather not send away a healer to find the herb we most desperately need. It would be a great service to us for you to find some, at the waterhole your friends have reached, and bring it back for us."

"Collect you some mudwort?" Amber checked in relief. "I do not know quite the 50 I should—but I know 20 very well. Mudwort I could find blindfolded." Her eyes shone with the truth of it. It wasn't a boast, but an assurance. And a plea.

Nzizi was gazing imploringly at Inqe, and Amber continued quickly; realising how important this was. "I've walked in the wilds long enough, and you've taught me more than you know these past weeks," she urged. "I can do this. I'm ready."

"You have made a start, and a good one," Inqe conceded gently, fixing Amber with an appraising look. "I am not sure it is wise or fair to ask you for more. Still, you are good with Sand Giant tracks," the Harpy leader admitted. "Our Sand Giant will need to find another water source, now that our pan is almost empty—so she will be heading to the same site as your friends. I will give you guidance to reach it, but we cannot go with you. And we must ask you to return immediately with the Mudwort. We do not have much time."

"It will be several days from here," Amber acknowledged, trying not to balk at the thought of tracking so far alone. "But I told you I would help you in any way I could, and I meant it. I'm only relieved to be able to do so now."

Inqe's smile was both grateful and guilt-filled. "I should be urging you to return to your friends for good, not hoping you will come straight back."

"I have friends in more than one place," Amber promised. "And I will race back, as though my footsteps can summon water like the Sand Giants'."

Inqe bowed deeply. "Then you are ready for what we shall give you, in preparation for your journey."

Chance and Choice

The matriarch drew a series of deft directions in the sand for Amber to commit to memory. After that, Amber packed hastily, trying to squash down the sense of loss as tightly as she was squashing down her sleeping mat into her pack. The urgency of her mission couldn't quite eclipse her sinking awareness that this would be her last assignment for the Harpies. Once she returned with the Mudwort, they would need her no longer. The candle of this memory would burn bright all the days of her life, and a candle it would remain: it would never burst into full and glorious fire, but neither would it ever dwindle away to ash.

Amber swallowed against gathering tears. She'd miss everything out here. She'd miss the *light*. There had to be a different name for such luminosity as was found out here: she'd never seen such hues elsewhere. In contrast to the harsh rays that pierced the desert, these splashed radiantly across the driest grasses, as though in compensation for the lack of water. It wasn't a dying light: it was a blaze of glory. And if the light was golden, the memories were even more so.

Nzizi appeared at the doorway, her movements as urgent as Amber's. The room felt suddenly crowded with things unsaid, but Nzizi's breath was hot as the desert as she closed the distance between them. In a smooth motion, with a scattering of dust and powder-down, Nzizi plucked a shaft from her wing and held it, not in clutched triumph, but in tender-fingered offering.

"Until I see you again, keep this."

Amber stared at the feather: as long as her forearm, as mottled as the drought-clung veldt and clung with as much residual power. She took it reverently.

"A part of me will always be with you," Nzizi promised. "I am not so much a pathfinder as Inqe—but I hope this feather will guide you, should you ever feel lost." The Harpy smiled, fierce and fond.

Overcome, Amber hugged her tightly. "I will carry it always, as I will hold you in my heart." Anticipation of her journey writhed like a snake within her, but she felt now in addition surrounded by a powerful calm, which lifted her like a vulture's wings above such exhaustive passions.

"You are ready," Nzizi accepted. "Follow me."

Amber knew she would come back briefly, but still, it felt like the end of an era as she cast a final look around the simple cell that had quickly become a well-loved home. A sombre air permeated it now that late-night laughter no longer smoothed the angles. But memories floated like sunmotes into the rafters, and the baby birds that had woken her in the soft pre-sun hours would grow up here. Nzizi would move into Inqe's quarters, and in time someone else would stay here.

Nzizi smiled restoratively. "Do not be troubled. There is one gift left."

Wonderingly, Amber followed her along a path she didn't yet know, to where the secret might be found. Hastening through the bush, she realised painfully how much she would miss this.

"Antelope! Spiral-horned. You haven't seen this one, yet." Nzizi grabbed her arm in excitement, and for a moment Amber forgot all talk of a gift: the present was enough in itself. For a second, she still couldn't discern anything amongst the blur of bracken and bramble—but then she glimpsed it, and the whole Realm seemed to come into focus. The twenty yards or so between them seemed to disappear, and all her anxieties about leaving vanished too. The creature's presence seemed to invite the watchers into a parallel, timeless zone they were privileged to inhabit.

"They frequent only places no-one else has been for weeks," Nzizi breathed.

The knowledge stuck like an emotion in Amber's throat, and she nodded her pledge to remember it. With a snorting huff, the antelope moved away, holding his proud horns against his back to duck under the cover of the vegetation. But she breathed the air it had breathed. What a time to be alive!

"They come here more often than we do," Nzizi explained. "Our ceremonies are less frequent than they used to be, now our workload is heavier." She looked spirit-lightened from the encounter, and Amber hugged her in celebration.

With her attention refocused on her surroundings after the antelope's departure, Amber realised just how wild a section they'd arrived at. Tangled within the thorns and hanging seedpods, nestled beneath branches of all descriptions, waited a dilapidated lean-to as awe-inspiring as any temple.

It housed, as an antiquated library might house an accumulation of the most ancient and venerated texts in a jumble of haphazard prestige, a phenomenal collection of earthenware jars and amphoras packed ramshackle together upon endless precarious shelves.

Amber tiptoed into the dusty shade after Nzizi, mute with curiosity. Her gaze wandered in astonishment across the piles of vessels stacked together snugly. She felt as though she were stepping into a company of wisdom dating from the earliest days of the Realm.

"This is where we keep our most prized possessions." Nzizi smiled at the Fairy's suitably open-mouthed expression. "Not even Inqe knows everything on these shelves," she admitted, her voice warning and welcoming in equal measure. "We keep our best grain, reserves of medicine, incense: everything of greatest value here. The vulture presence keeps away the small creatures who would take the shelter's harvest for their own."

Amber swallowed. She realised she would even miss the meat-and-acid stench of the ever-watchful raptors. But, veiled in cobwebs and settled with dust, the indefinable collection before her drew her eye almost like the antelope had, and she felt within her a sense of reverence similar to having been in its presence.

"Take care: for you can take one pot only, and I cannot tell you what is inside," the Harpy intoned, as though selecting her words carefully from memory to perform a sacred duty correctly. "I cannot help you choose, but if you allow yourself to be guided by your heart and all you have learnt from us, you will not go wrong."

Amber nodded solemnly and approached the treasury with some trepidation. The vessels seemed truly primeval. There were some tall and elegant, some squat and fecund, some with indecipherable symbols—even some with face-like features. She wandered entranced, caught in their spell. Touching each pot lightly, tapping it gently as though she were merely admiring the artistry of such tactile treasures, Amber continued slowly, as though in deep consideration, until she came to one which felt hollow.

She lingered and thought fast. The heavier pots must surely each hold within themselves something valuable to the Harpies: she had no way of guessing exactly what, but she certainly couldn't countenance claiming any of them. So, instead, her fingers curled protectively around this lightest one. She could almost imagine the look Jasper would have on his face when she came back empty handed, so to speak, but that couldn't be helped.

Nzizi answered her hopeful grin with a beaming smile. "You have claimed your choice?"

"Yes, and I thank you for offering me any at all," Amber promised. The more she looked at her gift, the more she loved it. The vessel was small enough to be helpfully portable, enticingly round, dual handled, sturdy enough to survive a rough journey, and covered in pleasingly symbolic decoration. It wasn't a lie to admit wanting it.

The Harpy apprentice regarded her, her eyes as clear and far-sighted as only a vulture's could be. "And if I were to tell you that the others held food, water, medicine, seeds, gems?"

The words came easily to Amber. "It would not sway me. Everyone here has deeper need of such things. I would still take the empty one and be grateful for the hospitality shown to me."

Nzizi's eyes twinkled. "Well spoken. It remains to be seen whether it was well chosen."

Amber hugged her and cradled the vessel delightedly. "I chose it to remind me of you, and my time here," she assured the herb finder warmly. "I could not want for anything else."

Nzizi beamed. "When one learns to be content with little, one gains everything they need."

"When one has found such contentment, one needs little else," Amber countered, emotion catching in her voice as she tried to convey the depth of her gratitude.

But, as she took her leave of the woman who had been her mentor, her heart felt as light as the pot. She drew herself up gratefully and cradled the gift a little tighter in promise. Time to prove she could track.

Striding through the patchwork scrub following the sand-scuffs and bark-rubs she could recognise as clearly as her own footprints now, Amber felt as though a weight had been lifted and a path cleared. Perhaps it had: ever since that day when the Sand Giant had come stumbling into camp and crashing into her heart, she had dreamt of tracking one by herself. And now she was doing so, alone and for real. She could do this. She could find the Sand Giant and return with the Mudwort. She could be a herbfinder for the Harpies. She could stay and complete the training. Pass the tests and make it her job. Make it her life.

Amber smiled unselfconsciously. Long ago, she had run similarly through a storm with no way of knowing where she was going or how it would end. Here, now, she knew it would end well.

If there was still a life to look forward to afterwards. If the rains returned.

Kill or Cure

With the sand slowing his steps and the sun slowing his thoughts, Jasper felt he would be sick. It had been days. He assumed it had been days. It might have been forever. There might no longer be any water left in the Realm, save for what they carried—and that was draining away rapidly.

The distance between the three companions and their serpent guide was shrinking likewise, mirroring the diminishing levels of hope they could sustain. At first, they had spread out: Yenna in front, scenting the way, Racxen next, reading signs, and Jasper finally, carrying the main supplies. But gradually the severity of their predicament had encroached like sand into lungs, and they walked now together almost in a huddle, all but clinging to each other: their companionship the only safeguard against the cavernous, predatory void of the desert.

Pushing his worries further down into his chest with every morose step he took, the Prince spared a worried glance for Diberkati. The serpent no longer slid supplely but dragged herself through an ever-drying Realm as though she could no longer bear the effort of bolstering it. It wouldn't be enough, this time, to dig into a dried riverbed and be grateful for the scant moisture that seeped. Diberkati was dying. They needed water: real water. The kind Zaralathaai had revealed and revelled in. The kind that might never grace the Realm again now that she was dead.

Jasper felt himself salivate with the remembrance of rain, and the sensation was searingly painful. Fairymead had been gifted with four seasons, and he had to admit he'd never considered how lucky that was, until each had dysfunctionally dwindled away. Now, no-one in the Realm had drunk their fill for months.

Dehydration made his thoughts drift further. No-one had been granted any warning of the drought. If he had known, all that time ago, that the rains which had fallen so frivolously were to have been the last, he would not have cursed them for having made it difficult to fly; he would have taken the time to watch Yenna snap her jaws at their offerings in abandon. He would have laughed with Ruby as she danced, and he would have been stalwart in his refusal to join her, but he would have been pleased to have been asked none the less. He would have felt a quiet joy in watching Hydd and the Selkies swim in solemn splendour, the droplets dappling their coats until they merged with the waves.

He sighed, with a longing deeper than thirst. Had any of them known, they would all have acted differently. But it was the way of these things never to be anticipated in advance, even should they perhaps have read a forewarning in signs that only now made sense.

Jasper gathered his resolve; it achieved no end to persecute himself for what no-one had predicted, and he could feel his thoughts begin to unhinge his mind. He tried to count himself grateful for the mercy of having out here been spared the sorrow of bearing witness to the encroaching drought. Walking the tinder-dry fields of Fairymead past the withered flowers hanging in brittle remembrance across the meadows had begun to infect him with a kind of survivor's guilt, as well as a sense of dread at what was yet to come. It had almost been in contrast a relief to reach the immutable, enduring swathes of desert, where nothing was supposed to grow and where struggling to survive was the norm and not the symptom of some unconquerable malaise infecting the Realm. At least out here the dryness wasn't sacrilege: the desert was as stark as usual. Out beyond the remnants of the lands-that-were, here stood the land-that-ever-would-be: the sand the grains that the Realm would grind down to, and which would remain in the end.

"You're becoming delirious." Yenna's voice at his ear was steadier than any thought he'd had for hours, and calmer than anyone had the right to be in this predicament.

"And you're not?" He managed a fond, jovial smile.

"Actually, I am," the Wolf Sister admitted. Between the shade of her veils her brow was sheened with more sweat than usual. "I haven't picked up any kind of scent for a while now."

Racxen dropped back alongside. "And I've lost the tracks."

"What?" Jasper stared at both of them in rising terror. He almost wished he was alone with his miserable thoughts still, instead of being confronted by these truths.

"At this rate the Goblins will close in on Diberkati if we leave her behind, and if we don't find water soon, we'll die before we reach it," Racxen admitted briskly. "But we've lost tracks and scent, not hope and reason. It's simply time for a new plan."

"And I suppose you've thought of one?" Jasper managed tersely.

"Of course we've thought of one," Yenna scoffed with an amused growl.

Racxen's knowing grin mirrored the Wolf Sister's, incomprehensibly untroubled. "We just need you to execute it."

A protest, pleading and petrified, stalled upon his lips. Jasper couldn't let himself speak it. His voice would have sounded too loud, swollen with fear in the sudden silence that ground against his soul—but that wasn't the reason. He owed both the Wolf Sister and the Arraheng many times over, and anything they could possibly ask of him would be less than they deserved.

"Of course," he pledged solemnly. Still, he shivered to say it. What could he offer, truly, if his companions found themselves wanting?

Panic pressed, but the fact Yenna remained unworried gave him strength.

Glittering between her veils, the Wolf Sister's eyes spoke more clearly to him than anyone else's voice. She had put her faith in him on the battlefield, many seasons ago. And she hadn't asked him, back then, any more than he was capable of. Any more than he knew exactly how to do. He had spent so much of these quests falling back, letting the others take the lead, worrying privately that he was only there as a fool. Whereas Yenna's blazing-calm gaze was telling him quite clearly that his only foolishness lay in not realising the worth others recognised in him.

What a difference a new perspective made.

He swallowed dryly. *What a difference a new perspective* would *make.*

"One moment, if you please," Jasper managed in relief, going for grandeur, as Racxen rolled his eyes companionably at his belated enlightenment and Yenna grinned with pride.

Lightheaded, Jasper sprang to the air. He'd barely flown these past months: all across Fairymead the need for flight was becoming reduced as Fairies' bodies readjusted to the limitations of lacking water. So, of course, his movements were laboured, his breathing heavy. He was too weak for this, in truth, he berated himself. But let it never be said that the Prince of Fairymead put such considerations above the welfare of his subjects, let alone his friends.

Grimly, he strove higher; wingbeats pulsing arduously through air that no longer felt recognisable, let alone readable. As his mind fought the thrall of fear a superstition squirmed, as visceral as the simultaneous lurch of gravity: that a day might come when the currents of the air would fail as the currents of water were failing now.

All the more reason to get this right. A sense of duty had always given him security, and he gave himself over to it now, and felt better for it. After all, shimmering below him, mere specks upon the sand now, waited three whom Jasper could never stand to lose: the woman to whom he had pledged his life, the man he still owed his life to, the serpent to whom they had unknowingly owed so much for so long, who had only just finally asked for a fraction of the assistance she deserved—and there were so many others waiting unseen beyond the sands.

At first, it had felt uncomfortably as though he might be running away in leaping to the air, but in fact it gave him strength to return to himself, clarity to reorientate himself, and opportunity to remember he was still in a position to help them all. The sky welcomed him, even though his efforts felt clumsy and his limbs leaden. He could think up here, with the air cooling as the atmosphere thinned. And when it thinned too much, the currents wrapped around him strengtheningly, became his ally against the fickle visions playing out below, shimmering in the throes of sight-breaking heat.

Everything was easier to discern from up here. The dunes that had seemed insurmountable shrank back to their true sizes, and he could even glimpse the sprawl of the Harpy settlement before the horizon. Had they really managed to travel so far? Perhaps the vastness had tricked them. After all, the desert played with perspective even as it played with their lives, Jasper thought, his old moroseness creeping in.

In that frame of mind, he assumed the approaching patch of abyssal shine beneath him to be a protrusion of sand-bare rock when he first glimpsed it: anything else had to be a fanciful glitch in perception too cruel to be entertained. But the textured scatterings around it weren't rock: they were scrub. That much was undeniable, and not as risky to countenance. And with the scene contextualised, suddenly the site made the kind of sense that couldn't be sullied. Jasper stared and stared, struggling to remain in the sky with his shock. But, as sudden a shock as it was, his soul knew salvation when it saw it: he'd found water.

The gleaming urgency of it brought tears to his eyes as he swooped in closer. His desperate eyes drank in the view: the pool's darkness a blessed relief amidst the scouring swathes of blinding sand. A jewel of an oasis, picturesque in its perfection and gleaming its desperately needed promise from between fringes of almost painfully vivid green lifted as though in celebration by the trees ringing the water, it was a gloriously impossible sight, even before he glimpsed the tiny, barely recognisable figure approaching it. But no time to consider the potential consequences of that now—he must first return to the others.

Triumph roared through Jasper like the desert winds as he raced back, wingbeats pulsing effortlessly in exhilaration and his speed scouring away the stresses of before. With his vision shuddering with overreached effort, he almost mistimed his landing in his haste, but he fixed his eyes on Yenna—her steadying eyes stabilising him amidst the vicissitudes of a capricious Realm as always—and managed to correct his course.

He landed a little more heavily than he'd intended, and he instinctively tried to brush it off by dusting his sleeves down and looking smug, but relief outflowed from him like a cloudburst. He didn't have to say anything, for his companions could read it in his face. They were saved.

His friends embraced him, and he felt like he was still flying. Exultation bloomed for this one ability that the lack of rain hadn't stolen from him: not flying in itself, but being able to help those he cared about. Although, he did have a wild moment of fearing he deserved rebuke for not doing it earlier.

He steadied himself again beneath Yenna's gaze, and a flood of understanding passed between them.

"Being your full self was ever your greatest gift to me, Jasper," she promised, her voice as quiet as sand-sunken footsteps. It filled her heart to see him as much in his element in the air as she was in the desert, and he could feel her pride in him.

Racxen grinned in delight, and clapped his shoulder, breaking the spell. "Would you like to take the lead to your new discovery, Prince?" he teased. "In case you feel like you've nearly forgotten how to do that, as well?"

Jasper afforded him a smirk, sniffed mightily, and swept forward. "After me," he managed, getting his breath under control, and steadying his legs.

His friends, serpent and all, followed trustfully, and Jasper found himself humbled.

Then, he remembered he still had a reason to feel smug. "You won't believe who's there ahead of us."

Plant Wisdom

To walk amongst such viridescence as the oasis after days of aridity was a joy, but Amber couldn't let her focus slip. She had to find the Mudwort, and return.

Suddenly, amongst the swathes of unidentifiable strangeness, a certain twist and coil of growth made sense, and Amber ran through the checklist in her mind, just to be certain. *Overall impression of tangled protuberance. Swollen, fleshy leaves. Latticed colouration. No latex.* Elation bloomed. She'd found the plant.

Now, to pluck the leaves in the right way, so as to promote regrowth and preserve the leaf-sap for the long journey back. She felt pleased with herself that she'd chosen the little clay pot: it would protect her precious cargo nicely.

Gingerly negotiating the crowded clutch of reeds and rushes jostling joyously around the edge of the oasis, she next needed to get right to the base of the Mudwort's stem, where the newest growths were sprouting—protected, of course, by the most insistent thorns.

Grimacing in apprehension, Amber wrapped her sash around one arm and crouched, reaching tentatively towards the plant upon whom her entire attention was fixed.

Suddenly a cracking of twigs that was not of her making froze her, despite her vulnerable position, unable to see or even move without betraying her location.

Fear sluiced instead of rain, hammering like her heart, as she considered her predicament. For a moment, the tremblings set up by the dry grasses mercifully overcompensated for any sound she might make, and she seized on the moment and threw herself into the undergrowth.

Racxen froze like the rest of them at the noise, but the grin that split his face betrayed his joy. "Amber, it's us!"

"You blundering fool, she could have been a Goblin," the Prince rebuked tightly. "They're going to catch up with us eventually."

But neither Racxen nor Amber paid him the slightest heed as they closed the distance between them with the same disbelieving joy that Jasper had reserved for approaching the waterhole. They were each other's sustenance and sanctuary, and they were reunited.

It seemed only seconds later that the Prince cleared his throat. "If I can beg restraint for a moment, we need to go back for Diberkati and guide her to this water," he reminded pointedly. "There will be time for . . . indulgences once you two return home."

Realisation twisted in Amber's gut: she hadn't told them yet.

Racxen watched her knowingly. "How was your time with the Harpies?"

"It was amazing," Amber blurted with a grin, struggling to put it into words. "I learnt herbfinding. I learnt tracking. I helped a Sand Giant . . ." She raised the lid of the amphora to reveal the Mudwort inside.

Yenna's golden eyes flared appreciatively. "They sent you here for herbs, alone. You've done well."

Amber let her heart swell at the Wolf Sister's recognition. She wasn't used to feeling this proud yet, but it was growing within her, so she gathered her thoughts and her courage. "Apparently well enough to return," she admitted. She heard the certainty in her own voice as she spoke. "It doesn't have to be over. I asked Inqe if I can do an apprenticeship. She said yes."

Eyes shining, Racxen reached out, and of course not to stop her. His hands linked with hers instinctually, in celebration and solidarity. "I will never say *don't go*," he promised proudly, softly. "I will always say: *come back*."

Jasper frowned. "Several months in the middle of nowhere, in the throes of drought? You can't."

Amber rolled her eyes. "Imagine if that wasn't your go-to response for everything."

"I'm just saying, it might not be the safest option, and you don't exactly have a track record of sticking with apprenticeships," the Prince reminded bluntly. "But you don't need to worry, because you don't have to decide today."

Amber eyed him sternly. "No—I don't need to worry, because this is my decision, not yours, and I'm not going to be backed into a corner. And as far as I'm aware, how many apprenticeships I've tried doesn't affect you in the slightest."

Jasper sighed. "I'm just trying to protect you, Amber: you've blundered into things and got hurt many times before. And you can't tell me you know how this is going to end, either."

"No, I still don't have the answers—but this time, I'm fine with that," Amber corrected obstinately. "This time, I've got more resources. My head is clearer, my heart is surer. So, I have every reason to hope for a better outcome and, if it all goes wrong, I'll also deal better with the consequences."

Jasper watched her closely. "You've never mentioned herb-finding before."

"No—because I was never going to notice a path to the side when I had to watch my every step through a quagmire. Coming out here gave me a chance to consider what I'd never yet even contemplated."

She glared at him and tried to let her anger override her disappointment. Did Jasper really not know her by now? But her confidence, as cautiously as it had begun, was strong and solid now: hewn from ice initially and then expanded in the bake-heat of the scrub. So, she stood her ground. "I've finally got a plan *I've* decided on, and however it ends I'm not letting it pass by."

"Well, then." Jasper smiled, smugly benevolent again. "That all sounds clear enough."

Amber hadn't felt quite so irritated by him in ages. "You don't just get to—"

"I merely wanted to know how you felt about the situation," he appeased, spreading his hands as Amber growled in frustration. "Although I did a moment ago think Racxen might hit me."

"It's not him you're at risk from," Amber warned treasonously.

"Look, you've never needed my permission before," the Prince rejoined seriously. "You don't have to want what everyone else wants. For goodness sake, Amber—the struggle is deciding what you want and going after it, not inventing a thousand reasons to prevent yourself from doing so once you've finally worked out what it is. You don't have to wear sackcloth all your life. You know what you want, and you've an opportunity to go after it."

Amber grinned in acquiescence. "Maybe I'll come back after all, then. After several months."

Jasper hugged her. "You'd better. And I suppose you'd best be getting those herbs to the Harpies. Is there anything you want to give to us, to ease your burden?"

The Prince was looking somewhat covetously at the vessel. Amber tightened her grip protectively. "This was given to me by the Harpies," she reminded firmly.

"I just thought such a priceless artefact should go in the castle vaults, instead of being kept at risk of breaking," Jasper sniffed defensively.

Amber rolled her eyes. "I'm not going to keep the vessel. What would give me the right? As a wise man once told me: the entire Realm doesn't revolve around me. I'm bringing it back to Inqe." She took a breath and slowed down. "When I return to begin my apprenticeship with the Harpies. Because, yes: I'm going back to the desert now."

Jasper watched her. "You mean: for good?"

Amber chewed her lip. "I mean: for a good while." It was an admission, yes—but also a warning. Her life was her own, to do with as she saw fit.

"Perhaps what Jasper meant was: can *we* offer *you* anything, before you go?" Racxen corrected smoothly, intercepting her gaze and closing the distance between them as decisively as he closed the conversation to the Prince, preventing Jasper from saying any more about it.

"Several months, you say?" He couldn't deny the gravity of the words, but he kept his voice upbeat as he encircled her gently with his arms.

"I think." Amber grimaced gratefully. "It might not be that simple."

Racxen's gaze intercepted hers. "And you know that it doesn't need to be. Life can be an adventure to be lived, instead of a struggle to be endured."

She wrapped him in her tightest hug, not trusting herself to speak. "I'm not sure there's much point to beginning an apprenticeship, when the Realm seems fated to end in ash and fire upon the sands," she admitted. "But thank you, more than I can say, for supporting me to try."

"We have learnt enough about fate to know it can always be challenged," Racxen whispered in intimate reminder. "And even if it can't be changed, we can still have amazing adventures along the way. I will be there, with you and for you, through it and after. So . . ." He kissed her decisively, with a grin. "Go have an adventure. When you get back, you tell me about yours and I'll tell you about mine."

Amber grinned her pledge, she couldn't help it. But then tears shimmered as reality intruded once more. "It feels wrong to leave you, when we don't know how much time we have left."

Racxen brushed her cheek lightly, the smooth back of his claws catching her tears and cooling her skin. "We've never known, and we never will. It doesn't lessen what we have. Now more than ever, when we don't know what the future holds, we need to live our lives," he promised, and Amber felt suddenly unsure that he couldn't read futures as well as footprints.

The Arraheng smiled, with the certainty of one used to reading cycles longer than the span of lifetimes. "I'm not asking for anything other than what is in our grasp, Amber. I don't need it to be different. I want what we have—and I love how we are. Besides," he reminded. "Your eyes lit up when you told me about it. You're supposed to love a path as well as a person. You've a chance at an apprenticeship here that makes you feel alive, as well as lets you have an impact. It's what you've always wanted."

Amber's smile spread, tentatively. "It felt so different, being with the Harpies, contrasted to the other apprenticeships I've tried," she agreed softly. "*I* feel different. It feels more real, and I feel more authentic. They let me be me. They need me to be me."

Racxen nodded back, the emotion in his eyes overflowing into tears as he rested his forehead against hers. "We all do."

"But now you're crying too," she pointed out miserably.

"Because I'm thrilled for you: that you've found it, after all this time," he managed to laugh huskily. "Not because I don't want you to go."

Amber's smile split her face as joy burst from her heart, and she pushed all her goodbyes into a kiss.

They parted ways full of memories and motivation: Amber to return with the Mudwort to the Harpy encampment, and the others to return to Diberkati and bring the serpent to the water-swollen sanctuary of the oasis.

Retracing her steps back towards the Harpy shelters, Amber found her journey passing with encouraging speed. She remembered with quickening heart how difficult she had found it, how overwhelming it had felt, when she had first begun learning to traverse and trust these lands. Now, the dangers hadn't changed, but even commencing the Harpies' training had changed her. And, to think she was returning to complete it!

Days blended into night and into days again, as Amber's waterpouch lightened and her heart did likewise. Finally, substrate solidified beneath swirling sands and the desert gave way to the scrubland again, and Amber breathed in a sense of coming home. She walked the dust route in peace and with purpose, as she recognised more and more of her environment, listening gladly as the chatter of birds stretched wide the sky and the thrum of insects tangled amongst the spikegrass and thornbush. The browns of the bush blended with the blue of the endless sky, and despite her urgency Amber felt steady as she strode on. The feeling spread like sunshine and was enough to sustain her in her sweating-with-effort solitude until she recognised those final twists and turns that cut through the scrub as deftly as an antelope's path towards the Harpy settlement, and were just as effective at keeping those within safe.

The clearing spread and Inqe stood before Amber now, silhouetted like a tree, her smile speaking for her. The matriarch stretched out her wings, and the Realm seemed to stretch in response as she did so. The rustling of feathers settling into their rightful place instilled in Amber an unmistakeable sensation that rightness had similarly returned to the Realm, despite the undeniable trials to come. Wings half-folded, inhabiting the kind of duality Amber could only long for, Inqe was a vision fierce and fear-quenching: the kind the Fairy could imagine once prompted thunderstorms to break easefully into rain. Okay, Amber admitted, that was beyond even the matriarch, but being back in her presence prompted the same shuddering relief.

Inqe enfolded Amber in an embrace: all feather-brown robes and hawk-keen eyes, and near-skeletal hands that never clung or grasped, never acted like they didn't have enough. "Welcome back."

Amber grinned, feeling a weight lift off her mind as well as her shoulders as she relinquished the pot full of precious Mudwort and returned the embrace warmly. "You knew I was coming?"

"I could not know. Still, it was one of the few things I was sure of." Inqe's strong features creased in a smile as she scooped out the sticky, succulent leaves and summoned a passing companion with a message-filled glance to spirit them away to the shelters as needed.

"I have not seen the future for several moon cycles, now," the matriarch confessed, turning her attention back to Amber. "But we do not need to see it, to meet it with courage. You have done us a great kindness, and we will continue your training gladly. Keep the vessel—a gift can have more than one use, and its learning is an offering to the giver."

Amber beamed eagerly in gratitude. Her heart was already awash with what she had learnt from Inqe and Nzizi, and she wanted to take in more of it yet. When she had arrived the first time, she had worried her mind would not manage, but instead her capacity had burgeoned along with her comprehension until she had found herself feeling a little bigger and acting a little bolder.

"I will study everything you are willing to teach, and use all I learn to help in any way I can," Amber pledged with fervour. The impressive, impervious gaze of the Harpy humbled her, and not unwillingly.

Inqe smiled, pleased. "The Realm grows ever drier, but kindness is a well that cannot be depleted. We need all assistance that can be offered, now more than ever."

"For as long as you'll have me," Amber promised, grateful. In these times of pressure and paranoia, she knew she needed this diversion, and the new direction it gave to her life, as much as the Harpies needed it from her.

Inqe looked into the distance with reverence, deciding. "You have done us a great kindness, Amber. Rest in your quarters for now—Nzizi will be with you soon enough to guide you through the next stage of your journey with us. And then you will see if continuing your training still seems a kindness." The Harpy matriarch's eyes were gleaming with something of Nzizi's mischief with those last words, before she clutched her hands companionably in farewell, and left the Fairy to follow the worn route that had become familiar, to the hut that had become home.

Once inside, the inimitable quietness out here, filled with elusive living noises instead of intrusive artificial ones, crowded companionably around Amber, and she refamiliarized herself with her surroundings with quiet joy. She took the opportunity to scan through some of Nzizi's plant books and re-read her own notes. There weren't many other options, as she didn't want to intrude on the Harpies' duties. So, she waited peaceably. Amidst the vastness of the landscape and the depth of isolation the settlement was surrounded by, what she had filled more space, and she did not find herself wanting. Everything out here required more and took less. And she found she needed less, to feel satiated and satisfied. The harshest environment contained contentment, if only one had the privilege of choosing it freely as she had, and she knew how lucky she was and determined never to forget it for a moment.

Studying attended to, Amber shoved back the flynet and flopped onto the bed that felt like hers and let herself rest. The heat made it easier to not do anything and, while she didn't want to succumb to ennui, she knew she needed to take the opportunities that came her way—including this one.

She felt as light as the sun streaming through the window, and as settled as the squat lizards that had tucked themselves away in the corners. The heat curled around her like a blanket, and she drowsed, conserving her strength.

Nzizi came to her in the silence, needing to say nothing. Amber woke and greeted her feeling as though she were still dreaming, but Nzizi embraced her as though she had never doubted her return, and maybe she hadn't. Amber returned the gesture tenderly. The Harpy felt all bones and feathers, and so, so alive. She'd missed her, even this short while.

Now and over the next days they started simply, Nzizi taking Amber further and further out into the wilds to test whether she could identify this plant or that one, those tracks or the others, and filling the narrowing gaps in her knowledge. Amber applied herself diligently, and the Harpy responded in kind, pleased the Fairy was so committed. Every day Nzizi would choose further signs for Amber to interpret and find her more trails to follow.

Amber lapped it all up. Once she stopped listening to the voice inside that told her she couldn't, she realised she could. Under Nzizi's tutelage, the once incoherent swathes of scrubland grew recognisable, and richly rewarding. The grasses began to whisper of the life they supported, and the thornbush tangle transformed from an impenetrable maze into a decipherable map she had as much access to as any animal.

The landscape became her dearest treasure: tapestry-like and tempting.

She learnt more about the animals, too, and grew to especially love the vultures. The drawn out, throaty cries, flung encouragingly from their watchposts became as familiar to her as her own voice, and just as welcome. They accompanied her triumphs as well as her trials: they crowed over the herbs she gathered ever more efficiently, and they sounded their solidarity and turned their harsh voices into waymarkers when she feared herself lost during a navigation task.

Of course, as the distances Nzizi roamed, with Amber clambering after, lengthened and lengthened across dried mud as hard as the granite outcrops the Gargoyle Rraarl frequented, so too did the pans that they found to gather water shrink and shrink.

Nzizi took it in her stride. "It's an ideal place to learn tracks and signs," the herbfinder promised decisively as they arrived at the latest one, gesturing with a bangled hand expansively towards the prints surrounding the meagre puddle. "The animals must drink even in deepest drought, and the mud clings to their feet and forms their tracks as clearly as an answer to a question."

And for the next few minutes, Amber forgot the troubles of the drought, as Nzizi differentiated five separate antelope tracks across that perilously dry mud, and Amber thought she might remember four. Eyes dancing as she tested her, Nzizi clapped her approval, and it felt as though the noise chased away the ghouls stalking the rest of the Realm.

It felt to Amber too good to last, but days later she was still as stoked. This amount of energy, this level of happiness, began to feel the new norm. There need be no going back. There *would* be no going back, until she wanted to. She could stretch her resources for longer than anticipated because she didn't need as much to live on out here. She didn't need anything superfluous, and that gave her freedom. In a place where she had so little, she knew she had enough, and she had found a bottomless source of contentment just to be. Each morning she drifted awake into warmth, and red sunlight, and felt like she was home, and every evening finished with setting herbs into their appropriate storage in what was rapidly becoming Amber's favourite ritual.

"Today's gathering shall be different," Nzizi announced, the next day after several. "We shall see how much of tracking you can put into practice when we are staying out overnight." Dark eyes flashed in conspiratorial challenge. "You shall pick up the trail of one of the antelopes and see if you can follow it somewhere auspicious to sleep."

The thrill of the idea raced through Amber, but her smile faltered as Nzizi started packing for a night in the wild with practised ease. "I'm not sure I've reached that summit, yet."

"No," Nzizi agreed, with the ready smile of one sharing a secret. "But look how much better the view is already."

Amber had to agree. There might not have been any water left, but the sun's first tentative rays flooded the scene so generously that Amber felt anointed and refreshed at once. She got to spend her days in this landscape, and still dreamt about it at night. What could be better?

The excitement of spending a whole day and night in the wildlife-filled wilderness of the scrublands was still sinking in as Amber followed Nzizi, crossing the wide scuff of trodden-bare ground that ringed the settlement and continuing into the tinder-dry grass beyond which reclaimed the space as wild.

Amber wasn't sure she'd ever get used to these moments, but she'd quickly grown to love them. As she strode into the unknown the initial frisson of danger faded, drowned out by the relentless buzz of insects, and kept at bay by the constant avian conversations that flitted around them, confirming the lack of predators if even just for now.

Nzizi slipped readily back into guiding Amber, pointing out the next 30 plants Inqe would need her to learn, and before dusk the Fairy had begun to recognise most of these. Some had a distinctive smell, some she could link with the animals which ate them, some reminded her of locations. She was just beginning to feel confident, when she remembered the issue of where to spend the night and Nzizi, by way of encouragement, brought her to what could only be described as an antelope dancing ground, smiled sweetly, and gestured for the Fairy to pick a track.

Such a jumble of trails would take a while to unravel but, before long, Amber realised Nzizi had dropped back and let her take the lead. Silence here was not a deficit of sound, but an absence of distraction, and Amber focused on everything she had learnt with everything she had in her.

"You're picking up more than just herbs out here," Nzizi noted proudly. "You haven't lost the Spiral Horned's tracks amidst the others for some time now." She watched the Fairy closely. "Remember: the antelope can be your saviours," she reminded protectively. "Their eyesight, their hearing—everything of theirs is better than ours. Out here, death is only ever just around the corner, beneath the next tree, or amongst the next reeds," she acknowledged, but her smile stayed warm and her voice unperturbed. "Out here, that feels far enough away," she explained simply.

Amber stared at her in astonishment, for she knew Nzizi's words to be true: she felt the same. She let the realisation settle in her bones and was calm.

Nzizi grinned playfully. "Perhaps it's even further away for you: your tracks are unusually light. Even Inqe would have trouble trailing you."

Amber grinned back, embarrassed. "I can't claim credit: it's down to hollow bones." Something caught in her chest, but she spoke through it, trusting Nzizi. "It's probably the only Fairy trait I've still got."

The Harpy took her words in gently. "Without wings, the thickets won't slow you down, like they do us. And, while we use ours to shade, not to soar, and so have less need of hollow bones, it would prove useful out here to evade trailing while finding the herbs. After all, we do encounter Goblins on occasion, at the pools. They drink as we all must."

Amber was silent, and after such trauma Nzizi could well imagine why. So the Harpy took her hands, as though she could better imprint meaning with her touch. "I will let you in on a secret, Amber," she insisted, her dark eyes overflowing with a truth as celebratory as it was serious. "We are only teaching you—we are not healing you. You are not broken—you do not need fixing."

The pulse of what she said repeated through Amber's soul, heartbeat-soft.

Nzizi's smile grew light again. "Besides: none are found wanting, who can find water," she pointed out, splicing through the Fairy's tangle of thoughts with a gesture that seemed to part a veil.

Amber almost shrieked to glimpse the restful glimmer of water gleaming behind the grasses, as temptingly as a certain gem had shone beneath the silted surface all those seasons ago when Amber had reached to claim it from the mud.

The Fairy stared as she rushed forward, as elated as she was astonished. "We found it!"

"*You* found it," Nzizi corrected, her voice as encouraging as the water. "You followed the Spiral Horned's tracks, and they drink much more frequently than the other antelopes, so they led you to water." She regarded Amber appraisingly. "How do you think you did?"

Amber turned to her, her eyes agleam with the energy of what she had achieved. "Pretty good. I just need to—"

"No, no, no. That will not do at all," Nzizi interrupted, firm and fierce and full of vulture sternness.

Amber swallowed, certain she had done wrong.

But the herbfinder only laughed in exasperation. "Don't tell me you need to improve this or that. You did amazingly," she insisted. "Recognise it. And not only for once: from now on."

Amber's heart swelled. "Thank you," she managed.

"Thank you, too. You found us a very suitable place to rest," Nzizi countered, completing an expert scan of the area before advancing. "And rest we shall. But the sun will be sleeping within the hour, and all kinds of creatures may come for water before, so we must prepare ourselves and our site."

The Harpy's soft voice barely disturbed the thread of silence that had woven itself around the scene, so Amber simply nodded, wordlessly and readily.

The preparations Nzizi spoke of were almost as restive as sleep. Firstly, in the last rays of almost-light after their long day, they sat amongst the scrub to observe the pool: far enough away that their shadows wouldn't reach the water and so, Nzizi said she'd been told as an initiate, nothing from the water could lunge out and reach them either.

Knowing this step could not be rushed, Amber settled down to watch and wait beside the Harpy. The quietude was hypnotic, and she let it permeate her as she contemplated her place in this vast wild expanse. Out here, huge things were rendered somehow more manageable, and small things manifested themselves mightily. As though to illustrate that point, a cluster of host-birds fluttered down in chattering convergence to settle in the reeds for the night and Amber watched them, entranced, as their murmurings expanded fit to fill the evening. The soporific rustling of the grasses lulled Amber further as the wind picked up in the wake of the gathering darkness, scudding the surface into a memory of another lake many seasons ago, in tempestuous weather, when Amber had been running towards an uncertain future. Now, despite facing similar uncertainty, the birds around her nestled peaceably and she felt herself drift towards a sense of peace as well.

Feeling she was half dreaming already, she watched a feather of Nzizi's lift into the wind and alight delicately on the pool's surface as though testing the fabric of the Realm. The feather shivered and played entrancingly, caught in a dance of its own creation. So as not to break the spell-sacred silence, Amber simply stared.

Nzizi, of course, saw, and the herbfinder's eyes seemed to slip into a middle-distance accessible only to those of her ancestry. Her voice evoked the enduring wisdom of the vultures as she whispered in response:

"Scales may fly and feathers swim
Hope can water lifeless sands
But can a way be forged through fire
When one must fall where none can stand?"

A shiver traced Amber's spine despite the night's heat. She was about to question Nzizi when the Harpy clutched her arm in silent thrill.

The flock of host-birds lifted from their roost in a flurrying cloud, parting to reveal mud-crusted swathes of skin shifting across the familiar, heavyset bulk of a Sand Giant.

Watching the animal approach to drink, Amber promptly forgot everything else. It was the same one from earlier: the one the Harpies had rescued. The creature's skin folds were as uniquely wrinkled as the whorls of her own fingerprints. Amber would have recognised her anywhere. Those deepset eyes twinkled peaceably now, glinting with a light beyond troubled times, older and more precious than the most ancient gems of Fairymead. Endearingly small ears, funnel-shaped and petal-edged, swivelled cautiously, and that hulking square head lifted in delight to scent the precious water.

Amber breathed out in deep satisfaction, feeling the Realm come into focus as she beheld one of its most primordial denizens. Fingerlike trunk tips snuffled along dust-dry dead grass and curled exploratorily around tougher reeds as the Sand Giant navigated short-sightedly towards her goal.

Amber drank in the opportunity to watch such a creature at close quarters. That busy trunk looked delicate and snufflesome, and made the Sand Giant look worryingly vulnerable.

"That proboscis helps them breathe in sandstorms," Nzizi whispered. "It prevents sand reaching their lungs. And in the cold desert Restës it allows the air to warm before reaching the lungs." Wistfulness pulled her voice into a thinner strand for a moment. "Or it did, when the Realm was making sense."

But her melancholy dissipated as, arriving at its destination and welcomed by the sucking squelches of mud, the Sand Giant squealed like a hoglet and rolled with abandon, her wrinkled face dissolving into contortions of pleasure and her grunts reverberating with contentment.

The peaceful, rumbling susurrations of the Sand Giant were like the shiftings of the Realm itself moving back into alignment, and Amber watched in hushed awe as the Sand Giant stomped and wallowed, churning the silence and the sediment.

The encounter lasted only moments, and then she was gone, with the suddenness that belonged only to wild things, but those moments were so full of meaning and experience that they thickened to support Amber; solidified around her to hold her up and carry her onwards through the uncertain times ahead. The silence now seemed to comprise of more, having seconds ago contained such a creature. Amber let her vision, like the pool, take its time to settle.

"She has used up almost all of the water," Nzizi murmured, the softness of her voice belying the solemnity of her words. "It was no more her intention than it was ours, the last time any of us truly drank our fill. But the fact remains."

Shock sank into Amber with a stone-like chill. But while it shook her resolve, it could not shatter it. She looked to Nzizi instinctively and saw in those hawk-sharp eyes that the Harpy's adaptability was more agile than the future was fragile.

"For now, we must remember that while there is less, there is still enough. So, let us prepare for sleep," Nzizi reminded. "Some needs remain as fundamental and within our control as ever."

So, Amber cleared their sleeping area and refilled their water, as Nzizi prepared the simplest of dried meals. Attending to their joint tasks in an amiable silence soothed Amber. Their parallel contributions and completions—the platonic exchanges of two souls flickering flamelike and unquenchable in a vast and vibrant night—felt like all the intimacy she needed right now and spoke of a deep and sacred unity bound by these experiences. She wondered if Nzizi felt it too. Between the glances, smiles, and touches they shared, she hoped so.

"I will keep first watch," pledged Nzizi after their companionable meal, her soft voice permeating the silence without puncturing it.

Gratefully, Amber unrolled her sleeping mat, smoothing out her cares and untangling her thoughts at the same time. She lay back and settled into the luminous night. She couldn't drown in this darkness, she realised. The stars had risen silently and now pinned back the sky, holding up its corners and stretching it out until morning, and she felt so grounded that even the stones that pressed into her back simply reminded her of her connection to the Realm even as the skies above elevated her equally. Listening to the quiet, conversational crackle of the campfire, Amber stared and stared until she felt her soul spiral and it seemed as though the great expanse above her were actually close enough now to rest over her, and she nestled amongst it and felt connected with all things, as the night folded itself around her in a promise that although everything was different, all was far from lost, and much could be better again.

She should probably have tried to sleep, but instead Amber lay there, her thoughts stretching and spinning, wakeful amidst a night she didn't want to miss a moment of, willing herself to absorb everything as her soul swelled with her surroundings and her eyes sparkled with the stars.

Glancing to Nzizi, she realised the Harpy felt the same. Nzizi's silhouette sat sure and serene nearby, outlined by stars. "I used to think I only realised how big the Realm was when it rained, and I heard it falling in all the places I couldn't see," she murmured into the darkness.

"I remember those times," Amber whispered back in solidarity. "And I know the vastnesses are still out there."

A resolute peace swelled in Nzizi's voice. "Reminding us that though we are small, we have survived thus far."

Amber smiled and held her gaze in agreement. Feeling safe on the ground, she drifted towards slumber.

When Nzizi woke her to take watch in the most velvet of darknesses, Amber realised in exultation it meant she had managed to sleep. She roused herself feeling as though she belonged to this landscape and prepared herself for the watch feeling as though she'd never get tired again. The stars looked like they had sunk down during the night and were now close enough to be nestled amongst the trees surrounding camp. The moonlight felt brighter than back home—brighter even than by the sea.

As Nzizi settled to sleep, Amber let her senses expand to encompass as much of the night as she could. Beneath the pale starlight, the ground lay split into sharp contrasts of silver and shadow, across which myriad silent, subtle creatures had left their prints scattered as though in muted greeting while she'd slept.

Even now, antelope of all descriptions were continuing the business of their lives all around her. As they delicately picked their paths and conducted their nocturnal navigations, the brightness of the moon and the depth of the night confused Amber's eyes and turned the creatures to paper cutouts, daintier even than during daylight hours. Their silent approach, and the unconcerned glances they cast towards her before continuing, swelled Amber's heart. The pool was drying even as she watched it, but still the creatures came, and found sips of sustenance, and here they stayed until nothing else welled from the mud.

As the antelope left with the water, Amber refused to let fear take the place of their company. She'd already refilled the waterskins, she reminded herself. She'd even filled the tin pot Nzizi had gifted her. And, while she knew herself to be still reliant on Nzizi, she was never truly alone out here, she'd just witnessed how there were so many unseen animal lives constantly playing out, brushing against hers. The drone of the cicadas was muted in these hours: a background lull and no longer a rushing warning, but it filled the night and stopped her falling. There wasn't a non-animal soul awake for miles on miles, and yet the heat pressed like a crowd, the insects buzzed like voices, and the constant interplay of nightbirds spinning above made her feel seen. As the hours stretched, she'd rarely felt less lonely.

Suddenly, the air changed: filled with the presence of something large and wild and close, and all at once time contracted into this moment. A mature male Spiral Horned antelope, the tallest Amber had ever seen, arrived in silence with a majesty that filled the night. Amber's shallow breath shivered with the evening breeze as, walking stiff-leggedly and holding his heavy neck high, he picked his way carefully along the edge of the bush and advanced towards the waterhole. Amber grimaced in frustration. The *empty* waterhole.

She chewed at her lip, wishing she could do something. More delicately than a bicorn the antelope moved, head bobbing cautiously. His liquid eyes met Amber's, and she instinctively looked aside: not wanting to frighten him, but also not wanting to trap him with her gaze or make him any less wild than he was.

Her glance landed on the vessel she'd left nestled beside her sleeping mat. Acutely aware that an ill-considered move could send her companion fleeing, Amber inched sideways, staying lower than the cover afforded by the sloping bank's silhouette and the trees reaching protectively towards her, and carefully felt around for the vessel. She wondered if the antelope would find her efforts enough. She only had the one pot, after all, and a tiny one at that. Still, she curled her fingers around it resolutely. She would do what she could with what she had.

Antelope and Fairy tiptoed towards each other. Trembling with hope, Amber crouched, with as much reverence as caution, and tilted the vessel.

The splash of water against desiccated ground sang with its own music, elating Amber. But, from her sweaty hands, the vessel slipped and rolled noisily down the bank. The antelope flinched but didn't run, and Amber didn't want to send him fleeing by retrieving it.

Cursing her clumsiness, Amber resigned herself to losing the water. They weren't that far from camp, and they still had their waterskins. She glanced back instinctively to Nzizi, and saw the Harpy stir.

The antelope, meanwhile, cast aside his earlier caution and darted eagerly to drink the precious water now lurching in rapid spillage from the fallen amphora.

Lost in the moment of witnessing the antelope's relief, Amber didn't notice the Harpy stealing up next to her.

Nzizi clutched at her shoulder, and for a wild and terrible moment Amber feared she'd seen a predator approach. But the reality was far more unexpected.

"Look," the Harpy urged in wonder, in the birdlike voice that predator and prey alike felt safe with and ignored. "The water, Amber. The water is still pouring."

Enthralled, the friends clutched hands in silent delight, their faces creasing into boundless smiles. The joy they couldn't voice danced in the air and infused the land, for Nzizi was right: water was brimming out of the overturned vessel still, spilling hope as much as anything. The small, unfinished pot, squat and uneven, which Amber had chosen and treasured and carried with her ever since Nzizi's gifting, now lay glowing ethereally in the blush of moonlight, unbelievably pulsing forth limitless water.

"Zaralathaar's last gift," Amber murmured. "It must be." Hope rose like a Renë tide. "She told Diberkati she would alter the curse!"

Nzizi beamed, breathless. "That is ever the way of enchantments, no? They must be happened upon, instead of sought out. And once revealed, they must be acted on, in greatest haste."

Amber held very still, listening to the joyous gurgle of the growing pool, as an idea swelled in her urgently. "Someone needs to fill the pans. And you have been kept from your duties by training me long enough."

"Your training was an extension of my duties, not a diversion from them," Nzizi promised loyally. "And together we have been far more efficient at herb gathering than I could have been on my own. But you are right. The pans must be filled—as far and as widely across the Realm as possible." Nzizi's farsighted eyes slipped into another distance as she considered. "Maybe you were never meant to stay here, and do as I do," she mused softly. "Maybe you were always meant to come here and do what you have done. And what you have the chance to do now."

Then her gaze grew fierce and focused. "Still, we do not know how long this enchantment may last," she warned. "And plans made in haste are the most dangerous, out here. They are deadlier than any wild creature."

"But you have prepared me well, for this," Amber reminded, steady and certain. "I cannot thank you enough."

Nzizi swallowed. "I have been preparing you for nothing other than being yourself," she promised. "You need not thank me."

Amber grinned shakily. "I know. But you cannot dissuade me."

Nzizi sighed. "I know that, too," she promised softly. "You tread this land more lightly than me," she added impulsively. "But you have left a print upon my heart."

Amber hugged her tightly. It suddenly felt vital that Nzizi understood how much their time together had meant to her. She had the fleeting, shocking realisation that by leaving now she might never see the Harpy again. But a second realisation slammed into her, just as forcefully and infinitely more reassuring: that these moments would shine brightly for the rest of her life. And she would shine brighter because of them.

Nzizi smiled because she knew: not in the preternatural way of the Harpies, but in the simple, no-less-true way of a friend.

"You have taught me more than you know," Amber promised, snuffling the words out through tears that somehow managed to feel like strength. "I'm not going to say I will miss you—because instead I will never forget you." She swallowed painfully against the constriction in her throat. "It was a lie of sorts to myself, to think I could stay. Yet I'm glad I believed it, for what it has given me in bringing me out here."

"Not all journeys need to meet their expected endings, to be proven worthwhile," Nzizi reminded gently. "It doesn't have to be more than it is, to be enough."

Amber nodded fervently, steadier now. "It doesn't have to have been forever, to have been a dream come true," she agreed, grinning fondly.

Nzizi beamed and hugged her as though infusing her with strength. "You will go, and I will stay, and we will need nothing else from each other," she promised. The Harpy thrust a generous portion of supplies towards Amber and stepped back decisively.

The Spiral Horned antelope, embodying the delicately-charged stillness of the night, had observed this whole exchange without moving, as though instinctively recognising the true focus of the companions' attention. Nzizi grinned in gratitude of its continuing presence. "Like I told you the first moment I met you: the antelope are my heroes, not the predators," she admitted fondly, following Amber's gaze. "If I were them, I'd keel over from nervous exhaustion before the sun had finished rising. And yet they live out their whole lives in full scope and in all their splendour, as though they were the main characters. I suppose they are, really. They are in more scenes than I am, certainly."

She lowered her voice solemnly for a moment. "Never ignore the antelope. They can show you more than any map. They will tell you about the water, about the wind, about predators, about the Goblins that might—"

"I promise." Amber hugged her tightly, knowing she must get moving. "I'll be fine. And I won't rest until I have filled all the pans."

Nzizi beamed. Then she reiterated the locations and their landmarks to Amber as though she could turn it into a protective mantra, urgency vying with pride to witness her apprentice's readiness. She couldn't bring herself to say goodbye, and in truth she didn't need to. They both knew what they had shared; what they would always hold on to.

So, the Harpy simply blinked back tears and clutched the Fairy's hands to her chest one last time, as though gathering Amber close to her heart to keep her safe. And then she released those hands, infused now with her heart and her hope, and retreated back along her own path as she entrusted Amber to hers.

Alone, Amber sucked in a steadying breath, in the hope that it would settle her skittering heart. But she must push on now: on through the night and on through the heat. She orientated herself from Nzizi's whispered instructions and strode out towards the first pan.

The feeling that chased at her heels—the nostalgia for something that had barely started and could not continue—was not something she had expected, and certainly not something she had the luxury of sparing attention for now. She must in the future think of her time with the Harpies not as something lengthy cut short, but instead something perfect and complete within the little time it had, which would shape her whole life henceforth. As for now, she must think of nothing save for how to reach the waterholes.

With the rest of Nzizi's gifts tucked into her pack, she raised her close-clutched vessel decisively to the antelope—now a watchful speck in the distance—and took her leave of him, heading into the unknown once more.

Kindnesses and Cruelties

As she left the antelope behind, the sky seemed to darken in his absence, and at first the night felt so deep that Amber half feared she might disappear into it entirely, or else be swallowed up by the innumerable shadows cast by the jagged silhouettes of the scrub, which seemed as she rushed past to crouch in anticipation of attacking her. But out here she had learnt to assess darkness and shadow for what they truly were, and so panic could not rise. The wind flapped like sails in the vast expanse of wilderness, and she set her sails accordingly. She kept up as much speed as she could without breaking the cardinal rule of no running amidst a landscape populated by predators and, as she advanced through an endless night, her mood became as buoyant as her steps. She had something concrete to contribute, finally. Lives depended on this water, and the opportunity to journey out here completely on her own, let alone for something as important as filling the pans, was utterly thrilling. And there was a reason Nzizi had let her go in the dark. With the stars above to guide her, she could adjust her course with confidence. And surely she couldn't feel all that frightened, having only just taken her leave from her Harpy mentor.

So, Amber continued in good heart, drinking in the hypnotic quality of the experience. The moon was fat and the horizon far. Her senses expanded, her mind calmed, her ego shrank, and just for a while she felt part of the natural way of things. She got to walk in the footsteps of the animals; following the natural paths they trod, listening for the alarm calls they were attuned to. Once she'd removed the protective and comfortable barrier of being able to rely on Nzizi, the separate components she had enjoyed learning—following tracks, interpreting signs, understanding the interplay of behaviours—all stitched themselves together into one expansive, ever-changing tapestry wherein things started gloriously to become relevant and make sense.

And there was much to make sense of, navigating that night: from the early arresting scent of a bull Sand Giant just out of musth, to the reverberating groan of a sow not 100 yards away later, everything became immediate and meaningful as she put her tracking skills into practice. Treads from ages past sank their soft shadows into waypoints beneath the moonlight, illuminating the path as her vision acclimatised to them, and soon she was again picking up the recent tracks of Nzizi's most beloved antelope—the ones who needed to drink the most frequently. All the signs converged: she glimpsed the pan, and she'd reach it in no time now.

But no sooner had she formed the thought than she ducked behind the tallest tussock of grass, as though its spindly blades were any defence, and froze. She might feel safer walking alone than before, but she was alone no longer. There was a Goblin ahead, on the other side of the pan.

At first she couldn't process the scene in her terror, and for a wild and horrifying moment she thought he was stalking towards her. But, as that panic-induced misperception faded, she had to admit that the reality was even stranger: a lone Goblin stumbling loudly, as though oblivious to both her and the pool he was approaching, his gait erratic, his grey skin blurring in and out of the night-blended shadows hovering at the edge of vision.

From between the scissored fronds of grasses Amber peeped, mind racing, discomfitingly aware that Fairies could not see half so well as Goblins at night. Could he be aware of her, and be laying an elaborate trap?

Amber ran through her options quickly. He was as alone as she was, and he hadn't seen her yet. Hopefully. But she was in far more an exposed position than he—she couldn't stay here and be discovered, any more than she could stay here and delay her quest. The far trees reached out of the darkness, offering her their sanctuary, their long thorns shining silver. But she couldn't retreat to them. She had to fill the pans, and the first one lay ahead, vulnerable and exposed.

As a compromise Amber adjusted her course slightly, but she still managed to lose the Goblin. Skin prickling as she advanced regardless, she didn't know how to feel when the rustling that heightened her vigilance collapsed into a curtailing thud. In the resulting silence, Amber dared not let slip her best opportunity. After all, the noise had been too far away to affect her. There was no-one but the wind to witness what had happened, or her indifference to it.

So, she stole towards the pool, heart racing. There could have been a hundred Goblins here and she wouldn't have heard, so loudly did her pulse thunder against her temples. There were no antelope to keep better watch than her, no birds to sound the alarm should anyone approach, but there was still her first real chance at helping to heal the Realm from the drought, so all other considerations rushed into inconsequentiality as she darted forwards.

As she pushed through the denser grasses fringing the pan, her heart sank to see that the waterhole lay utterly empty already. The rough, cracked-crust remnants lay bare, a shocking ghostly pale beneath the wan light of the moon.

No time to lose, then. She climbed down into the hollow that should have been a pool, kept the lip of the vessel low, so it wouldn't shout its secrets, and tipped it quickly.

The resulting splash and gurgle as the water surged and swirled filled Amber with an adrenalin-like frisson. As she watched the level rise, murmuring encouragement to the water and gratitude to the Nymph who had conjured it, her hope rose also, and she scrambled up the bank again elated, paying no heed to the scuffs the rock-hard clay wrought upon her skin.

She paused, gathering her breath and her thoughts as she let the night settle into silence again. She'd filled the first pan—that would save some lives, for a start. But if she were to reach the others, she needed to shake off the Goblin from her trail. And she'd let her mission distract her: she couldn't hear him anymore, let alone see him. She needed to check if that thud earlier had been him—or caused by him.

Clinging to the patchy shadows afforded by the scattered scrub as she slunk towards where she'd heard the thud, her mind went back to Nzizi's advice about lakeside predators snaring the unwary by their shadows. But every moment wasted here was more water evaporating from the next embattled pool. So, she crept forwards, the dry grass rustling a brittle warning.

A crumpled supine form, all angles and arms, invaded her vision, no less startling for its stillness. Of course it was the Goblin. She watched the motionless figure cautiously, trying to remain dispassionate. His collapse could have been staged to lure her in and lower her guard before catching her unawares. But, seeing him slumped in the kind of aspect impossible to affect, his skin even greyer than the Goblin norm, her heart went out to him. He was utterly alone. His lamplike eyes, staring and unseeing, looked overlarge and vulnerable, and the nearby water might as well be another Realm away from him. He was nearing unconsciousness, and so far from help.

Unless.

She would never be someone to withhold aid. The Goblin was only here for water, in the same way the Sand Giant and antelope had been. His life was in her hands, the situation as delicate as the drying scales of

Diberkati when they'd first found her. She had helped, then. Why should she not, now?

Gathering him to her as she checked for breathing felt uneasily like moving a corpse, so cold was he despite the scorched earth. Her own pulse raced fit to prevent finding his, but the feeble huff of rotten-flesh stench through jagged teeth was proof enough that he was still alive, if only just. He was clearly in a bad way from the drought: his dehydrated skin was as flaky as the bark from a dying tree. And who knew what else might have happened. So, she moved quickly. She'd set the vessel on its side next to her in her haste, so it was clearly empty, but she tipped it with full confidence and again gave murmured thanks to Zaralathaar as her trust was rewarded with a thin steady stream of water issuing forth so she could drip the moisture against the Goblin's gradually responsive lips, careful not to flood his mouth and risk choking him. It didn't feel entirely different to when she had given Racxen water, all those seasons ago when he had collapsed. She knew just as clearly now that what she was doing was right.

"Witchcraft." The word speared her, thrown from the lips of a Goblin behind her.

She twisted, weighed down by the one she had been trying to save, as sallow eyes gleamed in rapacious realisation around her.

Mutterings closed in, from all sides:

"What are yer doing here, out all alone?"

"Don't yer know that it's dangerous? Come with us home."

"So far an' so fragile, so lonely an' scared—"

"Our lair isn't far—yer can take respite there . . ."

Hands swarmed around her, and a terror more rancorous than could descend in the presence of any animal began tightening its grasp.

The Goblin man in her arms, strength regained, pushed himself into standing, staggered back, and shoved his compatriots bad-temperedly away in the process. His rasping voice tore roughly through the mob. "Step back. Have yer forgotten who I am? Explain yerselves."

Fear spread to fill the silence. And it wasn't only Amber's.

"She saved yer wi' witchcraft," one Goblin managed. "She muttered over yer, an' the water kept flowin' while yer drank."

Scenarios wrestled through Amber's mind in the darkness: surely he wouldn't believe it, surely the mistake would never stick—but the possibility gleamed like a far-off raincloud suddenly within her reach.

Stoking the belief that it was her magic, controlling the water, instead of the vessel, could secure her survival.

The first Goblin looked her over, his stare burrowing into hers as though he could gouge out the answer from her eyes.

Amber held his gaze; returned it with every bit of lofty arrogance she could muster.

The Goblin let the silence fester and grow sinister. "Then she is useful," he hissed. "Fer now."

It hurt that his voice hissed like Diberkati's, but Amber drew herself up grandly: there were a dozen Goblins surrounding her, and more circling beyond. She couldn't escape them, couldn't outrun them, couldn't lose them in the dark when their nightvision was better than twice as good as hers. "Then I'll go with you," her voice murmured like thunder. "For now."

Then the hands she'd held tenderly seized her roughly, and she fought the urge to struggle and make the situation worse.

The stars seemed to spiral away in despair as the treacherous company wended its ever more capricious way through the night. Amber lost all track of her location, but she knew when she had the chance, she'd take losing herself out here over staying with the Goblins. Until then, she tried to walk imperiously. She was supposed to be a sorceress, after all. She tried to channel the haughtiness of Zaralathaar, the dignity of Inqe, the loose-limbed grace of Yenna, the confidence of Ruby. She concentrated on it so hard it almost staved off the growing realisation that the Goblins hadn't bothered to blindfold her. They really were that sure they didn't need to.

But they had to be reaching the lair soon, surely, for the pack that had crept silently enough across the veld to have ambushed her was now cackling and whooping fit to wake the dead, triumphant in their capture. The cacophony made it hard to stay calm and think, but she had to, to stay alive. The situation was still playing out, she told herself. She had time to work out what she was going to do about it—if she could keep her head in these vital early stages.

As the journey lengthened, her captors began to relax. Amber was still surrounded, but eventually she was walking by herself. This was her chance. She would flee into the waiting darkness.

Or: she would, as soon as she had got rid of the Goblin she'd assisted, who, as though having read her mind, had decided now was the exact time to fall into step with her. The imposition of it irritated her almost as much as her entire predicament. Still, she took some comfort from the fact that his eyes gleamed as suspiciously as her own. She felt strongly as though she were not the only one vulnerable here, and the sensation was as strange as the territory they were now stumbling across.

"Why'd yer help me?"

Amber couldn't tell whether the question was more guarded or goading. She coaxed her shoulders and neck into cracking, as though that was all it took to shake off the impact of his treatment of her, while in her contortions she stole a glance at how far away the others were. For good or ill, she was probably out of earshot of all but this Goblin. But what would a sorceress say?

"I'm regretting it now, if it makes you feel on safer ground." It was probably too honest, and not at all what a sorceress would say, but she snorted it tiredly. A mask might be imperative to survival, in this situation. But she also needed to remain herself, to stay sane.

To her surprise, he laughed in response: a throaty, not entirely sinister sound. "I'm Torek." He held out a sharp-nailed hand.

"Amber." His handshake felt normal. Was that wrong of her to think? It had sounded like he had some standing amongst the group. Could she convince him to let her go?

She swallowed. She could barely form a thought right now, let alone a plan. Now was not the time to ask questions or presume intention. For now, she would play the part of the self-possessed sorceress. She couldn't control his responses, but she could control her own.

More immediately, it seemed as though Torek was wrestling with a question of his own. "What is it?" she urged. Perhaps she could pretend to be on his side.

"Yer could have flown away. Yer didn't. Yer wanted ter be captured."

Any hope of alliance froze with her blood then. Nausea itched along her skin like one of those venomous centipedes Nzizi was always warning her about. "You don't capture a sorceress," she spat. She bit back the rest of the retort; she couldn't bear to confront the emptiness of any threat she could make here.

But her mind raced. Nzizi had taught her to always make a plan. She needed something to soften if she was to survive. So, she needed to find something *to* soften.

And then she noticed it: an awkwardness in Torek's gait, as well as in his manner. The way he was compensating, as he walked. He was in significant pain, and he was hiding it. Only a healer would notice—the other Goblins certainly hadn't, or they would have torn him apart. Her heart leapt.

"You should be glad I stayed," she advised cuttingly. "You need to take good care of me. The moment they forget about *me*, they'll remember your weakness back there and turn on *you*."

He straightened as though she had struck him.

She kept her stare gemstone hard, wondering if she'd overdone it.

"You can't hide an injury once it gets worse." She quietened her voice this time. It was more than he deserved, but she needed him to need her alive. "You were really in trouble out there, before I found you," she reminded in an undertone. She swallowed. She was only goading him to learn his weakness, not out of genuine concern, she told herself. It wasn't like she'd trust any answer he'd give her.

Torek studied her a long moment, and suddenly pulled up the tattered sleeve of his jerkin. "I've hidden it this far, ain't I?"

Amber almost felt his agony; almost cried out. His forearm was a savaged mess. "You're lucky you can still use that hand," she managed. "Are you not in horrendous pain?"

It was a genuine question, but she supposed it deserved the smirk it earnt her. "You don't survive amongst Goblins if you voice your hurts," he muttered, snatching the sleeve down again. "If they find out, they'll kill me."

"That's horrible." She didn't need to fake concern.

"It's survival of the fittest."

Her mind whirred, contemplating why he decided to trust her with that information. It was too uncomfortable to consider, so she changed the subject.

"You don't think the serpent you're chasing will prove the fittest of you all?"

He stared at her then, dreadfully, and she wasn't sure whether his eyes on her felt more like tongue or teeth. But she had to defend Diberkati.

"Yer must be sorceress ter dare talk ter me like that." But Torek sounded more amused than threatened, and Amber's indignation vied with her relief.

"But yer don't know as much as yer think about that serpent." He paused and in the stifling heat Amber froze, not knowing what to expect.

"We tried ter mine," he began eventually, unexpectedly. "It's all right fer you lot. It's not like *you're* grubbin' around on the outskirts. The land's better fer you, everything's easy. Yer dig fer yer gemstones an' no-one cares—an' why should you have them and we not? But no-one told us how. We dug too deep. We woke something up."

Amber wanted to retort that this was exactly why the Fairies only mined sustainably, but it would have sounded privileged and pointless, so the words died in her chest. "That's how she got unearthed?" Amber managed faintly, shocked. "How she got hurt?"

"Guess so," Torek acknowledged gruffly. "We just kept digging, deeper and further. I don't even know what we thought we were minin' fer. We were fed up o' living like scavengers. We wanted real money. We wrecked the land. We thought it was far enough out that it wouldn't matter."

"And, in doing so: you angered a serpent." Hearing him speak thus of ignorance and poverty, a little of the anger had gone out of Amber's own voice. But only a little.

"We didn't know she was there." His reply spoke defiance, yet perhaps also apology.

"At first," Amber growled in correction. "But once you learnt better, you still didn't stop."

"Well, she tried ter stop us," Torek snarled defensively. "She burst forth from the Realm, seekin' retribution!"

"She shouldn't have had to—it wasn't her duty to stop you," Amber snapped. "And you talk of retribution? She was disgorged from the dying earth. All she sought was understanding."

"Well, if yer hadn't banished us, none o' this would've happened." The Goblin sought sanctuary in morose silence.

Amber held her tongue. What good would it do to claim *she* hadn't banished anyone, all those seasons ago on the plains? About as much good it would do for Torek to claim *he* hadn't done Thanatos's bidding.

While she was trying to decide what to say, Torek's eyes grew colder.

"I need yer fer what yer know about sorcery, not serpents, Amber," he warned leisurely, and on his tongue even the use of her name felt an uncomfortable intimacy.

She eyed him hatefully, hoping she looked offended by his imposition instead of panicked by her own inability to explain the absent. "You know if you speak of an enchantment, it vanishes. So I can't tell you how, exactly."

"But yer can do it?" he insisted. "Spill water, an' make it last?"

Amber nodded sullenly. "How'd you think I've been surviving out here, on my own?" Of course he'd think it could only be by witchcraft, not bushcraft.

Torek stared openly. "Good. 'Cause it's the only thing keepin' yer alive." His eyes gleamed. "Halt, yer maggots!" he yelled to the Goblin rabble. "Clear a way ter the pan!"

Amber retreated back into silence, as Torek offered a mocking bow. All she could do for now was fervently hope that Zaralathaar's enchantment would hold. Everyone's lives depended on it—her own most immediately.

The moonlight shivered uneasily as Amber scrambled down the clefted banks of drought-baked mud, towards the stagnant secretions belaying all that remained of the pack's clearly once-vast water supply.

Amber almost retched as she reached the remnants of it. The pan stank of water left to go fetid and the gas-bubbling algae which was the only thing capable of still living in it. It stained the landscape like blood; stark and desperate and sad. Night insects whined as though in warning, anxious to see what she would do.

Torek crawled towards her like a rumour she couldn't shake, and his breath rasped in her ear as his nails dug into her wrist. "Go on, sorceress."

"Get your hands off me, then, and step back," Amber managed. "I need to focus if I'm to get this right."

She snatched her wrist from his grasp and ignored the urge to rub away the pinpricks of pain. The Goblin horde was inching closer now; claustrophobically so. But the night's heat pressed around her, replacing Torek's touch with its own and soothing the skin he'd ensnared. Around her the surge of insects, strewn up by her approach, hummed in solidarity, fit to block out the Goblins' presence and her own fear. She stood tall again: claimed if not the space as her own, then herself as belonging to the space. *Remember*, she told herself. *The Goblins are passing through—but you have lived here.*

"Magic takes energy," Amber warned, gathering her confidence, and summoning what she hoped to be a sufficiently impervious voice for a sorceress. "Anything happens to me, anyone so much as tries to hurt me, I won't be able to summon the water."

At the resultant growl from Torek, the mob shuffled back reluctantly, and Amber tried to imagine it was just her and the elements, out here in the night. The heat pressed around her encouragingly, eager to be part of the illusion. She set the vessel down—the focus needed to be on her, and not on it. So, she presented her hands skyward, then pressed them reverently to the powder-dry earth. Next, she brushed her fingertips through the soft-scratch grass, and finally dipped them into the vessel. A sudden panic engulfed her: that inexplicably it wouldn't work. But she tilted the amphora and the silver flash of pouring water sprang forth, easing the pool below into fullness. The resulting shudder that gripped Amber wasn't pretend.

Covetous appreciation rippled through the watchers.

The deed done, Amber sank down onto her haunches; exhausted by the tension even as she feigned sorcerous fatigue. She watched furtively as the Goblins fell to the water, scooping great handfuls of it or kneeling face-first to drink. Staying slumped, Amber tried to scan her surroundings. If she stayed on the ground a few more moments, as though utterly spent, perhaps their focus would shift, and she could flee—

"I'm indebted to yer, Fairy." Torek's voice sprang more unexpectedly than the water. An odd look seized his face as he stepped unnecessarily close, and Amber scrambled to stand before he could grab her. She stared at him combatively. Of course Torek hadn't drunk with the others. Of course he hadn't lowered his guard.

And yet he had called her what she was, and that had felt oddly validating. And he must have said more than he'd meant to, because for the first time he pushed on by himself and left her alone—as alone as she could be amidst a seething throng of Goblins.

Revived by the water, the pack picked up their pace, and Amber's mind raced faster. Nzizi had taught her that she could adapt to every new moment in the wild. But she only had the route to their camp to work out a plan. She couldn't outrun the horde. She couldn't evade them. She certainly couldn't take to the sky and leave them behind. It was the first time she'd wished for flight in seasons. The thought almost felt like witchcraft in itself. Wasn't that the way of Goblins? They made you consider the taboo? She stole a glance at Torek, wondering.

He misinterpreted it, and slotted back in beside her, keeping step. "Have yer always had yer gift?"

Amber growled internally. Of course in his eyes it would be a gift, instead of a skill she'd cultivated, maintained and controlled. Still, survival here relied on being social, even though his proximity set her teeth on edge.

"It's not feeling like a gift right now," Amber renounced venomously. Then she took a steadying breath and threw herself from an internal cliff.

"But I gained it not so long ago—when I lost the ability to fly. Well, I didn't lose it, I gave it away." She smiled a genuine smile, and allowed herself that one truth before she wrapped her tongue around Goblin-ready lies again. "I suppose I traded one for the other. And the pressure was too much. That's why I left."

Amber paused. She'd thought the falsehoods would taste ashen, but she'd just heard the words trip off her tongue. She couldn't change what had happened—but she could control the narrative. She had made the incident her catalyst for years now—yet perhaps it was time for a rewrite. The words had come to her suddenly and swiftly, and not all of them had been pretence. But was it a travesty, to be speaking so openly about something so intimate? She hadn't spoken to anyone about it for so long, and here she was, spilling it all out to a Goblin.

Who, for all his faults and for whatever reason, was listening and, so far, hadn't said anything bruising in retort. "Yer couldn't handle gaining the one—or losing the other?" he pressed lightly.

Amber tried to stop her eyes from searching for the answer around the veld. "Ask me in a few weeks."

Torek's bulbous, searching eyes flared at those words. "Yer recognise it's best fer yer ter stay with us, then, as well as inevitable?" he confirmed, quietly approving. "Good. It'll be easier on yer. *They'll* be easier on yer. There's those'd kill yer fer yer ability, Amber. I just need yer help, is all, at camp. The less yer fight, the better it is fer all of us. That's what yer've got ter focus on, now."

Every response she wished to throw at him burned unspoken in her throat. She knew she must keep her responses under control and contort them for her own ends. This would be a long game to win, but it was the most vital of her life. "If your thirst outweighs your hunger, I've no quarrel with you," she managed firmly, although her skin prickled to say it.

Torek laughed throatily. "Why should I hide my nature, ter avoid offending yours? Just don't make me have ter do anything unsavoury."

Amber bristled. "What you choose to do is your own responsibility, so don't blame me if it leads to your ruin," she warned coldly.

He chuckled quietly and the sound was like sand rolling down a dune: soft and unsettling, and hateful enough to steal the footing of the unwary. "Fae means fickle, remember?" the Goblin retorted, giving as good an impression as any of feeling hurt as he threw her a searching glance. "I'm not supposed ter trust yer any more than yer've been taught ter trust me.

But we might just both have ter learn if we want ter survive. After all, ye're full of surprises, Fairy. Yer might just find I am too."

Amber eyed him cautiously. She was beyond bothering to analyse his speech, and she was done caring if she'd offended him. But she also owed herself more than to cast away any opportunity of improving her chances, so she shoved her misgivings aside, refused to let him know how much he'd shaken her, and went on with the business of surviving by releasing her frustration with a sigh instead of a verbal assault.

Torek took that as assent and smiled casually. "So, yer didn't go into the desert ter court temptation, like they're sayin'?"

Amber rolled her eyes skyward. "Not quite," she snorted. When would this night end? "But then, I'm guessing you weren't actually out hunting down luckless travellers for meat."

"Nah, we don't need ter eat fer a while yet."

Amber huffed as though amused, as though unafraid. But gradually smoke befouled the wild wind, forcing through the uneasy companionability that had begun to knit between them. A change swirled in the air—and seized Torek.

Amber instinctively tried to drop back, as the pockets of shadow that had been inconsequential clumps of scrub began to translate into the trappings of a vast camp: bones and bedding strewn in equally chaotic disarray, the thick smog of meat-burning fires hanging low and menacing.

Amber swallowed. A pervasive, primal terror pierced the chronic fear that had coated her like a skin throughout this ill-fated journey.

"Yer quarters, sorceress." Torek gestured mockingly, to where the darkness had congealed.

The sweat encasing Amber chilled. It was literally a cage, although a nearby thorn tree was trying its best to scratch its way inside. A cage in full view, in the middle of the camp, with the firelight already licking it licentiously.

With nothing else to try, and eager to get away from Torek and the others, she ducked inside. After all, she'd never learnt to fight well. Get indignant and stand her ground, yes. Actually fight in any real capacity, no. And what would be the point in fighting one Goblin, when dozens lie further in wait?

Torek snatched the pack—containing the amphora—from her shoulders before she could turn and slammed the grate.

The betrayal of the theft screamed louder than the shock of captivity, and she fought to keep composure as she spun to face him. She couldn't afford to appear vulnerable. So, she fixed him with a stare she fervently hoped would seem deeply disdainful instead of desperately panicked. "A sorceress's supplies are not to be meddled with," she bristled, trying to imbue her words with a sinister foreboding.

But Torek came dangerously close to seeing through her then. Not quite to who she was, but to how she felt. "Yer think yer can fix everyone, Fairy," he warned, his voice strangely flat now. "That it's just a case of getting to know how they've been wronged, an' how yer can put it right. But there is nothing yer can put right here. And there have been far too many wrongs."

Amber's anger flared to heat the air between them: anger at him, anger at herself for ever having cared about his fate, and most of all anger that she now had to pretend to care still, to even hope to survive.

And there was far too much at stake for her to waste energy on his mindgames. "At least give me the food that's in there," she managed, changing tack. "I don't feel well." The pulsing headache of earlier had long since dissolved into a dizzying sense of otherness and dissociation. She almost felt like she didn't need food anymore: like she would float away without it and no longer be chained and bound and stuck here. So, she knew she wasn't thinking straight enough for survival. And she knew the only emotions stronger than the temptation she felt right now were the worry Racxen would feel if he knew it, the indignation Jasper would express if he heard it, the sorrow Ruby would bear if she learned it. So, she owed it to them to stay strong.

"I wasn't lying, earlier," she insisted. "I need to keep my strength up to manage the sorcery you're after, and if I fail, we'll both be in mortal danger."

Torek fixed her with a scornful look as he rifled through her knapsack, and she almost felt his nails along her back as he did so. "Yer've nothing in here ter speak of, Amber. I'll give yer what yer need."

Amber stared mutely, her heart plummeting as Torek stalked away. Could she dare hope that he would be called away, become embroiled in Goblin business, forget to come back with anything? Without him, she could fold herself around the pain of hunger and nurse it alone. Denying the need on her own would be infinitely preferable to succumbing to it in his company.

She perched restlessly on the edge of what passed for a sleeping mat and tried not to think about the fate of the last prisoner to use it. Then she lay down bad-temperedly, trying to will a barrier out of the incessant, headache-wringing heat.

She thought back to the evenings in the bush at the Harpy settlement, amidst the grunting roars of full-stomached predators and the proud alarm-barks of the myriad antelope who had out-danced them. The night had sounded so much fuller, then. And yet so much less frightening. So, she wrapped the memories around herself and tried to lose herself in them.

But Torek did return, with meat blackened by char as well as shadows. And he stayed to eat with her, too. The threat of it almost closed her throat, but he wasn't wrong: she wouldn't survive here without eating. *I am not this,* she told herself. *This is something I will do to survive, not something I will ever become.*

The firelight turned everything fickle, as though in recognition of the taboos she might be breaking, both unwillingly and unwittingly, in accepting the meal. The flames crawled over flesh and food, imbuing the scene with uncanny animation.

As their eager tongues licked across Torek's face, Amber wished miserably for the campfires of the Harpy settlement, or the torches that danced across the shadows of Arraterr's cave walls, or a moonless night in the middle of nowhere with no illumination at all—anything would be preferable to this. She kept a baleful eye on Torek through the bars. He had stolen her freedom; he'd stolen her supplies. He couldn't steal her plans, but she needed time alone to make them, and she wouldn't get that until he left. And if she didn't eat, he'd never leave. So, eat she must and eat she would.

The pulsing glow from the fire pressed everything closer; pushed a false intimacy which she resented. But at least the inconstant light worked its own mercy, confusing flesh with food and turning shadows into sustenance.

She chewed without tasting and swallowed without thinking. Fuel: that's all it was. She wouldn't serve anyone by dying out here. She had to fill the pans as far and widely as she could, and then she had to get back to her friends. After she'd got away from Torek.

"So, Fairies can't survive on air," the Goblin drawled smugly as she finished eating. "Yer need earthly pleasures, same as the rest of us. And if there's anything yer need, my lady—anything at all—I am yours ter command."

"Anything except that which I desire, I presume?" Her eyes hardened. "My freedom."

"The horde needs water. I'm looking after my own." Something in his manner changed. "But I owe yer, so I'm tryin' ter help yer, too. I'm going ter leave this with yer."

A knife, thrust between the bars. That was what it took for her gaze to finally tear from the Goblin. She stared in foreboding at the blade—as ordinary as it was assaultive, saw-toothed and sullen, dulled in shine but not in sharpness—and felt her blood chill to behold it.

"Yer think Goblins have no compassion," Torek growled. "But this is the kindest thing I can give yer. Yer'll learn, Fairy. The only way out o' here is kill another, or kill yerself. We'll make a Goblin of yer yet."

Her stare snapped back to him, and she kicked the blade under her mat, as though terrified to even glimpse it. But her spirits soared unseen, for Torek had just given her not just a weapon, but also a tool—and she now needed to distract him from realising it.

The only way she knew how to do that was to annoy him. Another argument, then. "You talk of compassion, and kindness," she argued. "But come dawn you will denounce these precious, strengthening attributes as weaknesses your kin cannot abide. It is only to me you can speak of such things."

Torek stared as though unsettled but rallied quickly. "At least I have kin," he grunted. "Where are yours?"

Amber sniffed. "Scattered across every land, and I'm glad they're not here listening to you."

Curiosity caught him a moment. "Family would not stray so far."
Amber gestured encompassingly. "Friends may roam as far as they like, knowing their hearts will remain as true, and their support will remain as steadfast."

His resulting confusion seemed genuine. "But they're not blood."

"Of course they're not. Wouldn't it be boring if blood was the only thing that could bind you?" She was on firmer ground now and would fight him over it.

"Ah, so you're talking of bond mates? To further the line of your ancestors?"

Amber snorted in exasperation. "No."

"Then yer kingdom will fall ter ruin, and you will bear nothing but blame."

She felt safe enough to roll her eyes jokingly. "And this is why you know nothing of friends."

The amusement snuffed from Torek's eyes, and bitterness seeped from them instead. "And what would you know?"

Amber was about to retort angrily, but something akin to genuine pity stopped her. "That they're more vital to our survival than anything else," she murmured. "That with some, the connection develops over years, and others over moments. And that either way the bond holds true and remains long after you are parted."

She was speaking calmly, now, her knowledge transcending her situation. "Some people you really can trust," she advised simply. "And they make everything better. They help you endure when survival is not guaranteed."

The irony of her saying it now seemed lost on Torek. "But secrets shared are vulnerabilities lain bare. Ye're saying it's worth the risk?"

"I'm saying with the right person, there is no risk." It felt important to say, even to him. Especially to him. Her gentleness wasn't a pretence, now.

"When they've seen your weaknesses, and they show you you're still strong: you know you have a friend. Torek thought for a long while. "It must hurt," he suggested.

Amber thought he was going to add: *to be apart from them*, or something, but he didn't. *It must hurt.* She tried to work out how to respond.

"Look, I know why ye're getting stressed," Torek soothed dismissively, mistaking her silence again. "Yer own kind have put too much pressure on yer, fer too long. But ye're absolved, here. Don't yer see? Yer don't have ter worry about that, now. Yer don't have ter worry about anything, anymore. It's not yer responsibility. Nothing is. There's no pressure."

No free will. Amber kept the correction to herself. *No agency. No liberty.*

"There's more pressure than ever, for those of us who care about more than just ourselves," she insisted. "I'm not trying to hurt you or your people, Torek. I'm not trying to keep the water from the Goblins. I just can't keep it only for you, or only for me."

She fought to keep her voice steady, but the rage that had been simmering this whole night gave her the energy to continue the conversation far beyond what would no doubt prove safe. She had to survive, but she couldn't keep silent. "There are pans several days' walk from here that will dry without aid—and you're willing to let people there die because of some messed-up notion of me being a commodity you don't want to share?" she challenged him. "You could just let me go there, and kill me after, if you truly dared pit yourself against a sorceress."

Torek laughed: a grating, humourless sound. "Yer can't save everyone, Fairy. Attempting to will kill yer. Yer have ter look after yerself and yer own, an' that's what I'm doing. It's not pretty, but survival rarely is. Yer'll come to see this, staying here, sooner than anywhere else."

Amber hesitated. Responding like this would either build a relationship or set herself up for ruin. But she needed to know what drove the Goblins, to get out of here alive. And she needed to speak her truth, to some extent, to stay sane.

"You know there's something wrong with what the clan are doing, or you wouldn't be spending your night talking with me," she risked. "You're unsure, and you're lonely," she acknowledged evenly, as he leant against the bars of her prison in response. "That's not a crime. But you've got to know that keeping someone against their will is."

"Not in our society. It's survival of the fittest. The mistakes of the weakest are the boon of the strongest."

"Of course," Amber retorted, her voice dripping with sarcasm. "In a 'society' that renders its citizens unable to trust their own, translates 'survival of the fittest' into an excuse to overpower everyone else, and mistakes anything other than sadism and savagery for weakness, that would make sense."

Torek rolled his shoulders and adjusted his stance, unperturbed. "The more isolated yer are, the less you can rely on others. Yer've got ter put yerself first, Fairy. Especially here."

"No," Amber insisted. He hadn't killed her yet; she'd last another night whether she argued with him or not, she decided headily. "The more isolated you are, the greater a duty you have to support others."

"Not ter the detriment of yerself," Torek contradicted flatly. "It's the last taboo of survival. And the first rule."

She willed the heat of her indignation to overcome the coldness of his statement. "But followed to its conclusion, there would be no healing. No kindness."

"No." She thought he was contradicting her, until he added bleakly: "There isn't."

His eyes hooked into her, and Amber tried to tell herself that they couldn't drag her down as she forged her answer.

"There could be. We both know you need my help."

Torek's eyes flashed, unhinged and unmoored. "I'm not going ter owe yer, Fairy," he snarled.

"And I don't want anything you're offering," Amber promised in a returning growl. "But if you don't wash that wound it won't just be me whose life is at risk out here."

"Yer don't have ter worry about me, Fairy." She wasn't sure whether he was pretending to misunderstand her, or whether he really was arrogant enough to believe she cared about him. Either way, his mood had changed, like the clouds scudding across the moon. "I'm stronger than most," he rebuked lightly. "I'm the Prince of this clan."

Amber raised her eyes skyward. "Of course you are." Her laughter wasn't even mocking. "Thanks for making me feel better."

He couldn't find the malice in her words and left, confused.

Hope rising in his absence, Amber breathed away the past moments, and settled into being alone again. She took grateful refuge in the deepening of the darkness that folded around her. It couldn't keep out the Goblins, but it could shield her from their eyes for a few moments while they were busy gorging themselves and bickering around the fire.

Her only company for now was the night itself, and she welcomed it. Thunder snarled petulantly across the sky, but although the clouds remained tight-clenched fists that relinquished nothing so easeful as rain, at least their noise covered her own.

Quickly, she scanned the cell she was being held in. She pledged to stop thinking of it as a prison and recognise it for the refuge she could make it. And she felt more vulnerable without her supplies than she did behind the bars, in truth.

So, trembling, she tied a knot with a strand of grass through the latch, and turned her boots outwards towards the threshold, as though that would keep anything back. Then, to busy her hands against the adrenalin she sought for something else to do. It smarted that she had no way of getting a message to her friends, but no matter. The land here had grown into her friend. She took a handful of dirt and sprinkled it around her bed. Let the Goblins think it was sorcery, or bewitchment—they wouldn't guess at the real magic it wrought here: the sense that the land was on her side.

She felt in her pockets. What did she have with her? Treasures from her friends: Mugkafb's piece of chalk, a bandana of Yenna's for the desert dust, one of Ruby's bracelets, and a piece of numbing soul root from Racxen which she might even be able to use to barter with Torek for her freedom if the right moment could be carved.

Spirits rising, she placed each of these items at a different corner, as though they could conjure a safe space between. Let the Goblins see, and wonder. Her continuing existence depended on them thinking she was some sort of high priestess, after all. She scuffed a few signs in the dirt at the threshold for good measure.

It would still be dark for a few hours, which was a relief. Torek prowled a distance away—too close for comfort but too far to keep eyes on—but, for now, she was thankful for the prisonlike nature of her cell. She wouldn't be disturbed, because she couldn't escape. And, while she couldn't escape, she could plan to.

She lay down, mind whirring, but any answers eluded her like the whining insects that complained incessantly at her ear while hovering out of reach. And, sharp as the knife under her bed was, she could hardly slice through iron bars with it.

Before the bleakness of current reality could overwhelm her, she drew the curls of darkness around her like the coils of Diberkati and tried to breathe herself into sleep.

Slumber brought solace, despite all things. She slept in snatches, dreaming of a surging, spilling torrent that could outlive and overtake and sweep her far away from here.

Of course, when she woke, she was drenched only in sweat, but she felt imbued with strength. Yet she couldn't have slept for long. The darkness was still sticky and thick. So, she lay still, staring at the cage of shadows erected around her, as she tried to interpret the sounds around her just as she had done in the bush with Nzizi.

The heat, which around the Harpy settlement had spread spaciously, squeezed itself anxiously here, as suffocating as Goblin-breath, but noises still carried. A quietness constructed around the crackle of the fire reigned on the outskirts, for apart from a few on watch, most Goblins were sleeping. But Torek, unsurprisingly, wasn't. He was blundering around like a blinded Sand Giant, systematically decimating the silence. She was surprised the others hadn't turned on him—he must have been telling the truth about being a Prince. And it sounded like he was heading straight for her.

Scrambling out of bed was as close as she could get to preparing a weapon.

"Wash your wound," she hissed explosively when he was near enough for the words to reach only him. If he kept this up, she'd never get any sleep again. "I can't believe you haven't washed it."

"Washed it?" She might as well have said wipe it with gravel. "That's fer the weak," he growled. "The toughest will live, regardless. That's what keeps the horde strong."

"That's what keeps the horde one step from breaking apart from the inside out—with you all so on edge that you dare not trust another soul," Amber retorted. "You're spending your night next to me because you trust my eyes more than theirs. You're not looking out for them. You're doing whatever you can to survive an abusive relationship."

"If they see me tending a wound, they'll kill me," Torek retaliated, his terror bleeding through his bravado.

Amber rolled her eyes in exasperation. "That is literally what I'm telling you, and yet you're still wasting your breath arguing with me? Way to aggravate a sorceress."

Torek bared his teeth, but then shut his mouth. "I'm a Goblin. I have to survive by any means necessary," he mumbled, finally more subdued.

"Including letting me help you," Amber insisted bullishly. "If that wound gets infected, it'll kill you before they do. There's no valour in letting something simple contain more suffering than it needs to. I helped at the Recovery Hall back home, even before they knew I was a sorceress. I have supplies." Urgency seized her like adrenalin. "Get me my bag."

"You speak of valour to me. Interesting." His eyes opaque, Torek stalked off.

Elation buzzed through Amber. She dared not think beyond this, but she was a step closer to escaping.

Of course he didn't bring the key when he brought her bag, but no matter. Let her think she was more focused on the latter than the former.

"Just lean against the bars like you're guarding me or something," she grunted; as though she didn't want to arouse suspicion, as though they were on the same side. "And hold still while I clean the wound. It's going to hurt. Not that you'll care."

He wordlessly shoved his arm against the bars and hissed appreciatively at the bite of the fluid.

"Done," she pronounced in triumph. She pushed him away slightly, and he let her. "Now. This root helps with the pain." She pinched off a tiny piece and pressed it into his hand. "It'll give your body's defences chance to rally."

"Thanks." Amidst the ambiguity of the night, something floated. Amber didn't know whether to grasp it or grind it into the ground. It crawled around nauseatingly, like an insect she didn't yet know the toxicity of.

The Goblin didn't go, just yet. "Amber?"

Something prickled along her neck. It still felt like a warning, to hear her name on his lips. "Torek?"

"You know this new gift? Don't give up this one. Not fer anyone."

Amber stared into the darkness after him and thought.

Until she saw him reach the fireside and throw himself down bad-temperedly. Then, she leapt into furtive action. She needed to stash provisions quickly, now that she had her bag back, for who knew what the dawn, or even the rest of this night, would bring.

And so Amber opened her pack, feeling a little like she was reconnecting with her heart. She took a breathless inventory as she forged a plan. What would a sorceress have? Feathers. Hail Nzizi! She had gifted Amber a magnificently vulturine one. Next: herbs. She found more than she'd remembered picking, none the worse for drying for a few days in unchecked pouches. Under the cover of darkness, she curled herself up as though sulking, and between the safety of her hands went through her supplies. Tooth Grass, Wolf's Tears, Mudwort, Night Root, amongst others. She chewed her lip thoughtfully as she examined them, and then she stashed a little of each beneath her pillow, in case Torek thought to take her bag again.

For now though, she held herself still, and willed that stillness to calm her. Finally, in this quietude she had created, she could think clearly. She had been reunited with her resources and regained her reserves because she hadn't lost hope and hadn't stopped looking for options. And now a possibility undreamt of was unfolding before her: because, combined in the right quantities and with the right treatment, compounds in the herbs parcelled in her bag and nestled beneath her pillow would corrode the metal bars that bound her.

The realisation seized her with an urgent thrill. And, while this night wouldn't last much longer, the last dregs of darkness still shrouded her mercifully from the Goblins.

Working quickly, she split off the husks with her fingernails and ground the herbs together, adding her own saliva to make the paste which she daubed pleadingly against the base of two bars. Better to do it beneath a Goblin's eyeline, after all. She must have got the components right, for she burnt her fingers in the process, and felt glad even as she spat and soothed her skin and scuffed the remnants of her efforts into obscurity.

She paused instinctively when finished, in fear that her furtiveness would somehow have carried a signal to the camp, but her small act of rebellion seemed to have gone unnoticed. Hopefully the meat-stench, that was beginning to drift around the central fires as the Goblins stopped snoring and started stirring, would mask the chemical smell of the paste.

She didn't know how long it would take—and she didn't know how much time she had left. But she had taken steps towards her escape, and so for now she lay back if not easefully, at least filled with the thrill of secret endeavour. For now she had her supplies back, and she had set her plan in motion. She had her hope back. So, she could afford to let the paste do its work.

She watched the clouds scudding impatiently past the moon and just hoped the time would pass as quickly.

That hope was squashed almost beyond reshaping the next morning. Pleased with themselves over their capture of the Fairy, the Goblins' smugness made them indolent, and they lost all urgency: lazing around in self-congratulatory slovenliness chewing bones and drinking enough water to make themselves sick.

The inertia scratched at Amber's soul. She'd assumed they'd drag her off to the other waterholes the Goblins might frequent, where she could at least start orientating herself and planning an exit route. But at this rate, she'd be stuck here forever. And with the Goblins prowling incessantly around the cage to which she was constantly confined, her ruse with the bars would be discovered.

"There's no rush," Torek promised languidly when she challenged the wisdom of relying solely on one water-source. "Ye're not going anywhere."

His certainty made her shudder, but her own determination wouldn't drain away as quickly as the water. The horde might have lost all drive to move on now that their only aim seemed to be drinking her own endless supply dry, but there was more than one way to move a plan forward, Amber assured herself. She still had certain things under her control—and she had one façade in particular to maintain for, should the Goblins figure out that it was the vessel and not her with the power to govern the water, it would be all over.

So, with the horde drunk enough on their own good fortune to relax a little, she sought out conversation with Torek until his ebullience and arrogance combined fit to respond to the flattery of her pleas and she found herself, as planned, permitted the run of their camp—albeit in the shackles that Torek took delight in deeming necessary.

Let Torek think mere iron could constrain her—she would show him how wrong he had been before the end. After all, stumbling around camp in chains, no-one would pay attention to the wringing of her hands, and no-one would notice a few errant specks under her fingernails. She was free to put into play the various tricks Nzizi had shown her to illustrate various aspects of herblore—tricks she could now use to if not devastating, at least unsettling, advantage.

She would take every opportunity to do so. Day by day she made as much mischief as she dared, in the hope it would instil both an agitation enough to drive the Goblins on to further waterholes, and an unease enough to establish her status as a sorceress and render her reputation incontestable. She knew, after all, just which bark would flare the fire into eerie violet hues on a restless night. She knew which sap would make water froth and bubble with bitterness and render it undrinkable. She knew which stems you could wipe over a bed or cloak to leave undetectable tiny hairs and induce ceaseless itching for at least 3 hours. She knew which leaves, if you took them in your mouth and chewed them a minute before spitting them out, would dry with the lingering stench of rotting flesh.

All these she used to her advantage, and more. She almost began to believe about herself what Torek put around camp: that she was a worker of witchcraft and possessed of unhoped-for power.

But she was forced to recognise that while this seemed to be keeping her alive, it wasn't giving the Goblins a reason to let her go. Time blurred and bled, and she lived for the brief respite of the transition between the days ending and the nights beginning, when she could sink into the solace of dreaming of the company she couldn't keep. While these sacred visitations couldn't stave off the mornings to come, she woke imbued with the strength and steadiness they instilled in her. And coiling through her dreams always, like a guiding silver thread, was the foil-sheen of surging water, and when she woke the memories guided her like the tracks Nzizi had revealed to her and she gathered them to her to find her path and make her preparations.

Shoring up her reserves in this way, she shrank her thoughts into getting through each day, focusing on the practical. She could do this: she might hate every minute of it, but she could do it. And each night, when she was returned to her cell, darkness fell quickly in reward. Not fell, Amber corrected herself: returned, to reclaim the land as her own. Prowled around and settled in over her like a bushveld shadowcat.

This evening, though, felt different. A new restlessness had seized the horde, and Amber didn't know why. She searched her mind quickly. What were her options? Here at camp, imprisoned or not at, four-dozen eyes were on her constantly, and she was beginning to lose faith in her attempts at corroding the bars: at this rate she would run out of herbs before the iron so much as started to discolour.

Still, she did not have to feel positive to take positive action, she reminded herself. So, she applied the paste again, well-practised as she was now. It helped her to think, and she came to the only conclusion plausible. She'd have to orchestrate time alone with Torek, because there must be more chance of outwitting and escaping one Goblin than the entire horde. For now, her best defence against whatever group hysteria was infecting the camp would be to stay in her cell and feign sleep while she could, in order to rest up and be ready for when she could next take action.

As though in affirmation, darkness came and drew its soothing veil across the land, lending Amber a shield until morning.

Daylight prodded her gently, and she realised she'd actually slept. For a moment, she felt elated—until the cacophony of chaotic sounds that had woken her registered. The entire camp was noisier and more animated than on previous mornings, possessed with an urgency as yet incomprehensible. Amber lay still, pretending to still be asleep, while her mind scrabbled around for what it could mean.

"Up." The key thrust into the lock pierced any sense of safety and Torek jarred open the door and kicked her bed, intrusive and unnecessary. "Ye're going to fill more o' the pans."

She kept her triumph tightly checked, but it filled her whole being as she scrambled to her feet and prepared, stuffing the precious water vessel into her equally treasured pack as she glowered and glared.

As she stumbled out of the cell, Amber saw the Goblins had armed themselves with stout thornbranch sticks. Revulsion vied with revelry: whatever they were planning, they thought they'd need weapons against her. She had been playing the part of the sorceress well, and the game of her life was now afoot.

"Don't get too confident," Torek warned sourly. He toed the ground she'd been pacing for days spitefully, to prove an unsettling point. "For all yer powers, yer can't make a mark on this Realm," he whispered venomously. "Yer leave no footprints. No proof yer've been here. Nothing to track, nothing ter find. No witness ter whether yer live or die. So yer'll stay with us, because yer'll see there's no alternative. Just so yer know, before we head out."

Amber felt something in her tighten with resolve against Torek and his hateful moods. *Nothing for* you *to track*, she promised to herself. In truth, just being outside made her feel closer to her far-away friends. Something buzzed inside her, to be heading out into the wilds again. The Goblins were expecting her to feel outmatched and overwhelmed. They didn't know that every scent on the wind, every print on the ground, would call to her and help her.

If Torek would stop posturing and let the horde get moving.

"Then take me to the pans and I'll show you what kind of mark I can leave," she declared, as though merely eager to meet the challenge in his words. "Take me to the water."

He sneeringly pushed his face into hers as though to punish her challenge and Amber squared to defend herself, but his voice lowered unexpectedly.

"Once yer've filled the pans, there'll be no more use fer yer according ter the others," Torek warned brusquely in an undertone. "Stay close ter me."

A pair of Goblin men slunk forward with the shackles as he stepped back, but Torek swatted them away irritably.

"I told yer: don't play along," he snarled. "She doesn't need chains." He looked her up and down, scornfully. "There's nothing out here she can outrun."

Amber sniffed, unperturbed by his blustering. "There's nothing out here I'm scared of."

Torek growled and shoved her forward unceremoniously and at this signal half of the horde lurched into animation and broke camp, chaotic as a troop of monkeys as they followed her from the sprawling, bespoiled clearing and away into the bush.

Riding high on this new version of freedom, Amber refused to be intimidated. Let the Goblins wonder how she knew where the water was: they didn't know which birds flew in decipherable patterns searching for it, they couldn't discern the scent of waterweeds amidst dustclung air, and they wouldn't glimpse amongst the myriad general tracks the subtle ones leading to pans.

As she relaxed into the journey, Amber shot an arch look at Torek. "I'm surprised you dare leave me untied."

A leisurely grin flashed in response: even his mood appeared lifted by a change from their slovenly campside lazings, and he seemed to have put to one side his previous resentment. "It'll be noonday before journey's end: I'll have no shadow for yer ter steal."

Amber rolled her eyes good-naturedly.

Torek's own eyes settled on her seriously. "And I want yer ter trust me."

"I'm sure you do," she assured him evenly. "For your own reasons."

He looked almost sorrowful at her words, as though conveniently forgetting how often his own had been flecked with cruelty. "Might do yer good ter realise yer owe yer life ter me," he admitted now, more softly. "Might someday blossom into allegiance."

Amber thought quickly. 'Someday' indicated there would be several more days before all the pans had been filled. And despite what she might want to claim, he wasn't wrong. She had adopted a kind of truce with him. More to save her own energy than from any change of feeling, but let him think as he wished, if it kept her alive. After all, it would be exhausting to second-guess every interaction and battle through its complications in her head. Instead, she would simply let it be, and keep her strength for things in her control.

Like the water situation. It was nearly time for her to put on her show, for the horde was approaching what must have at one time been a stately, slow-flowing river. Behind the brittle stems still clumping in shivering solidarity, the empty bed now lay in silent testimony to the waste that had been laid to the land.

Seeing it in such a state shocked her more than she had expected, and so in Amber's haste to approach first as would befit a sorceress, she managed to trip over her own ankle as she navigated the baked ridges leading down the bank and spilt a little water as she stumbled. Torek's hiss struck out snakelike towards her.

The parched ground wheezed at the water's touch, as though sucking an intaken breath at the fulfilment of a need long left unmet.

Amber covered the noise with her own growl of frustration, but an idea spilled out also, and as she averted her eyes downwards to think, the ground suddenly made sense. A Sand Giant had walked through here. Recently. She went to scuff the sign into obscurity but found Torek watching her curiously.

"Yer don't have ter," he promised gruffly. "I revel in what is dangerous. I wouldn't dream o' killing it."

Amber eyed him cautiously. "And I revel in what is wild. I wouldn't dream of killing it either."

An uneasy understanding, prickly and awkward, crackled warily between them.

The Goblin's smile was teeth and knives. "Seems like we might have found our common ground, Fairy."

Amber grunted in acknowledgement. "Except you want the Sand Giants to be deadly, and I ask them to be nothing other than what they are."

Torek smirked in return. "And here was I reckoning we might be getting somewhere."

I am, Amber promised herself. *I just need to come back here a few more times to get orientated and set a few more waypoints by spilling water. By then the bars will have corroded, and I'll break out that same night and find my route out and away and back to the others.* As a plan it left a lot to be desired, but it was all she had so she must consider it enough.

"Yer might want ter use this for yer sorcery." Torek's interruption sounded surprisingly tentative, bringing Amber back to the present and setting her on edge agian. He held out a flagon, squat and fecund, and she realised the Goblins were waiting for her to work her magic. "'S the most precious vessel we have."

Cold sweat slicked Amber's skin. "Then you'd best not trust me with it." She hoped she sounded self-deprecating, instead of desperate. She tried not to stare at what he held: for what was clutched in his hands now held more terror for her than any weapon, representing as it did the unravelling of everything.

He didn't look at her, then. "Thought yer said that's what friends did, though. Trust."

Amber swallowed. "My own vessel is imbued with my energy," she tried to explain. "I work best with what's mine." It might have taken her too long to come up with the retort, but hopefully she'd managed to make it sound a challenge instead of a plea.

"Perhaps what's yours is more than yer think."

She managed to not flinch, but she didn't manage to smile.

She made her preparations fearing they might be her last: the pan contained not one droplet to start from, so instead she raised the amphora to her lips while murmuring incantations and let fall her saliva surreptitiously inside. As her heart beat a frantic tattoo, she tipped the vessel and gave real thanks as it spilled its bountiful contents into the waiting waterhole. Feeling almost sick with relief, with great ceremony Amber finished by pouring some into Torek's flagon. She tried to ignore the sweat creeping along her skin as he drank silently, eyes fixed on her, and then marched them all back to camp without a word in such tightly packed formation that escape was once again impossible.

Still, before dawn the next day she was awake and eager. After all, being taken to refill the pans granted her the most freedom she had yet been permitted, and it also provided her only chance to learn a route out of here. At first, Amber feared the horde must realise the risks they were taking, but covetousness overcame caution. The Goblins wanted more water, and more again, until Torek was bragging around the fire that keeping this pressure on her it would not be long before she had filled every pan ever slaked by Goblin tongue.

Amber heard her time running out with the rushing of his words, but she honed her plan and nursed her hope, collecting glimpses—of notable trees, of unusual boulders, of anything that could waymark for her—as urgently as a Goblin would collect gold. The landscape pieced itself into a near-completed puzzle as, despite the different route by which they reached it, Amber realised they were returning to the first pan the horde had ever asked her to fill. She glimpsed, where she'd spilled the water before, a tiny glimmer of green, tentative enough to go unnoticed by the Goblins, who had no reason to take heed of it. But to Amber, it was a lifeline. It would begin the breadcrumb trail to guide herself out and away.

That would have to be a few nights hence, though, for the Goblins showed scant interest in returning to camp. As though intent on both demoralising and disorienting her, the night dissolved into a chaotic cavalcade of Torek's insistence as he constructed a nightmarish forced march intent on reaching every waterhole, however ravaged, remaining in the Realm.

In no position to challenge him, Amber instead focused on making sure her stumbles and spills became more judicious: a reminder, here and there—to form a map she could read later, whatever the depth of the darkness to come. Every time Torek derided her clumsiness, she would renew her lamentations against being elbowed and jostled by the pack and argue so protestingly that it soon seemed simpler to ignore her weaknesses and push on. And, if the antelope stared a little harder than usual, they kept their secrets.

Eventually, after a hissed consultation amongst themselves, the Goblins blindfolded her, and Amber knew she must be nearing civilisation. She spilled out all her senses. She might not have had her sight remaining, but what she did have was a birth-right relic: a vestigial ability that would never forsake her. That same uniquely orientating ability that enabled a Fairy to fly unerringly through a starless, depth-distorting night sky now let her stumble less-than-blindly whilst blindfolded.

"Only 20 miles northward from where you were captured," Torek mocked at one point, interminable hours later on the most torturously circuitous route. "Might as well be hundreds."

The closest point she'd yet reached, then. She stared skyward as though she could sear into her memory the stars' specific alignment, although knowing her luck the Realm would have shifted them out of view by the time she could make her escape. Feigning tears, Amber slammed her amphora down angrily enough to send a good deal of water sloshing commemoratively over the sides onto the parched ground, and she threw herself and her bag down in a sulk for good measure.

As she'd hoped, Torek's attention was drawn. Although not for the reason she'd expected. Her rucksack had loosened when she'd flung it down, exposing some of the contents.

"What's this?" Torek pounced on the bag, was already going through her possessions. She'd repacked some of the trinkets she'd placed around her cell, in a sentimental attempt at symbolically keeping her friends close by. She regretted it now most sorely, as the Goblin rifled through carelessly.

"So many who purport to care fer yer, yet they haven't bothered trying ter find yer," he murmured leisurely. "Might be time ter put them behind yer and find some new friends."

"I didn't want anyone coming after me, remember," Amber lied mutinously. "I didn't want the responsibility of being a water priestess." But she couldn't stop a certain sadness from sinking into her sigh. *I really won't have anyone coming after me*, she admitted to herself wretchedly. *They think I'm still with Nzizi—who thinks I'm happily questing to fill the pans.*

She rallied her thoughts. At least she was doing the work Nzizi had hoped, and she had taken a further step in plotting her escape today, by waymarking a route between the pans. Now she just needed to exact her escape as soon as the herb concoction had taken its effect on the iron.

But she felt a sudden terror that her duplicity had shown on her face, for Torek leaned into her suddenly. "Yer responsibilities lie here now, Fairy. Remember: I can outrun yer, and I can overpower yer," he whispered predatively. "Don't get any ideas."

I've already got the only one I need, she retorted in her head, trying to ignore how much he'd shaken her. She must hold fast to her plan and not let any inkling of it spill with the water.

But Torek's eyes had already flicked back to amusement, as though expecting Amber would somehow think she'd imagined the previous moments. "What's the matter?" he taunted lightly. "Don't like yer men a match fer yer?"

Amber snorted in frustration, refusing to let anything of his stick to her. Her silence was probably a dangerous response, but she didn't care. She'd never reach the level of hopelessness he'd need in order for her to rely on him or accept how he wished to treat her. Torek thought he was her whole Realm, out here—but he wasn't. She was surrounded by the whirring of wings and the warbling of birds, the rustling of scrubland grasses, and the metallic flickerings of insects about the ground. They bolstered her, held her up, kept her together—just as they linked the sprouts of green that were interlocking the sprawling pans.

Amongst them, Amber breathed more easily, thought more clearly. It would make sense that the Goblins would only trust her to go further—get closer to home—once they believed she could have no hope of escaping, she reminded herself. So, the time she had taken thus far, in creating this attitude within them, had paid off—indeed better than she'd hoped, for she had even lain a trail out of here. She was now ideally placed to enact the next step in her plan: she must return with the horde to the camp, hope that the bars had finally become as corroded as the Goblins' caution, and finally make good her escape.

The magnitude of it shuddered in her. So much was at stake: she would have to move more carefully than ever as she crept unseen towards claiming her freedom, for she could not afford to jeopardise it now. She must put in short-term patience to achieve long-term progress. After all, once she was free, the time it had taken would fade away. The success of her plan would be worth any amount of preparation.

And the best preparation now would be to start heading back. Surely the horde would soon. No-one had eaten properly for days.

As though reading her mind, an antelope doe picked past carefully, cropping quick mouthfuls of drought-crisped grass. Her glance brushed Amber's. As sentimental as the idea was, Amber found herself trying to convey her plan to the gentle creature. *The next time I see you, I will be alone,* she promised silently. *I will have broken my rusted bonds, and I will run past you untiringly and wish you well.*

Those liquid eyes shone as encouragingly as refilled pools, and Amber risked a smile. She felt lighter, no longer burdened by carrying the knowledge alone. Her plan had been made real now that she'd told someone. She'd bought the Realm time by filling more pans—and her own time was approaching.

But the horde was approaching too, and the antelope showed scant signs of leaving, even as her Goblin escorts pressed closer. "Why aren't they scared of you?" she asked Torek, genuinely puzzled.

He looked at her oddly. "We don't hunt them."

Amber frowned. "I've never seen anything but meat on your tables."

Torek grinned, delighted now. "Indeed. Think on it, Fairy. We can't all survive on air."

The antelope fled, as though in realisation, and she was alone with the Goblin horde again. Dusk bled across the damaged land, and the torturous route back wasn't long enough to shake Torek's comment from Amber's mind.

By the time the camp crept into view, the darkness and her exhaustion were both complete, and she didn't complain as she was led back to her cell. She wanted the protection of the bars as much as she wanted to test their strength as soon as the horde turned its attention away from her and towards whatever nefarious plan it could cook upon the fire tonight.

After so long without sleep, the edges of the Realm seemed to shiver and blur, as though warning Amber she was straying too close to a flame. It sounded like the other Goblins had been busy in their absence, and reunited the horde was back to full strength, but she was too tired to pay that fact much heed. All she could think about was collapsing onto her mattress. The anticipatory relief of nearly being back in her prison, where she could finally lie down and be touched only by the pressing heat of the night air and not by fetid Goblin breath, was almost overwhelming. She didn't even say anything combative to Torek as he ushered her inside the cell and took his time over the lock.

"Yer want ter be in here, tonight," he promised tersely. "In our absence, the others caught scent of another Goblin pack. There will be a hunt."

Amber watched him, guarded. She wasn't going to give him the satisfaction of asking questions. But she could feel the change in the air, the tension in the murmurings around the fire.

"I don't want yer ter get hurt," Torek offered.

"By anyone other than you, you mean," Amber spat. She realised she felt safe enough with him to show that anger, and she wondered fleetingly what that meant. "You'd last longer without food than water, remember that," she warned heavily.

"But now yer've given them water," Torek hissed accusingly. "Think on this, Fairy, as I prepare fer the hunt: yer've filled all the pans. *They* don't need yer. Only way yer stay alive now, is if *I* need yer."

He took his leave and revulsion flooded, infecting her like a fever. Urgency reared up and fought back, but what chance did she have? Four Goblins, at least, impaled her with their stares at any given moment. She shook the tampered bars, as though in frustration, and they barely moved. She was out of herbs, and out of time.

She felt her Realm shrink as she waited numbly for Torek to return. A sickening headache warned her how many days ago it had been since she'd eaten. She didn't suppose they'd waste decent food on her, now that they didn't need her. All the stories about the Goblin Markets from when she was little reared in her mind. She needed a plan. But this badly weakened she could barely think, let alone fight.

As though sensing her leaching strength, Torek re-materialised. "See, it's best that yer accept this calmly," he noted approvingly. "Yer'd die out there, anyway. Everything out there wants ter kill yer."

"No," Amber corrected faintly, rallying slightly. "Every*one here* wants to kill me. Every*thing out there* is indifferent to whether I live or die. That's a better set of odds." Wait: couldn't she appeal to the Goblins' love of gambling? She had to find a way of taking her chances out there. She tried one last thing. "If you're all so keen on hunting, why not let me loose?" She summoned a sorceress's voice, halfway between a growl and a purr. "Have some sport at least and give me a fighting chance to take my freedom before you take my life. You know you'd enjoy that better."

But Torek ignored her bait and pressed on regardless. "Yer'll thank me one day, after, fer this gift of suffering," This was his voice as she'd never heard it, and she'd never felt so wretched. "It will be the making of yer. It will elevate you above yer fellow women."

Now Amber was glad of the bars between them. "Nothing in your power can shame me, or need strengthen me," she snarled. "I will not become strong through surviving you; I will survive you because I am already strong. It is not trauma which toughens, but transformation. The trauma is of your making and belongs to you, and I will leave it behind along with you. The transformation shall be of my own creation, belongs to me alone, and I will carry it away with me. You will never touch nor taint it. You will see, Torek. What you do is nothing—what I do is everything. I am forged by the strength of fire in my own soul, so I am immune to any way you try and burn me."

She palm-struck the bars in anger and emphasis, and Torek stalked away, his silence unreadable.

Amber's breathing clattered against the bars for a long time after he had left, replaced though he was by enough other Goblins to render escape yet again a fallacy. She sat with her soul-storm of outrage, and gradually willed her heartbeat to slow. After the speech she had thrown at Torek, she was left with an incendiary need to prove to him it hadn't been empty words. But she needed to think her way out. And she couldn't do that while trembling with emotion. She needed a fierce, clear focus, and something to attach it to. Something to work on.

So, amidst a performance of such stereoptyped sorcery that the Goblins averted their eyes for fear of looking like they actually believed in her pitiful theatrics, she managed to daub more herb-paste on the bars. But after, the effort felt like a hollow waste, for she no longer had the time it would take to wait for further corrosion. She scrabbled in strangled silence for a new hope to cling on to now that the Goblins no longer needed her for the water. What use could the hunt be, tonight? It wasn't as if they'd leave her unsupervised during it.

But, for the sake of keeping herself sane, she convinced herself to hold out just a little longer: told herself that every new development, even this one, presented a new opportunity to survive, if only she could work out how to exploit it. Maybe they'd let her out to cook the flesh, and she could poison it with her herbs. Or if they kept her caged, maybe they'd think it good sport to force her to eat the flesh, and then she could pick the lock with a sliver of bone afterwards. Or maybe an opportunity was returning already? Her ripostes and repartees, her retaliations despite his standing as a prince, were clearly something he didn't get elsewhere. And he was still seeking her out, so she had to believe that they might just keep her alive somehow.

Amber watched Torek narrowly as he approached. His sallow eyes were unreadable, but he brought what probably passed here for bread. "Peace offering?"

Amber accepted it guardedly as he passed it through the bars. "You're offering the bare minimum of human decency. It doesn't deserve fawning gratitude." She willed her mouth not to water as she eyed him stonily. "You do remember how you spoke to me earlier."

He grinned as only a Goblin could. "I was hoping we could move past that."

Amber bit back a sigh. "Yes." She smiled brightly. "I'm sure you were." Brightness turned to brittle. "And no. We can't. This isn't one of those insufferable books where the man is incessantly toxic to the woman the whole way through and then as soon as he gives her a sliver of understanding, she melts and excuses all his iniquities. I know you think that after all our bickering we should have somehow gained a closeness akin to friendship, but that isn't how it works. I'm not going to just—"

"You will in time," Torek interrupted, infuriatingly amused instead of offended. "We all must make sacrifices."

"How about I don't make a sacrifice, and instead you stop making excuses?" Amber shot back.

Torek smirked. "I don't need to. I'm all you've got."

"Says the man who can only talk to me instead of his kin," Amber countered icily. Even alone in the Realm, she'd never need him, and she kept up her scathing glare until he slunk away uncomfortably.

But then she watched in dread as the four guards resumed their positions and Torek rejoined the rest of the horde, his steps now infused with a strange fervour. With low, cackling orders she couldn't fully hear, he led the hunting party away, their eyes gleaming unreachably, their marching suddenly caught with ritualistic meaning.

Despite having taken sustenance, Amber suddenly felt light-headed. The whole pack was ready to set upon anything—anyone—they found. Torek was right, curse him. She really was safer in here, for now.

She kept to her bed to avoid antagonising the guards—who in the absence of the others had sprung into ghoulish reanimation, prowling in constant patrol around the bars that she dared not now test. Muttering about the hunt they were missing. In the absence of being able to eat they entertained themselves by instead pushing increasingly suspect morsels into Amber's cell to see if she'd take the bait. When she remained resolutely unmoved, they started up an uncanny crooning.

"Hush little Fairy, don't yer cry
Goblins will sing you a lullaby
Eat from our plate an' drink from our cup
And if ye're lucky, yer won't wake up . . ."

They showed scant sign of stopping, so Amber cocooned herself in her cloak despite the stifling heat, and even found herself wishing for Torek's return. From beneath a fold in her makeshift blanket, she scowled at the bars in despair as though she could dissolve them with her gaze. But she'd been applying the corrosive paste for days now. What if she'd got the percentages or even ingredients wrong? What if she wasn't even weakening the bars at all?

Inhuman shrieking infected the air, tearing away all further thought.

Even the Goblins guarding Amber scattered, as Torek stalked over swaggering with triumph while the rest of those returning from the hunt cavorted in wild glee around the fire, skimming handfuls of embers like stones and howling derisively as the sparks they flung found their mark and burned their fellows.

Amber eyed Torek warily. "Hunt's complete?"

Torek sniffed. "I didn't take part. I wouldn't."

She watched him for a moment longer. "I believe that you didn't. I'm just not sure that you wouldn't."

"Want me ter tell yer about it?"

"I don't think you need to." Amber shuddered, watching the gloating scene around the fire. Unintelligible sounds turned sinister, crowding into a night fraught with unease. The air thickened with things unspoken and unspeakable, and fear congealed in unseen corners.

"I know you caught someone." She'd prided herself on needing nothing from Torek. But, right now, she needed him to refute her.

He didn't, initially. It was as though his eyes were shining too strangely to be able to. "What made you think you know anything?" he countered finally, looking at her at last. "There was a death. From another pack."

"Past tense? Before you arrived?" Discord and anticipation jarred in the air as Amber struggled to reconcile reality. "But these preparations aren't for a funeral, are they?"

Torek grunted with amusement. "Yer know how yer keep the Gems of yer ancestors? Feel like it keeps them with yer, passes their strengths ter yer, that kind of thing?"

Amber grimaced guardedly. "Sort of."

"Well, we Goblins don't have many possessions. We're more physical than material."

Amber swallowed, unsure whether Torek thought he was imparting something sacred or sickening. "I see."

Torek grimaced. "Yer will soon. I can't make yer take part. I wouldn't. But there's nothing ter stop yer watching, 'though yer might tell yerself yer don't want ter."

He stepped back to unblock her view, and Amber held very still. Would she do less of a disservice to the deceased to look away, or to bear witness? Over by the fire, his form mercifully shadowed but the bent of his body unmistakable in intent, a Goblin crouched. Eating. Feeding: from another.

Awareness rushed through Amber: of the throbbing pulse in her heart that certified her aliveness, and of the shivers that alighted upon her skin as though seeking to reaffirm her boundaries and proclaim otherness from what was happening in front of her. But the tremblings that clutched her soul forced a question: was such a distinction inviolate, or illusion? She tore her gaze away in revulsion and sought sanctuary by staring into the scrub.

"Don't worry," Torek murmured, his breath close enough for her to wonder about the scent that lingered upon it, and the particles she was now breathing into her own lungs. "I'm not hungry anymore."

He moved away, and in his absence the sounds of eating were impossible to ignore, growing grotesque and all-consuming in the ambiguous darkness.

Heavy with horror, the hour grew later still, but at last satiation seemed to lull the Goblins, and they drifted from the fire to their erratic slumbers.

Torek alone stayed awake, of course, and predictably returned. Still, he seemed unusually preoccupied, even for him.

"Priestess?" He must be drunk on meat, or flesh, and his own success, to be calling her that. His voice held an urgency that she didn't understand.

"Is it your wound?" She tried to stick to what was safe. "Come here. I'll clean it."

"No. They're going ter kill yer." Torek blurted tersely, as though disgorging a bone. "Tomorrow. When dawn breaks, so will you."

Ah. That tenuous, all too fragile hope that somehow he would keep her alive—that she had any hope of convincing him to do so—died immediately. Torek's betrayal, if it could be called a betrayal when she'd always known she couldn't trust him, hurt savagely, and how could it compare against what would come?

"Why now?" Amber retorted shakily; as though keeping talking could buy her time, could make it any less real.

"Well, it's not now, is it. Because I bought yer time," he admonished thickly. "But someone's going ter kill yer, Amber. An' they'd draw it out, tomorrow. Thing is: I can do it quick tonight, instead. If yer want."

Panic overtook her. This couldn't be the choice she faced. Her last days alive couldn't have been these claustrophobic ones in this pitiful cell. She wanted to see those she loved again. She wanted to travel the Realm again. She wanted to feel rain just once more . . .

"Don't worry." She realised Torek was still talking. "It's better this way. The least I can do. The blade I'll use is sharp. Better than that rusted thing I gave yer."

Something else plunged into her heart, then. The thinnest of hopes. The knife. The knife he'd given her, that she'd kicked under the mattress. She'd saw through the corroded bars right now. She'd have to.

The possibility leapt, intense and animalistic, and she seized on it with desperation. "You'd do that, for me?" She didn't add a plea. She didn't want to push it.

"Mm." Uncertainty flickered; vied with arrogance. "Yer've got until I come back, ter make yer peace with the Realm. If I don't kill yer, they will. Like I say: it's yer choice."

A hatred colder than anything Amber had experienced threatened to overwhelm her. But he was leaving already and would be back any moment, so the seconds she had left spiralled into the speed of her scudding heartbeat.

She wasn't going to let him have anything of her. So, she threaded her spirit through the bars; sent it to tangle safely into the thorn trees beyond where the flesh-stench from the fire was already drifting and sending a palpable unease into the scatter-thoughted creatures inhabiting the branches, who set up a shaking and a shrieking. Amber felt a fierce thrill lift through her. The simian scrummage might provide something of a smoke screen for her escape and absconsion.

She risked a couple of seconds in exchange for the rising intensity of their squalling. The urgency almost overwhelmed her now that it came down to these few moments, so much so that the temptation was to give herself over to the anger: burn herself up in it so nothing would remain for when Torek came back. But that wouldn't free her. That would keep her trapped, immutably here, and awaiting his return. She must act, and act now. So, she scrabbled under the mat with fevered fingers and snatched the knife up triumphantly. But as she held it to the besmeared bars, her courage nearly failed her. How could she think she could saw through iron? She hefted the weapon grimly. What better option did she have? The blade was as snaggletoothed and savage as any she'd seen. Sawing was probably the only thing it was good for, if it was good for anything.

Anticipation swarmed ant-like across her skin, and as she placed her grip upon the first bar she felt the bite of the chemicals, as though they were clinging to her hand in hand, giving her all the strength they had. Time to find out if those herbal libations, offered in dearest hope and smeared in utmost secrecy, had been worthy of her worship.

The Goblins were still in their flesh-stupor, but it wouldn't last once she started hacking and hewing. She thought about what Torek said: that you had to kill another or kill yourself. That the only way to be free was to pick up the knife. But she'd show him: the only thing to do with a knife was cut yourself free.

She was about to draw her first stroke, when a cacophony of Goblin growls exploded in counterpoint to the tree creatures: Torek was fighting with someone, presumably about Amber, and the others in their meat-addled drunkenness were joining the fray.

Amber seized the opportunity and didn't stop, gouging for all she was worth. Corrosion flecked and flaked and flew away as she dug in with all her might. She sawed and sawed: sawed until the metal screeched and screamed in protest, sawed until the scrabble and struggle of it sheared away her skin.

Sweat and terror clung to her. The Goblins must be hearing her, even through their brawling. But finally, the blade seared through one bar and she dared not stop for breath before transferring her efforts first beneath and then to the side, until a section ruptured before her, brutal as a broken ribcage and with just enough of a gap to squeeze through.

Freedom finally within her grasp, a quick glance around her cell before she left was all she could afford. She couldn't countenance leaving Nzizi's feather in a place like this, but everything else—save for the blessedly small vessel—she had to abandon: she could barely squeeze herself through the gap, let alone her cloak or mat. So, she tucked the feather into her sash: for security as well as sentimentality, in the one act of indulgence she'd allow herself. She wasn't doing this alone, now. She had a vulture watching over her.

Then, gripping those hateful bars, she contorted herself through and finally she was outside: exposed and invulnerable all at once.

Everything leapt within Amber. The free air clung to her with enlivening fingers, urging haste. She would abandon the fractured façade of safety she'd constructed here and take her chances in the wilds beyond. But first she must evade the horde, riled and rampant and all around.

Expecting the ghoulish flare of Goblin eyes to light upon her at any moment with the explosion of each fresh volley of fighting, Amber scanned the stars, set a course she barely dared trust, and fled, darting low, keeping beneath the brightness of the horizon until she could reach thorn tree after thorn tree.

She stood shaking in the stoic, skeletal embrace of the final sylvan shadow at the edge of the camp, just out of the firelight's reach. The Goblins were still brawling and bellowing, but any moment the wind and her luck would change, and they would notice her absence and be after her, tearing across the scrub with the speed and ferocity of wildfire.

In this moment, though, she took her breath and felt aflame with a sense of freedom. She was alive and away, barely able to comprehend that after so many days and nights of planning and holding her nerve, bearing constantly the simultaneous possibilities of abscondion and annihilation, she had finally enacted her escape.

Worth holding on for, she told herself pointedly, trying to encapsulate her escape into those simple words and lay a mental trail back to this moment should she need similar strategy in the future. The future was what she must focus on first, she decided. She would process the past properly later, but for now she must leave her time here behind and not take it with her. She would consign the past terrors to memory, so as not to allow them to fester into trauma and infect the present.

And the present was about to demand her full attention, for she had perhaps nine hours of darkness to contend with. Nine hours alone, through the night and through the wilds. But there was a sacredness to her stealth, as she returned to the night and reclaimed herself with every step. The noises that crowded in around her—the twig-snapping tiptoes of antelope, the stifled rustles of cat-eyed creatures, the distant rumbles of Sand Giants—she welcomed back like old friends, relieved that they had overthrown the Goblins' proximity.

Once she was far enough away to no longer see the glow from their fire, let alone hear their unholy uproar, the horde seemed another Realm away, and Amber was back in her element. The weight of the recent past lifted, replacing itself with the focused, manageable caution of what lay in front of her.

Away from the trappings of camp, she could breathe properly again. The voluminous sky unwound in never-ending directions, and the unseen noises populating the vastness lent the night edges and angles, rendering it delineable and enabling her to orientate herself and navigate its stretches. The territory out here might be unknown, but it was far from unknowable, and she returned to its spacious, supple reaches with souldeep gratitude.

Staying her course by the stars, Amber walked hurriedly, as beneath a wide-eyed moon a strand of trodden-bare earth glowed palely like a silver thread guiding her towards safety. Such a path would be known, and walked, by everything out here. She had to hope her scent would be masked by that of something more pungent and powerful, so she couldn't be followed by the Goblins.

Amber's senses bristled as she waded through the nebulous darkness. The night smeared and smudged and grew endless. Despite a wan moon, the dimness was distorting: it felt as though with the light gone, a dimension had disappeared as well. At one point she walked up to a Sand Giant, and it was hard to say who was more startled. The encounter left Amber spinning through the Realm. How wonderful to find that the night was still populated by monstrous and undangerous things. Keeping the sweet company of an uninhabited night, Amber began to feel as though things might be okay.

Until they clearly weren't. Sounds skulked through the silence that were not of the scrub, and Amber was about to flatten herself into a shadow when she saw their source at the edge of vision: Torek.

Panic flooded, but she held her ground. He wasn't in hunting mode. He was fleeing. And as a far wind lifted, she could hear why. The pack were in fullthroated pursuit. And Torek was the only thing between her and them.

"They think I let yer go. They're going ter kill me." He took a few faltering steps towards her, seeing she was unafraid despite being as alone as he was.

Amber stood tall, claimed her space in silence, and didn't step back. He looked smaller now, somehow. She was too far away now, and he knew it. She had helped him once, and he knew how he had repaid her. She saw in his face everything he had lost—and everything she had regained.

"All I'm going to take from you is a few minutes' head start," Amber retorted evenly, needing say no more. "If you've got any sense, you'll lose my trail and hide out until the pack pass. If you keep following me, they'll be on you before they can even get close to catching up with me— especially having reawakened their taste for flesh this night." She hefted the vessel for emphasis and went to leave.

Torek stared at her, wild-eyed and wretched. Then he grinned crookedly, assumptive enough even now. "I'll hide out fer now, fer both our sakes. Until I can come fer yer. Can't stand against yer fae bewitchings, can I?"

But Amber was barely listening. "I never had witchcraft," she told him with less scorn and more pride. "I learnt bushcraft."

Away she sprang, and she didn't fear his eyes at her back. She ran until the darkness was a shield, she ran until the darkness was a sanctuary, and then she ran until the darkness was just darkness again: as indifferent and dear to her as anything else in the bush.

She let the heat of the veld cauterise the mental wounds the Goblins had left, then deliberately released a breath she felt she'd been holding for too long and released her past as well; let it tangle into the myriad thorns so that it could no longer follow her. The only risk now was the wild itself, she reminded herself. Hazardous enough by far, yet after the relentless mindgames of the Goblins, it was a relief to face something merely as it was. The wild wasn't mystical in its fierceness, it wasn't cruel in its dispassion.

And, yet. The balmy night chilled as she realised the depth of her danger. Fleeing Torek after his unexpected appearance, she had dashed headlong and hitherthither, caring only for the distance she was putting between her and the horde. Now she had left her pursuers behind, but she had also lost all track of where she was.

Terror clamped and spread inwards. Sweat clung desperately, as though it could squeeze the answer out of her.

The tattoo of her own footsteps harried her as she hastened even further. She thought she could remember the twisted silhouette of this particular tree, had definitely rounded the gnarled tower of that particular anthill. But she knew her mind was playing tricks on her. She wanted to remember so badly she was convincing herself of falsehoods.

She forced herself to stop. She wasn't going to randomly stumble upon her old route: she needed to pause, admit she was lost, interpret her surroundings, make a new plan. And she couldn't afford much time to do so. Sharing nightwatch with Nzizi, she had slept out here and felt untouchable. Alone, though, even standing still for too long could bring death. She couldn't just climb a tree and wait out the night without the Goblins creeping up on her, and she had to keep moving forward, if she were to have any hope of reaching the remaining waterholes.

She had to forge her way through, but she could no longer find even the stars: the clouds were scudding unsettlingly fast, and a capricious wind had picked up, blurring into obscurity all she could hope to recognise. It skewed her mind into similar unease, for with such tempestuous weather, she had no chance of hearing either the Goblins, or the predators the Harpies had warned her about. She felt herself catching the restlessness she'd seen infect antelopes before.

The antelope. Their forms suddenly made the only sense to be found amidst the shifting swirls of night, their cut-glass eyes glinting like mirrors through the darkness, emanating vigilance as though they could gift it to her. She'd never felt so relieved to be seen.

'Everyone talks about being captured by the gaze of a predator,' she remembered Nzizi counselling her. *'Yet it is nothing to meeting the glance of a prey animal and being trustingly ignored.'* Amber felt both heartened and humbled that the antelope now looked straight at her and behaved as though she were part of the environment. Offering a hundred gratitudes, Amber made up her mind to follow the herd to water, even if it took all night. She made herself as guileless as possible, so that they might read her intentions and not take fright.

Satellite ears swivelled and elegantly muscled heads dipped and raised in proud and ever-vigilant watch as the herd encircled her. Was it only in her imagination that those liquescent eyes recognised her? Was it folly to believe that the antelope knew her, as the bearer of the water they had imbibed?

Amber felt her spirits rise, embosomed and emboldened by the entire company of creatures. She had hundreds of eyes about her now, all looking out for the terrors her night-blind self couldn't hope to see.

She moved with the herd as though she were drifting in and out of consciousness: silent, stumbling and supported. Time passed like a dream, until the penumbra of pelage parted, and Amber stopped and stared at the sight before her.

A corkthorn tree, stark in its solitude, stood sentry beside a near-empty waterhole, its jagged branches reaching out as though to gather the meagre pool into such protection as its skeletal form could offer. Weather-wizened as it was, such an iconic specimen as this stood out like a beacon, instantly recognisable from Nzizi's description: deep-grooved bark, with pale patches flaking from the trunk, deep-grooved limbs branching into striking angles from which sprang needle-bright pairs of upreaching thorns. Having never seen one before, Amber knew it instantly—and she knew with an equal and absolute certainty that she had never been here. Beneath a cloud-veiled sky, she was utterly lost.

And she was utterly free, so she refused to let panic pierce her. Instead, she focused her full attention on her priorities, the first of which must surely be to repay the unassuming creatures who had brought her safely thus far. So, as the herd milled around peacefully, their companionable behaviours replacing the intensity of the darkness with an inhabitable intimacy, Amber threaded through the space left by the antelope and crouched at the sunken hollow where the oozing mud spoke longingly of the crystal waters it used to consort with.

Her concern spilling over with the amphora's contents, Amber poured steadily until the pool's level rose to swell the pan into shining abundance once more, and her companions at last drank their fill.

Amber joined them humbly, her saliva flooding as keenly as her relief. Staying seated in salutation afterwards, she decided to claim a rest and gather her thoughts, just for a few minutes, so she could navigate her way on with a clear mind. After all, she could no longer rely on following the antelope to the next waterhole—they wouldn't leave this one for hours now. But at least she'd just filled this pool, and so it was the only one for miles around she could be certain was uninhabited by amphibious dangers.

It was also most likely the only one for miles around at all, but she refused to dwell on that fact. Instead, she let her mind stray, listening peaceably to the heartbeat-steady lapping of supping antelope while she watched the scudding ripples of the surface skitter and sparkle in a subtle interplay of moonlight and night-breeze. She felt drawn by the water now, as she had been so many seasons ago when unsure and seeking answers. Perhaps it was the memory and meaning of all that had been set in motion then that now kept her lingering long enough to notice the strange tension that was swirling with the stirred-up silt and sediment. A single feather floated atop the surface, like a lotus rising unblemished above mud, and Amber felt a frisson brush her skin, featherlike itself, to realise it was Nzizi's pinion that must have freed itself from her sash.

"Scales can fly and feathers swim," Amber murmured. That had been the Harpy apprentice's premonition, hadn't it? Right before the Sand Giant had lumbered onto the scene and sent all such considerations scattering.

She watched, her breath light with wonder, while the feather twirled as though seeking true north and then held fast, despite the vicissitudes of the rippling breeze.

A curious reassurance descended, like a hand upon her shoulder. Perhaps Nzizi was guiding her, even now. Amber caught the bushveld scent clinging to the feather, unshakeable and unmistakable: a remnant of the wildness she now carried within her and had called home so recently — and a reminder of the preciousness of those months with the Harpies which could not be erased by any number of moments with the Goblins

Heart hammering, trembling with reverence Amber scooped up the feather and experimentally dropped it, just to be sure. A grin split her face as she watched it spin and settle, and she held very still. Even in her heat-addled state, she knew what to do now, with the feather as her pathfinder. There was only one thing for it: she must reach and replenish the rest of the waterholes, because who knew if the rains ever would? The darkness no longer frightened her, and she had a pledge to make good. Even if it took all night. She would, in all likelihood she assured herself, achieve a good proportion of her goal before the Goblins caught up. She had no food, of course, but she could indisputably last a fair while longer without that than the others could without water.

Amber steeled her resolve and brandished the feather determinedly. She had her compass. Now, to find the waterholes.

The antelope, of course, had more sense than to abandon their new-filled reservoir. They watched Amber opaquely as she prepared to leave. She wasn't returning home, or finding her friends; she was going further — even if it brought the whole Goblin horde after her, and the antelope stared as if they knew. Their eyes shone a warning, and even though she could not both heed it and complete her quest, Amber returned their collective gaze longingly, trying to pour her gratitude out to them. She had grown inordinately fond of the antelope during her captivity. At the edges of vision hey had watched her all the while: their silence at first bearing anxious witness, then imbuing stoic solidarity. And now offering farewell.

"Goodbye, my friends," There could be no 'until next time.' There could be no promises. But her breathing grew steadier, feeling their eyes on her. She felt seen, thanks to them. She felt certain.

Keeping the corkthorn tree carefully in her sight as a waypoint, she moved on, into an endless night populated only by the soporific stridulations of insects, the sounds scattering so distantly that she felt as though the Realm stretched out forever. With the stars spiralled away the darkness enjoyed dominion, and Amber's isolation was complete, yet she walked on with hurried steps but a tranquil mind. The quietude in her head declined to fill with thoughts, so grateful felt she to simply be alone again, after escaping the Goblins. With Nzizi's feather guiding her, there was nothing to fear. And eventually the clouds parted, and the moon bathed her path silver until it glowed, spooling out through the bush like a serpent. She wondered where Diberkati was.

Her heart leapt into her mouth as an antelope ram bounded past her, shattering the silence and utterly ignoring her in its urgency, the fruit he had been eating falling from his mouth in his haste. Amber froze, unable to decide between flattening herself to the ground to hide beneath the horizon, and standing tall and to stare down whatever had spooked the buck.

The silence stole back in around her. The antelope tiptoed back, showing no interest in the bounty it had dropped, its every hair raised and every sense heightened. The discarded fruit glistened between them. With only one dainty bite out of it, it looked passably clean and undeniably tempting.

Maybe her cervine companion hadn't been completely ignoring her, after all. Amber picked up the fruit, gave it a perfunctory slosh of water from the vessel, and raised it in a toast to the buck. It watched her inscrutably, aquiver as though ready to dart away again.

Juice and saliva flooded her mouth as Amber bit into the fruit. The sweetness clung strangely on her desiccated tongue. Ignoring the sudden wave of lightheadedness that sloshed against her, Amber surged to her feet again.

And stumbled.

The buck hadn't dropped anything. It had spat it out. *Goblinfruit. She'd eaten Goblinfruit.*

She vomited. The Realm stretched and splintered, distorting into fevered shapes as though reality were splitting and breaking like the dried — skin crust of the drought-ridden earth and letting nightmarish imaginings slip out through the cracks…

The buck stepped closer, and Amber staggered towards it, feeling somehow as though if only she could keep her eyes on the constants she could trust: the curve of those life-helix horns, or the shimmer of stripes streaming from sweat-soaked sides, solid against the shadows of the night, she might stay sane and safe.

But exhaustion took hold with sickly suddenness. Everything drifted into delirium, and in her increasingly unhinged state, as her vision betrayed her, she feared she was floating suspended in the night instead of walking through it. She managed to catch sight of the antelope again, and it seemed anchored better than her to the ground, so she tried to emulate its steps: one after another, placed resolute onto the dirt. But it felt as though her limbs were no longer attached to her feet. Maybe Torek had been right, when he'd taunted her for leaving no tracks and having no impact on the Realm.

No matter. The Realm had left its own impression on her. *You know this trail*, she tried to tell herself, even as everything lurched.

Why were the stars at a strange angle? Amber disjointedly realised she was on the ground, but she was too lightheaded to care. Yet even lying here, the sky akilter, she recognised this track. She could name these smoothened stones, she had seen before these specific minerals flecking ethereal colour into the powder-dry earth. She couldn't remember where she was, but she knew she'd walked here with Nzizi. It was a path of happy times. She would stay on it, and it would be okay. Wouldn't she? It was so dark, now. A drowning dark, far deeper than night.

She heard the antelope bark: a thrown, disembodied sound that rattled against her ears, and she realised she must still be part of herself, if only just. She was about to form a thought on that, but it drifted away with her consciousness.

Seeing her slump, a vulture stopped its circling, and swooped down.

The buck beside her snorted, and sidestepped. And stayed.

Fever and Friendship

She was back at the Goblin camp, lying on the ground, dreaming of the company she couldn't keep.

Except she wasn't. Not this time. Her friends floated through the darkness like points converging on a compass.

Dazedly Amber stared and stared, willing her eyes to stop watering and confirm what she most dearly desired and yet dared not after all this time believe.

Racxen reached her first. Safety flowed like water. His lips found hers in the darkness, and his kiss felt like coming home. He offered her soulroot, and she felt the effects of the tainted fruit ease a little.

She didn't need to ask how he'd found her.

"Prints are only part of it," Racxen promised, his eyes bright with starlight, his presence a solid shadow amidst a shifting night. "It's not just my senses I follow you with – but also my heart."

"Although it was by ill luck that we found your trail," Jasper warned, emotion overcoming awkwardness as he offered her the salt-cured supplies Yenna pressed into his hands and watched her begin to eat effortfully. Encircled by her friends, she felt safe again.

"I am sorry indeed to find you in such straits, yet full relieved to have found you," the Prince continued. "First we were tracking animals in the hope of finding a better waterhole for Diberkati, then Racxen was convinced one antelope out of the hundreds of them was acting oddly and followed that instead, upon which we picked up your tracks – and those of Goblins. I hope they didn't find the serpent."

"They found me instead," Amber began, feeling wretched. She inhaled quickly, steeling herself to spill out the entire story as quickly as she could, as though that might avoid it recontaminating her.

"Engo ro fash." Racxen forestalled, containing her distress even when he could not know its cause. "Your wild and precious life cannot be reduced to its most difficult days," he promised in solidarity, his words wrapping around her like a strengthening embrace. "Not everything that happens is part of your story; you get to decide. Tell us what and how you choose, in the way that would serve you best."

Amber felt the fire return to her soul. The truth was painful and she would always remember it, but she didn't have to relive it. Her narrative of it would be a tool through which to begin healing.

"I began my apprenticeship with Nzizi, and she let me choose a gift: one vessel, from their most treasured store," Amber began, the memory of that apprenticeship warming her like the bushveld sun. "I tried to choose the one the Harpies would least likely miss: a small, unassuming pot." She showed her friends. "Yet Zaralathaar had enchanted it – I soon discovered it pours water unceasingly. So I left the Harpies, with the aim of finding and filling as many waterholes as I could. Such an endeavour led to… direct conflict… with the Goblins. But when you found me, I had escaped and was attempting to make good my pledge. Before I mistakenly ate Goblinfruit and passed out."

A shadow slid away from her as she spoke, leaving her unshackled, and her smile was as strong as a Sand Giant now. "So: shall we finish what I started?"

"Indubitably. First, however, you need to sleep off the residual effects of that fruit," Jasper warned firmly. "We shall soon reach the camp Yenna and her Pack have sprung in the barrens nearby. You might not realise it, but you've wandered almost to the desert. Then, Amber: for once, do nothing."

He continued in soothing haste before Amber could argue. "You've solved the problem – let others now action the solution." He arched a regal brow. "Or, rather: you managed to accidentally stumble into possession of the Water Nymph's solution to the problem." He sounded for a moment more like the prim and prickly Prince she was used to. "But my point stands: rest. I will rendezvous with the leaders of all the lands, and we will work out the logistics of replenishing everyone's water supplies and sharing the vessel."

"More efficient than my plan," Amber admitted lightheadedly. "But what about Diberkati?"

"I have no doubt that once we fill the pans, she will find them herself," Jasper reassured. "But perhaps you were right about the serpent," he admitted philosophically, as the welcoming shadow of the Wolfren camp seemed to prowl protectively towards them out of the amorphous night. "Perhaps I was wrong to involve her. You always told me she wasn't the cause of this. She needn't be the cure, either. We should leave her be."

Amber nodded peaceably, relieved. Familiarity and friendship enveloped her amidst the sounds and scents of the makeshift settlement as the Wolfren welcomed the travellers back with howls and hugs, and Amber felt like she was home. Yenna sauntered over to greet her happily, Ruby threw her arms around her, and with Racxen her strength at her shoulder, she updated the Pack.

A Night Aflame

"Amber!"

She scrambled to her feet and froze, antelope-like. The recently refound sense of safety wrought by the Wolfren camp threatened to shatter as a hatefully familiar voice encroached.

"Did yer believe that nonsense about being untrackable? Did yer think bein' light on yer feet would be enough?" Torek hissed. "Amber! If it weren't fer me, yer'd be dead meat. Yer'd be linin' bellies. Yer belong ter me now. And I'm here ter take back what's mine. Show yerself, yer coward."

Hearing her name bellowed on an intruder's lips shocked Jasper. Racxen had already moved wordlessly to her side, and slipped a clawed hand into Amber's almost-not-shaking one. Yenna strode forth, flint in her eyes and a snarl on her lips.

"We have what we need to save the Realm," Amber promised. "There need be no bloodshed. I just need you to stand with me. I don't need you to fight for me." Torek had been a solid threat earlier, but he was a mere spectre now: floating indistinctly in the dark in contrast to the solid shapes of her friends standing firm beside her.

"You're not on your own," the Wolf Sister promised in return, her lilting voice smooth and her blazing eyes steady. "You're in no danger."

"They'll kill me, if yer don't come back with me!" The terror in Torek's eyes seemed real enough as his gaze finally fixed on her.

Jasper let his hand brush aside his robe, revealing the hilt of his sword. His green eyes turned to ice. "And I will kill you if she does."

The night settled, becoming aware of what it was witness to. Jasper remembered himself, and gestured imperiously to the waiting Wolfren. "Be wise, and doubt not the might of this Queendom."

Even Torek seemed to balk at the rows of gleaming eyes fixed wolfishly upon him. A mighty army of human and lupine forms claimed the night, and Amber's heart leapt to glimpse the legendary silhouette of the Centaur, Han, as well as that of her best friend Ruby, amongst them. An unearthly howl began to shiver through the Pack in an undeniably primal display of power, and the Goblin quailed.

Yenna snarled leisurely, and needed say no more.

"But I was good ter her – I never hurt her, not really," Torek whined, fixing pleading eyes once more on Amber. "She stayed."

"She survived," Jasper corrected in clipped tones, and Amber could hear anger more clearly in his words than she had in Torek's wails. "And if you think the latter suffices for the former you are an even more pitiful specimen than I first took you for. Save your breath and hold your tongue. No-one will let you take her."

With her friends bunched protectively around her and the might of the Wolfren behind her, Amber no longer feared the aggressor who had tormented her for so long. But something terrifying gleamed in his eyes, even as he saw the truth in theirs. "If I can't have yer, I'll take yer friend," he hissed, changing tack. "Yer owe me, Fairy. That serpent yer consorted with can't be far."

Amber froze. She'd dared hope Torek had forgotten Diberkati, that having a 'sorceress' to contend with had been diversion enough to at least buy the serpent more time and distance than this.

"She's not here." It was the truth, probably, and as near to rallying as Amber could manage. She'd sworn she'd never let Torek hurt her again, and yet here she was, answering too quickly to a question that felt like a knife.

The night sky seemed to bunch and darken as though in response, but the Goblin's reaction tore all attention from it. "The rains will return once the serpent is slain. Give her up!" Torek's scream spilled a rage that scorched worse than the heat.

"She is not ours to barter with; she goes where she pleases," Jasper threw back tersely. Murky as his understanding of the situation was, he could feel the deadly current of what had passed between this Goblin and Amber. In response, and a little rashly, he called out protectively: "she left long before you darkened this night."

"Yer expect me ter believe that, while yer summon a smokescreen?" Torek growled bitterly.

Amber was about to spit a retort when she noticed it too. The night was thickening, constricting: stalked by a danger subtler than the Goblins – one that clutched at her chest and squeezed into her throat, smarting her eyes, and stinging her lungs. In the absence of rain, moonlight had long been the only balm left for the Realm's sky, and now it was being snuffed out: by suffocating clouds of toxic smoke. Real and hateful, drifting in silent menace towards them, the deadly plumes were smearing through the night.

Amber's heart plummeted further as she realised the source. Distorted by distance, kernels of flamelight floated through the soot-thickened darkness, and it was not the sandsheltered plains they were spreading towards. The grasslands were on fire. And the Harpy settlement would burn.

Amber's fear flared fit to overtake the flames. Torek didn't need to flush her out. She would run willingly into this: for Nzizi, for Inqe – for any of the Order.

"I leave yer ter yer smoke, and yer serpent." Torek's incendiary voice pierced the miasma one final time. "P'raps it was right yer fled us. Look at what yer've created. Ye're a liability even ter yer 'friends'." He spat as he sprang away.

"The Goblins think you caused this?" Jasper muttered in disbelief even as Yenna regrouped and redirected her Pack, calling them back into human form and imparting to them a plan he was not yet privy to. His haunted green eyes stared past her into an ashening night. He desperately wanted to discount this nightmare as trickery, but the evidence was as overwhelming as the reality. "It's no mere smokescreen. It's a full-scale bushfire."

"And while the Goblins thought *I* conjured the water, not the vessel," Amber reminded brokenly, "it's obviously not *me* controlling the elements here."

Jasper stared at her blankly, uncomprehending.

"You remember the sandstorm?" Amber prompted urgently. The ground lurched as she thought of it. The whole Realm tasted wrong now, not just the air, and panic constricted as much as the smoke. Amidst the shifting sands of a slipping night, a fear long submerged was resurfacing.

"Of course," Jasper admitted. "I wasn't sure Diberkati didn't start it, unwittingly."

Amber swallowed, desperate to be proven wrong. "And what about this firestorm?"

"Oh, no." He stared in shock at the smoke-swollen sky. "You're right. I think she heard the Goblin. And that somehow, her anger coalesced into causing..." Jasper's eyes grew wild. "We have to stop Diberkati, to stop the fire."

"We have to *save* Diberkati, as well as stopping the fire," Amber corrected with a grimace, overwhelmed. "And we can't blame her, Jasper."

"It's not about assigning blame," Jasper promised hastily. "It's about finding a solution."

"We've no right to expect any solution from Diberkati," Yenna reminded him, her golden eyes fierce and focused. "But we can still offer her support."

"And the only certainty right now is the fire," Racxen interjected. "Whatever or whoever caused it, it will reach the Harpies in minutes, and they will need all the help we can offer to evacuate those they are sheltering. Diberkati is hurting, but those fires will hurt many more, if we don't intervene."

"Indeed," Jasper acknowledged contritely. "So—"

"We split up, and aid as we each can best." Amber urged, staring towards the Harpy settlement as though by doing so she could hold its inhabitants safe while she must plot a different course. Then she paused, uncertain. The Prince wasn't disputing her, but he wasn't heading off for the settlement, either. And he was looking worryingly noble.

"You are helping the Harpies, right?" she pressed, as he loitered. Even as she spoke she could hear the Wolfren rousing to their leader's barked words. "You are assisting the evacuation?"

"Yes," the Prince sniffed regally. "And yet no. Give me the vessel."

Amber balked. "What? You can't fly in this! You won't even be able to breathe – skin or otherwise. Nzizi spoke a prophecy which ended with a warning: 'One must fall where none can stand.' I don't want it to come true now," she added grimly.

"Even you know a Fairy's wings are heat-resistant," Jasper dismissed mildly, like he was fooling anyone that he believed this would be enough. "And it's falling, Amber: it's not dying. We none of us would get very far flying if we went around scared of falling – and anyway, I'm only using the vessel's water to put out the fire. It's no more dangerous than what you're about to attempt."

Amber glared her challenge. "You think you know my plan?"

Jasper gave a smile as proud as it was sad. "Amber, I always know. You're going for the source, as it were. You're going to track down Diberkati, while I douse the flames from above, and while everyone else rushes to deal with the destruction in her wake."

Amber rolled her eyes in reluctant concession. "Nzizi's feather will lead me to Diberkati, so it won't be as difficult as your enterprise," she argued, taking refuge in the camaraderie of their exchange. "As for the flames: they're in her wake, but not in her control."

"And *this* is in your wake, not in your control," Jasper reminded. "I'm not asking you to obey me, Amber. I'm asking you to trust me."

She hugged him in acquiescence, and the Prince's voice was gentle at her ear. "For what it's worth, I do agree with you: we need to protect Diberkati, not punish her," he reassured evenly. "And the rains may yet be linked with her."

"I don't think they have to be," Amber admitted. "But what if they could be? Historically, serpents have tended to have answers," she reminded.

"Historically, that's tended to have been problematic," Jasper retorted.

"We'll see," Amber riposted lightly as she stepped back. But there were real tears in her eyes, and Jasper looked, for once, truly shaken.

"I would say: 'don't go alone'," he mumbled stiffly. "And yet that is a luxury we cannot afford."

Amber gripped his shoulder in solidarity. "And I would say: stay safe, although that is a wish I cannot cause to come true."

She pushed the vessel into his waiting hands and he nodded unspoken gratitude.

As the Prince turned next to the Wolf Sister, understanding closed the distance between them and Yenna's eyes flashed her fierce devotion. Jasper drew a fortifying breath and sprang into the air as he felt her strength combine with his own.

Watching him soar to the sky, Yenna rallied and returned to the others in a few prowling paces. Her voice cut cleanly through the swift-swirling smoke. "My Pack will shelter the Harpies, and I shall ready our camp – but Inqe will need assistance in moving those at the settlement to this safety." Her blazing eyes searched out the means by which to make it happen.

"I will steer them through the smoke," Racxen pledged, his quiet voice certain. The simplicity of his words belied the complexity of his promise, and Amber grinned as she met his gaze. There was no-one she'd trust more in the darkness, even after all she had traversed alone.

"It is well," the Wolf Sister agreed, her eyes like warm embers. "It's a fair distance in fear, let alone frailty, to a sanctuary they do not yet know of. I would have them guided by the best."

Racxen's bowed his head in proud recognition, determined to see it done. Then his night-attuned eyes flared in proud recognition as two unmistakeable figures crested the dunes and sent optimism alighting on the company even amidst the smoke.

"You won't be alone," Han's lilting voice rang out, with the vibrancy of the ancient greenwood he was born of. "We will join with you, as safe hands and strong arms, to carry those who need it." Beside him Rraarl crouched in hulking readiness, Racxen's heart lifted to know the spirited Centaur and the stoic Gargoyle would be with him through the inferno.

It was Ruby's turn to draw herself up now quickly, turning to her best friend. "Hydd and I will help Yenna assist the evacuees." The Selkie's eyes were streaming in the smoke, but Amber knew the support he would provide would be absolute. Her heart overflowed with gratitude to them both.

As though sensing Amber's rising terror Ruby looked straight at her just for a moment, simply and surely, as though they were just winglets planning another gleeful post-bedtime out-of-the-window-escapade all those seasons ago when adventure had meant something different than the death-risking present. "And you'll meet us here – after you safely find Diberkati." She spoke as though creating this future so certainly that there was no room for anguish or alternatives. The way she twisted the hem of her fine silk dress in distraction betrayed a little of her fear in that almost imperceptible way only a best friend would notice, but the conviction with which she spoke anchored Amber hugely.

Ruby, of course, made no reference to her own fears, and voiced only the needs of others. "With everyone focused on the fire, the Goblins will be expecting to find the serpent unguarded, when she's at her most vulnerable," she warned Amber earnestly. "So, you have to find her first. You'll need to use the feather."

It wasn't a question, so Ruby didn't wait for an answer. She trusted Amber implicitly, and with time spilling like the sands she simply hugged her best friend, and dashed towards Yenna's Pack, the bright flame of her hair bouncing as Hydd strode after her stoically, the Selkie sweating streams beneath the pelt he would not be parted from.

As the company parted in preparation, there was no more time for goodbyes. And how could she say goodbye to the one from whom she could never be parted, in her heart? In recognition, Racxen padded towards Amber in reverence and readiness. He twined his claws between her fingers, kissed a promise against her lips, shared his breath with hers, and she felt stable amidst a spinning night.

Her heart swelled as she kissed him back; as though if she did so fiercely enough she could keep him safe, could hope to stave off the danger looming closer for them both. Because he was running into the fire, and she was chasing after its cause. And like the flames, the danger was licking ever closer.

Understanding sparked between them and they both drew back, pulled by an urgency even greater than their bond. They must part now, and face only dangers instead of each other. Amber had loved Racxen for years now; she could barely comprehend that she might never see him again. So she sealed the sight of him inside her soul now: his night-shone eyes, careful and relentless when picking up every detail tracking, which lost none of their eagerness when they rested upon her but dropped their hunger in satiation and found their refuge, his radiant skin dark as the earth the Arraheng near-worshipped and lived so close to, his tangle-black hair, clung with the dust of their adventures. The wholeness of him, from whom she never wished to be parted. She wanted to stare at him forever in case she never saw him again, but she didn't need to, she tried to tell herself. She knew him, bone-deep and flesh-real.

It's all right, she wanted to whisper. *We know what it is to love and be loved. I wanted all the nights hereafter with you, Racxen. I really did. Yet what we have had is enough for so many lifetimes, just in case.*

But they both knew they didn't have time for such goodbyes, so she didn't say it and he didn't reply. Still, his tongue spoke for his voice: imprinting every promise he'd ever made, making it so vivid it would never fade, never need be questioned, never retreat into memory, and would instead linger like a touch remaining, imparting all the love he had ever had for her and would keep forever, whatever happened after.

"Engo ro fash," he promised, his voice quiet and as sacred as the hidden stars as he sprang away into the murkening night.

Amber felt as though she could race the fire itself as she drew the vulturine feather from her sash and brandished it like a compass, trusting it to guide her true as she ran into the smoke.

***

The heat-haze from the encroaching flames shuddered as though in dread at what was approaching, and contortions of smoke roved spitefully across a constricting land, as suffocating as the confusion that was weighing down Nzizi as she plummeted from the Watch Tree and ran through the settlement to seek counsel with Inqe. "I have not seen Amber since she went to fill the pans – and the serpent, long before that," she admitted. The Harpy apprentice buried her head in her hands in self-reproach. "And now the Realm is not only drying, but burning."

The matriarch's farsighted eyes focused settlingly on her beloved and her weathered hands closed over Nzizi's. "Those out of our sight are not in our control," she reminded, swift and soothing. "But our future still is. What have you seen?"

"Smoke – and I didn't have to rely on my inner sight." Nzizi gathered herself quickly beneath Inqe's calming attention, but even her presence could not stave off the primal fear of what she must disclose. "I can tell the future clearly enough. A fire is coming – I see it on the thermals."

"And there has been no lightning this night to explain it," Inqe mused, her mind racing. The bush would burn like tinder, and where could they run to? Their one defence – their isolation – was about to prove their downfall.

But she must remain calm: for Nzizi, and for all of them. Membrane flicked across birdlike, unblinking eyes as the matriarch's sight and decision came into sudden focus. "Those who can walk, rouse them to doing so, and gather them outside. And send all our sisters to me, to tend those who cannot."

Nzizi nodded unquestioningly. The smoke was thickening already, and to evacuate everyone safely and suddenly would be no small feat. She must begin at once; there was no time for a strengthening embrace.

Knowing this, matriarch and mentor turned from each other, Nzizi rushing to the order's sleeping quarters as Inqe strode to the hospice beds.

Accompanied now by the anxious calls of the wheeling vultures who had caught her urgency as easily as they usually caught the thermals, the mentor swept through the lodgings like a vision, rousing her sisters who rushed as a murmurating flock to aid Inqe as instructed: each taking a different direction the faster to arrive at the matriarch's side.

Nzizi watched them go: Inqe would by now be rushing to the inner wards, to those whom it would take more than an Orderly's skill to rouse. And those who could not be bestirred.

The injustice of it all snapped at Nzizi's heels, as she hastened alone to the further chambers, on the outskirts of the shelter, to assist those who could be urged into waking and walking. Every Harpy here knew that those under their care had lived out their lives and had completed their journeys: it was not fair to ask any more of them at such an hour. Especially when the outcome of such an enterprise could not be promised; could barely be prepared for. She was not supposed to force the dying onto the path again. The Order had promised them peace.

But peace also meant protection from peril, and Nzizi knew a far more frightening death than should be waiting for her charges was closing in from outside – and from that the Harpies must defend them at all costs.

Above the paths the birds were already fleeing and Nzizi watched them go as she ran, feeling as though pieces of her soul were being torn away too. She knew in her heart many inhabitants would refuse to leave, and in response she would have to prove stronger than she ever had before.

As she reached the doors she met a vulture, hunched in silhouetted stature as though guarding those within: a lean image, thin and singular yet staunch in its stoicism, committing itself vividly to her memory. Unapologetically ugly and unwaveringly unshakeable, the sacred creature gave Nzizi courage to confront the unthinkable and so she took strength from its presence and threw the doors open.

Her abrupt intrusion was met with confusion from those inside, but instantly the ward's watchers joined with Nzizi's shared purpose, fluttering rousing whispers into into waking ears, and she found that the listeners mostly still trusted her as they ever had, even those who were further along the path than when she had last tended them.

Coaxing and cajoling, coercing, and commanding, Nzizi managed to convince everyone to move first through the corridors, and then out to the open courtyard. As the exodus gathered pace, urgency caught like the wildfire racing across the distance towards them, and by the time the smoky air greeted them outside everyone was jostling their opinions on the best route through the arid scrubland and away into the desert beyond.

Listening to them, Nzizi stalled, realisation congealing in the choking air. Not only would they have to abandon the only sanctuary they knew, but they would have to do so leaderless. For, feeling the weight of their expectations as crushingly as the current danger as she beheld her charges hunched huddled, hushed by pressing fear and darkening sky, only now did Nzizi realise that Inqe and the elders had not emerged.

Nzizi broke away in horror and rushed alone along the worn-dirt paths she could follow blind: to the centre of the settlement, to the order's inner sanctum. To that half-walled stone-cooled structure that somehow felt like a beating heart and treasured home, no matter how often death arrived as a guest.

Death might come as a friend to those ready, Nzizi knew, but she also knew the Realm of difference between the death everyone deserved and the one that was stalking towards them tonight. The only dark-cloaked visitor tonight would be herself, she determined. The others who had congregated with those in the innermost chambers might be Elders in title, but in truth they were barely older than she, and scarcely better prepared. To leave now would be to leave them to an infernal fate. Amidst the great sickening spumes of smoke sweeping the land, Nzizi could already glimpse the virulent flickers of flame lashing their way through the night as her beloved scrubland fell to the fire.

The half-wall surrounding the sanctum rose in familiar greeting, but at the windows beyond, wings spread to form a wall of their own. A living wall. A loving wall.

Inqe met Nzizi's shocked gaze silently, her stare lightning amidst the stormclouds, as steadfast as if she were merely holding the line before a Sand Giant: as though she were standing against an animal and not an incendiary monster.

In that moment, Nzizi realised two things: Inqe's intention to stay with those who could not leave, and her own responsibility to lead away those who could.

As she rushed back towards her duty awaiting in the courtyard, the apprentice closed her eyes, as though she could close off her heart, and forget all her hopes for the future. But of course she couldn't, any more than she could quieten the twin fears that lashed flamelike: that in leading the others away she was abandoning her beloved Order and her even more beloved Inqe – and that while supporting the evacuees outside was one thing, leading them into the desert was another. Where was there to go? The bushveld was burning. They must take their chances in the great void of sand beyond, of which Nzizi knew nothing. In which there was nothing…

"Nothing that can burn." The Arraheng from earlier was suddenly beside her, his skin the colour of red sand after rain and his presence just as welcome, his night-shone eyes blazing a route between dangers. "There is a Wolfren camp, equipped to help. Tell us how to help you prepare everyone — we'll take you there."

Nzizi stared in astonishment as his new companions stepped forward: a bronze-myth, flowing-haired Centaur, and a formidable, stone-carven hulk of a man she could only consider a Gargoyle: with sharp features and sharper teeth, but with a suggestion of supportive strength sculpted into his impressive stature.

The Harpy realised suddenly that she hadn't given a response, but the Centaur bowed fluidly, his long black hair cascading his shoulders as he did so, the plant-ink tattooed tendrils swarming his chest seeming to spark with life despite the snaring smoke. "Racxen will guide those who can walk, and Rraarl and I will carry those who can't."

"The journey is not so far," Racxen promised, trying not to cough as his dark eyes darted in quick assessment across the assembly.

"Then you must make it with those I have gathered. I thank you full-heartedly, I will follow where you lead." An idea flared suddenly and Nzizi drew herself up. Her far-sighted eyes swooped towards those Harpies who had clustered the crowd in the courtyard ahead, before alighting back on the dwelling within which remained Inqe and her most vulnerable charges. Even getting the words out against the smoke was a struggle now. She wouldn't waste her breath telling these new rescuers she wouldn't be coming with them. Let their attention be on the many they could save – not the few who would stay.

Racxen could barely see Nzizi in the swirling smoke now, but the Sisters she had summoned soundlessly swept him with all urgency to the courtyard and its crowd. "We Harpies are no strangers to ash and rebirth," one promised Racxen as she helped two residents onto Han's back and another into Rraarl's arms. "We will evacuate to this new camp. Lead on, friend and saviour."

Racxen bowed, and sprang ahead.

In a flurry of dark wings, the huddle disappeared into the smoke after him, and Nzizi was alone once more. She'd thought she'd know how to make it back to the sanctuary of the inner hall, but for once she couldn't orientate herself. Her vision splintered as, through the burgeoning smoke, lines of flame pulsed: thin and probing at first in the distorted distance, the intensity of the sight magnified against the depth of darkness being breached, before patches of burning scrub flared angrily in their wake and the fire gathered speed, tearing through the bushveld and spilling, virulently red as a severed artery, onto the open clearing wherein lay the settlement.

Everywhere she looked the flames were laying waste to the land, coursing the tinder-dry grass surrounding the sanctuary until its boundaries were scorch-ringed and ravaged. On the outskirts the Watch Tree fell to the flames, flaring into vibrant colours in a travesty of life before crashing broken and blackened like a smouldering skeleton as the fire raced on and the night descended into an inferno.

No-one screamed in the wild. It didn't help. But, for the first time in her life, Nzizi screamed.

Blindly, instinct-driven, she ran towards the surest safety she had ever known: the stone sanctum at the heart of the settlement. The oldest and most stalwart of her companions were staying, as well as the most beloved. Nzizi would, too.

If she could reach them. Streaks of fire sundered her surroundings and the congealing smoke formed such a misrepresentative miasma that retracing even the short distance she had taken the evacuees was now proving her downfall, the paths she'd called home rendered unrecognisable. Flames sprang towards her as though conjured by some dread force, consuming everything in their path, with a hunger as great as the thirst of the land, their greed unsurpassable and terrifying. A roar rose around her like the breaking of the Realm — and perhaps that night really was upon her, Nzizi feared suddenly, as the only home she'd known disintegrated inexorably around her.

Blanched paper-thin by a pulse of lighting against the burning night, the silhouette of a vulture flashed, swooping towards the crumbling stone of the once-secure shelter. The bird looked, to Nzizi's fevered mind, sharp enough to splice through reality and slip past its defences, and she seized the vision desperately, managing to follow this conduit of wildness untouched despite the firestorm before it left her with a harsh cry at the archway of the sanctum.

Inside, Inqe hunched her shoulders and waited, with the patience and presence of a true matriarch. Her bones were the stones of this shelter, and her passion its blood. The Order had carried out her directions exactly: the last of those wishing to leave had been carried out by the remaining Harpies, following the caravan of evacuees gathered by Nzizi and escorted by the Arraheng and his friends. Whether walking, carried or stretchered, the inhabitants of the shelter had all been safely relocated. She had seen to it, she reminded herself repeatedly to slow her racing heart. She had seen to it.

All who remained were herself and the wizened old man she now cradled, who when she had first approached to transfer him had unceasingly whispered what some would claim unintelligible things in urgent plea. Inqe knew his soul could take no more, could go no further, could not bear even to be carried. And the matriarch knew with equal conviction, in her great wisdom, that the only thing she could do for him now was to stay with him. He could not be roused to action, even in the face of death. And so, while the stones cracked from the heat and the shelter awaited ruin, Inqe hunkered down and stayed with him, while crescendoing mutterings of flame snickered in the dark.

But someone else was approaching now, much more quietly. Someone who had returned here after everyone else had left. Someone who had always wordlessly offered Inqe as much support as this shelter had ever shouldered. Someone she knew would stay with her, even after nothing else would be left standing, in demonstration of a love that had never been spoken.

As Nzizi entered, the darkness of the ward eclipsed the smoke outside for a moment. But it would only be seconds before the shelter was enveloped. The fire cackled mercilessly, and she could no longer tell how far away it was. She no longer had the energy even to hate it.

Out of years-old routine she pulled the sun shutters across behind her, protectively and pointlessly; and as she turned, she realised that she had shut herself in with the Harpy matriarch as though there were no-one else she'd rather be with, in her last moments in this Realm. As though she could bar the rage and hurt out, and spare Inqe. She wondered briefly if it was readable, what she had done, as she settled herself beside her beloved and the still form close by. Smoke stole any words she could say, and she stayed.

"Before the flames can touch you, I will enfold you in my wings, and they will take me first," Inqe promised, her lips finding Nzizi's through the darkness and heat. "And if our fate lies in fire and ash, I will lie down with you as readily here as I ever have in our chamber."

Then as the fire roared closer, Nzizi gathered the old man's prone body to her, breathing into his lungs even as the smoke tried to squeeze itself into her own. And Inqe, great shroud-like wings outstretched, mantled both of them as the flames reached out. "If a shadow falls on you, take heart and do not fear, for it will not be death, but only ever my wings."

***

Far away now, Racxen and the evacuees were wending through the desert, snaking across the sands as surely as any serpent. But Racxen was beginning to fear the smoke was stalking them. It should have lifted away long ago, but it continued to thicken unnaturally until even his steps were faltering. It drifted in sullen, heavy clouds, in a hateful travesty of steam over marshland, turning the cool night air into the most intimate enemy as it scratched inside his throat and clutched around his chest.

Beside him, the Harpies bore the same fate stoically, black wings billowing against blacker smoke. They should have been out of it, by now. The desert winds should have dashed it. But the Realm was no longer behaving predictably, and how could this be normal smoke, when it was not wrought from natural fire? It choked the air until even the Harpies with their preternatural vision could not see in front of them.

Racxen cast a desperate glance to Han, and the Centaur coaxed from his panpipes a tune fit to beguile the besmirching tendrils. For a few brief paces, the mirk lifted enough for Racxen to scan again for signs, and that was all the Arraheng needed to reset his course and forge ahead once more. But the smoke could not be tricked for long, and all too soon it descended anew, sullen and suffocating and so thick that breath could not be spared even for the Centaur's playing. Although Han strode on in silence as surefootedly as ever, carrying as he was a half-conscious evacuee on his back, sweat slicked his strong features, and Racxen knew he was not far from succumbing to the equine fear of fire.

"It's not so far, now," Racxen promised, hoping desperately he could provide the guidance he'd pledged well enough. But the Realm was being remade, amidst these ashes. What he had known could no longer be trusted.

He couldn't afford to close his eyes and return to the calm centre of his being, so he looked outside himself for stability instead. The elderly woman in his arms curled like Mugkafb used to, and another limped determinedly alongside him. Racxen glanced to her admiringly. She had urged the others on unceasingly, assigning herself almost as an extra helper, and he could no more let her down than any of the rest. He would walk to his ruin for any of them: as he would for Ruby, who was sharing stretcher duty with the Harpies, or for Rraarl, who was carrying one by himself.

The entire population of the Harpy settlement was now relying on him. Its inhabitants had sloughed off all sentimentality and abandoned their refuge, following him faithfully into the desert. Yes, the smoke hounded them grimly: thicker than he'd expected, harder to shake off than he'd hoped – but for all their sakes he couldn't afford to let himself succumb.

He could hear the confusion around him: the murmurs of evacuees seeking reassurance and the harsh-soothing, trusted responses of the Harpies, who would not voice their own anxieties for fear of worrying their charges. They had all been wrenched from their sanctuary, and been coerced into making a journey far beyond that which should be asked. They were trusting, but they were hurting, and frightened. He couldn't lead them wrong. But he also could no longer see, or sense, the way. The smoke blocked the sky, snuffed out the stars, smeared away all scents. And he owed them the truth.

But first, a new approach — if he could fathom one.

And, talking of approach, someone was coming: he could feel it. Between the chaotic hubbub of barely maintained calm, someone was running: streaming steady and sure towards them through the murk and miasma.

He felt the rush of pelting paws approaching, and ash-streaked tawny gold pushed against his legs in solidarity as Yenna made herself known.

Instantly he knelt, pressed his head against the Wolf Sister's grizzled muzzle gratefully, and exchanged a quiet breath with her.

In response Yenna opened her soul and howled against the threats of the night, sending a shuddering plea lifting high above the smoke. A wisp of answer returned from afar, spinetingling and undulating, and no explanation was necessary. Yenna's tongue lolled between fearsome teeth and her eyes gleamed fiercer still as she rushed onwards. *This way.*

With the Harpies' sheltering wings stretching wide as the evacuees bunched close behind him, Racxen strode on with new certainty, Han and Rraarl flanking him unflinchingly as the Wolfren sang home their leader.

Lupine songs dissipated the distance, and soon familiar spices curled with canine scents on the air, campfire smoke replaced the smog that had followed them, and the refugees were home.

The Wolfren slipped from the shadows to escort and assist, and Racxen shifted himself into the rhythm of caring, distributing water and blankets and the like with Yenna, as the Harpies did what they did best.

The darkness beyond danced with shadows, but the scattering of torches gleaming wolf-eye gold gave the night depth and stopped it spinning, and the site thrummed with the business of living. All around, quiet heroics were being enacted, as softly and unobtrusively as the breeze that blew soothingly across the sands. Hydd was tucking his pelt around a drowsing figure as Han knelt to provide support for a man whose cough wouldn't allow him to lie flat. Rraarl was dispelling night terrors as only his presence could. Ruby was tenderly brushing the locks of an elderly lady who was proclaiming her to be her daughter. Han was spilling such melodies from his pipes as would disarm the most tangled of nightmares and replace them with the most restorative of dreams. Racxen padded between the rows of figures, distributing the soul-root he always carried to numb the pains he could of those who were still awake.

Finally, when this was done, Racxen settled down to offer silent vigil, and gradually, he felt himself relax. The evacuees were settled and sated. They were safe, from the fire at least. The Wolfren pack encircled them protectively: some in human form standing distant and silent, the movement of their veils rippling in vivid contrast to the stillness of their posture, and others in wolf form walking stiff-legged between the sleepers, as though weaving strands of security as they kept watch between the Realms.

The wind rippled tidemarks across the dunes, putting Racxen in mind of the way the evening breeze used to scud across the sacred channels transecting the marshland. When first these verdant tributaries had shrunken and shrivelled until only churn and chaff remained, he had taken to visiting the drying remnants as often as he could: during that fluid hour between dusk and nightfall in which hope could still flow, as though if he could pay the earth the kindness she deserved it might heal her or at least ease her pain. But the drought had distended regardless, and there was nothing he could offer the parched earth, for what it required was needed more by the frailest members of society. So, instead he would simply touch his claws to the deepening rifts and ruptures of drying mud, and stay silent in his sorrow.

His steered his attention to brighter thoughts, conscious of the vulnerabilities woven amidst a drifting night. In his mind's eye, Arraterr lay as sparkling and welcoming as ever; and even in the state it truly was, it was still home. He had left his brother there, now that Mugkafb was old enough for staying without him and assisting in water gathering to be an adventure, and while he didn't know when he would return to him, he knew that he would. It would not do to dwell on all he was parted from when the Harpies and their charges had left everything behind and were enveloped by far greater loss and uncertainty. And, while Amber's absence chilled him more pervasively than a midnight audience with the Goblin King, in every likelihood she was currently faring better with the serpent, than Jasper probably was with fighting the fire.

As the night lifted unflinchingly into day, Racxen stared up searchingly and wished he could interpret from the final fading stars how the Prince was faring.

***

Certainty was falling away from Jasper like sweat. Flying into the fire zone meant flying away from everything fathomable: the air no longer behaved like air but like flame instead, the heat lifting and plunging around him like furnace bellows until he could barely stay in the sky. Great plumes of rising smoke drifted above him like snares, while below nightmarish lines of flickering red sheared through the darkness, stretching in ever expanding dominion across a splintering Realm.

Terror clawed at him like an aerial predator and Jasper struggled desperately to shrug off its clutches, his wings thrusting laboriously while the tongues of flame reached thirstily towards him as though, having dredged the last remnants of moisture from the land and air, they wanted now to steal it from his body in a final assault.

Amidst it all Jasper struggled to focus his vision, let alone his mind. Flying normally made him feel elevated: privileged to witness the splendour of the skies from a vantage few experienced. But now, as disorientated by his growing weakness as he was by the remaking of the Realm, Jasper felt, with the air barely breathable let alone buoyant, as though he were about to plumet to the ground in a fall from grace and an expulsion from everything he had once known.

Ragged and painful grew his quickening breaths, as the smoke slowed his thoughts as well as his limbs. What had been his plan? He couldn't fly further than this, couldn't reach the Harpy shelter. All he could hope for was to aim for somewhere he could dump the water and create a break in the fire to stop it advancing. It wasn't much of a plan even by his own reckoning, but he hadn't the energy to think any further than he could fly.

His own gasping frightened him, the air searing his lungs with every breath. And breath of what? There wasn't enough oxygen. Of course there wasn't, above the fire, he berated himself bitterly. He couldn't even draw enough air to cough properly, and on every attempt the smoke further invaded his lungs. Weak as a winglet he floundered on, fighting an insidious loss of altitude he'd never before encountered.

Blinded by the smoke, he could only hope he'd judged his positioning well enough. This would have to do, he decided blearily, tipping the vessel. He almost overbalancing with the effort; no longer secure in the sky, his actions and thoughts were as stunted as his breath. He was reaching his limit: it was like he'd forgotten how to fly, unable even to support his own body. At least he had done his duty: so much water would surely form a sufficient firebreak. Wait. He'd forgotten to pour it. He hadn't even the strength left to manage that properly.

Then horror lurched like gravity. It wasn't his strength that was the problem. He stared at the vessel and, in that moment, he cursed the sky and the earth and everything between. It was empty. And his heart, just as empty, dropped as well.

Of course the vessel's enchantment couldn't last forever on a dying woman's magic, he told himself savagely. It was over, and he was more alone even than Diberkati. He'd so desperately wanted to pay for past mistakes, and he'd ended up making his most catastrophic one yet.

One must fall. The words spiralled through his head, as uncontrollable as his descent. *One must fall. One must fall where none can stand.*

***

Anguish chased Amber's frantic steps as she raced the fire tearing alongside her and devouring everything in its path – as though its hunger could ever be sated, as though the great serpent could ever be appeased, as though the terrible wrong wrought upon her could ever be atoned for. White ash atop a coating of black charr amidst the infernal redness of the flames painted the landcape in nightmarish hues through which she struggled to find her way.

And where was Diberkati, amongst all this? Amber knew, bone deep, that the serpent would not have wished to risk the desert's most vulnerable inhabitants and, having seen that she had done so unintentionally, would have fled, with her path now guided solely by the determination both to limit the damage and punish herself. So, even without the guidance of Nzizi's feather, the Fairy knew the serpent was heading away from the Harpy settlement. But the surrounding scrub-scattered grasslands here held so many strands of burning that it looked as though Diberkati's anguish was still spreading, instead of dissipating.

Wisps of fire cackled around Amber like laughter, amplifying all she didn't understand, as she pushed on blindly. Being able to skin-breathe clung like a curse, now. She was as vulnerable as a frog in a polluted pool. She felt herself slow: the burning in her lungs repeating through her limbs. Brandishing Nzizi's feather as both compass and talisman, she stumbled through a disintegrating Realm. She knew there'd be a reason – embedded somewhere in her learning about wood density and such things – for why amongst the insatiable flames a handful of trees still stood, but right now they merely added a further sense of ghoulishness to the most uncanny of scenes.

On she rushed, alone and fleeing for her life, until the sand-strewn scrub deepened into true desert and, having run out of things to burn, the fire could go no further. Still, what use safe haven without finding the serpent? So, more slowly, Amber stalked on. The fire she might be able to finally leave behind, but the smoke clung yet like a mistake that could not be rectified, a stain that could not be erased. A crushing fear clutched Amber's chest in response: that Diberkati must be close, and cruelly hurting. Instead of diminishing, the danger had become more delicate.

Smoke-blind, she could only stumble on unseeingly, until she'd finally outdistanced the last streaks of the suffocating shroud. After coughing the smoke from her lungs, it was a relief to be able to breathe properly again.

That relief proved short-lived though, as through the clear night air her vision seized upon subtle, sinuous ridges in the sand. Hoping she truly had found serpent tracks and wasn't simply confusing herself with the ripples of the dunes, Amber tucked Nzizi's feather into her sash with a whisper of thanks, and began to tread more carefully. Slowing to afford such an endeavour the care it deserved, Amber dedicated herself to following a trail as erratic and destructive as the smoke.

She might have left one fire behind, but the one she feared she was about to find smouldering within the serpent lurking somewhere ahead would, she warned herself, prove more unquenchable. Diberkati should never have been forced into the Realm in such dire circumstances, let alone have been exposed to such hatred and anger and injustice as a result. It would be enough to consume anyone, even had they lived in the Realm for years. And for one newly birthed? She couldn't bear the thought.

But she had to bear it, for its manifestation lay before her now. Amber stopped, her heart in her mouth: for spilling into view, stretching like a stain against the pale moonlit sand, slumped Diberkati. Her sinuous tracks bled brokenly across the sands to where she now sank, lying listless, shudders coursing her body, burnt out like a storm cloud full of thunder that could never birth rain.

Despite her dehydration, tears pained into Amber's eyes. The prophecy had spoken of a serpent, certainly. But it hadn't said that she would be disgorged at the Realm's own breaking, and it hadn't said she would be left bereft, needing as much sanctuary and support as any. For Diberkati to have nurtured the Realm like an egg, and have been forced to witness its disintegration, seemed to Amber too much to bear. No wonder Diberkati had sought refuge in a place of such desolation and exposure that it embodied the vastness of her woes.

Amber's spirit stalled with her steps. This wasn't a problem the serpent was equipped for. This wasn't a problem any of them were equipped for. Why had she even thought she could go after Diberkati? She had no answers for her: she couldn't explain why this was happening, let alone promise it would stop.

But where there were no solutions, there could still be support. Amber held still, her mind racing through possibilities. Amidst the cavernous emptiness of the desert, she shrank her Realm to fit around just her and the serpent, and simply stayed.

Diberkati, though, seemed about to slither away, tensing at the Fairy's cautious approach.

"Everyone's safe," Amber called lightly in reassurance. "The Harpies evacuated the settlement," she corrected herself more honestly a moment later. "Racxen's leading them to Yenna's camp. And Jasper's trying to douse the flames with the vessel." Although shouldn't that have worked, by now? The thought intruded distressingly, but she swapped it for the trust he'd asked for and pushed that fear aside to make space for those of closer proximity. "Your anger is understandable," Amber continued gently. "But you don't deserve for it to destroy you." The sand sucked away her words, and she wasn't sure she could expect a response anyway. "I know you are hurting, but you can feel that pain without hurting yourself or others. With help – and I am here to help you."

"I didn't mean to start the fire." The desert itself seemed to shudder with the emotion in the serpent's words. "Yet not meaning to is not good enough, so I had to leave." Those elliptical eyes: keyholes surrounded by the glimmer of dying stars, flickered onto the Fairy. "And I have to leave, now. I'm not angry at what the Goblins will do to me, but at what they have done to you."

Amber held very still. She hadn't even fully told the others, yet. But she supposed it made a kind of sense that the serpent, nearby, would have picked up the vibration of her speech, however quietly she had murmured it to herself in an effort to render it down into mere words and so reduce its power.

"It hurts me that there's no changing what happened," Amber admitted. "But I don't want to carry that burden, much less have you bear it also. And my pain is not your excuse. I hope we are friends enough for me to speak this plainly."

Diberkati seemed to dip her head, almost imperceptibly. Amber stood her ground, feeling stronger for wielding her truth, and her heart overflowed. "Your own pain is deserving of attention, without comparing it to that of another," she promised. "You were at the centre of the Realm for so long that it is only natural for you to feel its destruction and loss more deeply than anyone. How could you be expected to partition off that pain, or protect yourself from it?"

Amber let her words sink in before continuing. "There is no power that can change the past. But that doesn't mean you don't have agency, or authority," she promised. "Our potential lies instead in changing the future; in deciding how to act now. I don't want to be remembered for what happened to me back there, and instead I'll make sure I'll be remembered for I do next."

The serpent's eyes swelled. "Well spoken, Fairy. But this time, what happens will also not be within your power."

Amber heard the warning in her words, but she refused to let it distract her. "Zaralathaar didn't expect you to save her," the Fairy promised, tears in her own eyes now. "She just hoped you would come to her — and you did."

The serpent's gaze shifted. "And you cannot save me – yet you came," she acknowledged. "I spent most of my time eschewing all company, since first I spilled upon these sands. And yet you followed me out here."

Understanding settled between them, reassuring as starlight, and the resultant silence gave Diberkati space to consider. Fury had overtaken her back there, faster than flame. The anger in the air had invaded her; seeped through her scales like pollution through skin. She couldn't excuse it, but she hadn't been able to stop it, either. So she'd fled where she could: into the desert, away from anyone she could harm. And now the Fairy was watching her, full of compassion and unknowing.

The pain in Diberkati's belly grew unbearable, as though there was simply too much hurt to be contained, and she howled in a manner the Fairy hadn't known she possessed. "I didn't mean to stop the rain. And I didn't mean to start the fire."

Amber was crying now, too. How could she expect Diberkati to feel things without acting on them? When one compared her time cloistered in the centre of the Realm with her time above ground, she was as brand new as a hatchling.

In the space of Amber's silence, the serpent spoke more steadily. "At first, I couldn't bear how the Realm was being treated. So, I became numb. That's why the rains stopped. I couldn't feel anything, anymore. I closed myself off, to protect myself from the Realm dying. And in response, the Realm began to shut down further,"

"But you're not numb anymore," Amber murmured. The serpent was practically still smouldering. She was probably standing too close, even now, but she didn't step back.

"No. You reawakened me," Diberkati explained, in a sibilant, suffering whisper, as she wrestled with what was inside her. "But the price of feeling what you have aroused in me is feeling everything. And I cannot bear it. I cannot bear what has happened to you and your friends, just now or in the past, or what may happen to everyone in the future. There is just too much wrong in the Realm," Diberkati confessed, her sides convulsing as though struggling to contain the serpent's sorrow.

"There is much wrong; that is true." Amber swallowed strengtheningly. "But it is not all there is."

The sands shivered at her audacity almost fit to steal away her words, but she spoke them anyway, soft as they were. The moments Torek had mangled would in time be subsumed by the magnitude of better memories she had herself made — some of which she had yet to meet. "The Realm is drying — dying, even," Amber confessed. "And yet some of my dearest memories I have only just made. Memories of sanctuary and safety — with you."

Diberkati's thoughts flickered with her eyes. "But I remember hearing that Goblin threaten you — and it was he who first threatened me and chased me down when I was just emerged and at my most vulnerable. Then I remember being flame-hot-angry."

Amber nodded. "True. But I remember also how, in the still of the desert evening, you coiled around us like a river and contained us against the cavernous vastness of the desert night. Your breathing rippled like water, and your length kept us safe. Your scales were cool and smooth as pebbles underwater. I dreamt of rain, that night."

Serpentine eyes settled on Amber, and felt settled in their turn. Perhaps the Fairy was right. She had been disgorged into desiccation, but she had also been met with acceptance. Even with love.

"But they say I will grow large enough to consume the Realm," the serpent warned. "There is so much going wrong, and it is all getting inside me. I wasn't due to be born. I was never formed to live above the skin of the Realm, and my own cannot keep my soul separate from everything that is failing. And so I am burning, because so many cannot see that the Realm itself is burning."

"I see that," Amber promised, her voice breaking with the heat of the air as she gave the revelation due reverence. "But I also see that many things are growing inside you, and anger is only one of them."

Diberkati's tongue flickered as she faltered. "I cannot come back with you."

Amber sighed softly. The snake's detachment haunted her, but she knew Diberkati spoke her truth. She couldn't assume she knew what was best for a creature as old as the Realm, and at least the serpent was no longer smouldering, so perhaps it was safe to leave her and return to the others to help them now.

"I didn't ask you to. I didn't come here to ask anything of you," Amber promised, trying to keep the sadness out of her voice. "I wanted to help you if I could. But I also wanted to say that, if I can't help you, it doesn't mean you can't be helped. The Realm is so much bigger than I am, and it is bigger than you even. It contains the help you need. One day," she promised Diberkati, "you will feel so much more comforted than you ever felt consumed. I know it might be a while away yet, but it is coming closer. And meanwhile, I wanted to try and keep you safe."

The serpent nodded as though in relief, and thought for a long while. The Fairy could speak all the kindnesses in the Realm, but her scales were drying. It was just a case of who would die first: she or the Realm. No need to affect her companion, though. She had paid her many kindnesses, and she would return the last one she could. She would leave the Fairy, now it was growing lighter and becoming safer, and once alone again she would burrow into the ground and wait for death, as she had first intended before the companions had stumbled upon her and filled her heart with hope. Perhaps, then, as Amber had said, one might fall where none could stand, and perhaps this could somehow save the others.

Thus resolved, and realising the Fairy was still watching her, waiting, Diberkati shook herself, and looked to the horizon for the first time, to suggest agreement and engagement, but she found herself staring into a rising sun that brought scant comfort, struggling as it did through a familiar smog. "I thought you said the other Fairy was dousing the flames?"

At her words, Amber dared take her eyes off the serpent for the first time.

Diberkati was right. In the growing light it wasn't so obvious, but an infernal glow still smouldered uneasily, amidst an uncanny swathe of smoke filling the edge of vision and creeping closer.

The Realm seemed to shudder beneath Amber. *It hadn't worked.* She trusted Jasper more than she'd ever tell him, and what he had attempted hadn't worked. He would have seen it through – for his people, for all people – had it been possible, even to his own ruin. So it wasn't that he had failed. But the plan had failed. The vessel had failed. And they were out of options.

"I thought the water would be enough," Amber managed wretchedly, broken.

The desperation in the Fairy's eyes brought Diberkati out of herself. Above ground, she might be as young as a hatchling, but below ground she had known the earth for eons. In comparison, the Fairy and her friends had lived so little time in the Realm. She found herself wanting to protect them, as they had tried to protect her. "It would have been enough to drink, for a while, yes." There was gentleness on her forked tongue as the serpent tried to phrase her words carefully. "But not enough to stem the fire. Not enough to replenish the Realm. Not enough to have things grow again. The land can't use water properly anymore, anyway. It has forgotten how to drink. The Realm has been hurt so deeply – to heal will take more time than we have."

As though in response to the serpent's torment the Realm began to rumble like far-off thunder, but Amber knew it was neither thunder, nor far off. The Realm was about to break beneath them. "Then, I will stay," she pledged decisively. "I might not be able to give you all the time you need, but I will give you all the time I have left."

"But I don't want the desert to kill you. And I came to the desert to die," Diberkati warned in anguish.

"The desert doesn't care if you live, and it doesn't care if I die," Amber responded. "But I see that you will not leave. I know you stayed with Zaralathaar." The remembrance shivered through Amber, despite the relentless heat. "And I will stay with you." It was too late to save the Realm, now. And perhaps she couldn't even save Diberkati from dying in fire and powder upon the sands, as that hateful Goblin had prophesised. But her blood hummed with chthonic harmonies, and the clarity of what she must do. There was no-one else out here: it was just her and the serpent, but it felt like the two of them filled the entire desert. And she knew the time had come to stay. Stay with the serpent who was as confused as she was, and who was hurting even more.

"I'm sorry I didn't come here to give you an answer." Amber swallowed hard, her lack of understanding suddenly as painful as the lack of water. "Not for some therapeutic reason, or because I think you can find it yourself, but because I don't have one. I don't know how we got to this point. I don't know what caused the Realm to dry. I don't know how we missed the signs. And I am so sorry for all of that. But I'm not sorry that I'm here."

"If you do not leave me before it is too late, I will be sorry you met me," the serpent despaired.

"I won't, and I never will be," Amber promised. "Not every story is destined to end happily. That doesn't mean you wish you'd never read it. And not every fight can be survived. It doesn't mean you haven't tried hard enough. It doesn't mean you gave up. It just means it wasn't a fight that could be won. It doesn't mean it wasn't life well lived."

"If you do survive, promise me something," Diberkati hissed suddenly. "And a promise you make to a serpent, it is always best to keep. Promise me: that if the rains return, you will look after this Realm better. Better than either of us knew how to, before this drought. Better than we let ourselves believe we could get away with, before we knew it could come to this. Neither of us caused this, but one of us could yet cure it."

"I do promise it," Amber whispered fiercely. "My improvement will be my apology."

"And so will mine be," Diberkati echoed softly.

The serpent's response was so unexpected that Amber stared questioningly.

"I was so angry, when I came out here," Diberkati managed to hiss, raising her sibilant voice suddenly even as desert winds gathered in screaming preparation for what might happen next. "But that's not what I feel now. You should have left me. You shouldn't love me. But I'm glad you love me – and didn't leave me."

A gathering rumble grew deep beneath the ground, as a crackle of tremors started to course across the sands like lightning. The dunes began to give way around them in shuddering release, as though the Realm were learning it was okay to let go. Amidst such cataclysmic change and seized of a threatening thought, Amber suddenly feared she was too far from, not too close to, her companion, at the breaking of the Realm.

The serpent was swaying amidst the shifting, sundering sands, as though preparing to strike an unseen opponent. "A gift is not enough," she pronounced, wild-eyed and wilful. "A sacrifice has to be made." Diberkati's eyes grew opaque as their membranes slipped protectively into place. "And a sacrifice cannot be asked. It can only be offered. A sacrifice, made in love." Her words were armour, before embarking on a war, and Amber's blood chilled, despite the heat sloughing from the serpent.

"No. Stop talking about sacrifice," Amber insisted, struggling to keep her balance and her calm. "It's scaring me. Talk of support, instead. Talk of what we shared." She was shouting now: shouting above the sandstorm. She saw whole sections of sand not far from them drop away. Time was falling.

"I remember it all," Diberkati insisted, shifting urgently to stay upright as the tremors intensified, her voice slipping through the sirocco as surely as her swirling scales had that night when she had wrapped herself around the Fairy and her companions and kept the desert night at bay. "And I will remember you, at the end."

The serpent lifted her great head now, ember eyes gleaming urgently as the swirling shroud of sand thickened chokingly. "But, Amber, you can't fly. You have to leave," she hissed as the winds rose to a scream. "Or one will fall where none can stand."

As the winds whipped fit to tear Diberkati from her sight, Amber rushed forward impulsively, fastening her arms around the serpent, as though that could shield her. In response, Diberkati shifted to coil her great lengths protectively around the Fairy, inch by inch becoming a living armour.

Encased in scale-smothered muscle, as the savagery of the sandstorm raged, Amber nestled her cheek against the curve of Diberkati's jewelled neck. The serpent felt cool to the touch now, as though the fire of anger had finally gone out in her.

Amber hugged her a little closer, relieved that the Goblins wouldn't get their hands on her, whatever else was about to happen. All around them great jagged sheets of sand began to shear away, as though the Realm were sloughing its skin. Amber felt the convulsive shudder of the desert beneath them, and knew it wouldn't be long before where they were standing collapsed: before the ground gave way and the Realm gave up.

She fixed her embrace resolutely around Diberkati. "That's the thing about me," she promised fiercely. "I'm no longer scared of falling."

Even as she said it the sand beneath her feet dropped. Wrapped in the embrace of the serpent, she could almost convince herself she was only caught in the heart-lurching tug of gravity within a downwards swoop of ecstatic flight, could almost believe the plunge would any moment surge into an updraft of soaring exultation. But almost meant nothing, and the moment never came. Hope fell as fast as she did and Amber plummeted amidst the hissing rush of cascading sand.

Just before every sensation blurred into the overwhelming awareness of descent, she felt first a shift in Diberkati's coils as though the serpent was seeking to protect her when the ground hit. Then, bereft, she felt a horrible unravelling: a loss of impossible magnitude as the serpent loosened her grip and fell away irretrievably.

Faster she fell herself now, gravity tearing at her in consumptive desperation as she hurtled through the cracks of a crumbling Realm while the dunes sluiced into ruin around her. The air reduced to dust, and the sand became both storm and shroud. Perhaps she would be trapped in this freefall forever – for what could there be left at the centre of the Realm, with no serpent to protect it?

As such thoughts spiralled and left her body, speed swallowed Amber like a snake, and she sensed no more.

But when a fullbody sting slapped into her in a reawakening jolt that surged through her soul, as she coughed and flailed and gasped, it was not sand she spewed from her lungs.

Awareness of a womblike warmth bloomed more sweetly than the flaring pain as her limbs pulled yieldingly through something and she realised she was floating. All at one she was wrapped in wetness and wonder, sound pouring in around her as she flailed ecstatically, caught in a river's rushing wave-swell. It wasn't deception, it wasn't a mirage. She was surrounded by – supported by – water. Crashing, cavorting water. It thundered against her; it thrilled through her. Although she couldn't fathom how.

A chuckling hiss rippled around her.

"Diberkati?" Amber spluttered, uncomprehending. The river, in contrast, seemed to have gathered confidence, and Amber no longer needed to struggle, for now the coiling water surged and sported with her, carrying her easily with a serpent-like strength. Everything sparkled amidst the stream's thrall as she was swept along.

"Is this you?" It couldn't be possible: that Diberkati had become the river, and had not only saved her just now from plummeting to her death, but was about to save them all from the ravaging drought.

"The Goblins said you would ruin us. And yet you have rescued us," Amber whispered, heart overflowing.

"Because I listened to you, and not to them. Suffering turns skin to scales," an unmistakably serpentine voice shimmered. "But not all suffering need be endured forever. Sometimes it lifts – or can be lifted. And a snake may slough her skin."

Conviction rushed with every syllable as the serpent-stream snaked vast and vital through the sands, but for Amber confusion vied with concern.

"But what's happened to you? Have you sacrificed yourself?" A tumult of emotions tangled within the Fairy.

The serpent, or the stream now, seemed to take it in her stride. "Is that what you felt you were doing, those seasons ago? Did you sacrifice your wings?"

Amber gulped, and not just to gather breath. Vibrations must have carried further than voices to the serpent, for her to have knowledge of that. But clarity flooded. "No. I transformed. I knew I could, deep down." Even amidst the sweeping suddenness of these rushing moments she was sure of it, sculling steadily now. "And I'd have done the same for Ruby. For Rraarl. For Mugkafb. For Yenna. Don't tell him – but even for Jasper. It's not about what Torek thought. It's about what I did."

"Exactly. It was an offering made in love and power, not a sacrifice made in obligation." Certainty rippled like warmth through the swelling waters. "And your transformation started before that. It all began with you running through the rain."

Amber began to feel that Diberkati's understanding was as deep and implausible as her current form. "How could you possibly know that?"

"You met me as the world-serpent, but I was also the water-serpent." Diberkati's voice sparkled like scales. "Once upon a time, and once more again." Gathering speed as she took her twists and turns through the land with joy, she surged like a great wave breaking. "And I knew because I *was* the water. I was the rain. I covered you and kissed you, and told you to run."

Amber stared speechless, caught in growing realisation as well as the roll and swell of the current.

"It took a long time, after the trauma of the Realm drying, for me to reconnect with my true nature," Diberkati confirmed. "But you helped me remember that I too can transform: and not only myself, but the whole Realm. This is who I am, now. This is who you taught me I can be."

Amber clasped those words to her, the realisation they sparked thrilling her as much as the rush of the river as it gathered in pace and swept her along, becoming a glittering arc of water swirling faster than flight, dousing everything in joy and wonder while her surroundings flashing past blurred and bloomed anew in the river's wake as it coursed at exhilarating speed through a remoulding Realm and forged a fearless way into the future.

Finally the serpent stilled. The water swirled and slowed, and settled as though sated.

Dazedly, from the intimacy of water-surface eye-level, Amber stared at the wholly alien landscape she had arrived into. At the touch of water after so long a drought, the earth around her seemed to hiss, to thrum and sing with the stirring of new life.

Hearing a hiss of encouragement, the Fairy clambered out, breathless and exhilarated. Trembling at the memory of recent moments still pulsing within her, as Amber crouched, wet-through and waiting on the serpent-slicked bank, a familiar and fearsome face reared, gem-sparkling, and sluicing water, more majestic even than the kelpie and twice as wild.

Diberkati gleamed, ethereal and elemental at once. "Today, you didn't run," she whispered, and the words fell from her tongue like water. "And I learnt I didn't need to, either."

"You didn't sacrifice yourself," Amber managed in awestruck realisation. "You reshaped yourself. You are reshaping the Realm!"

"And I have only just begun." The water rippled, swelling against its banks with a pride the extent of which was matched only by Amber's admiration for her friend.

Relief bloomed like the unfurling waterflowers within as Amber stared in astonishment from the side. As Diberkati flexed and flowed, she became a coiling creek, a playful brook, an easeful lake in turn – and this was just a flicker of what she was about to become, and bestow upon the Realm.

In witness to such wonders, any words of gratitude would have felt too small. In a dazedness of delight, Amber simply soaked up the restorative relaxation of the river. Even gazing upon it revived her, more than any river had the right to: reawakening revitalising recollections. The times she'd swum with Racxen through the passages of Arraterr, the moment she'd plunged into the Unquenching Well to save Hydd's pelt, even that first jump into the unknown, into the Great Lake after Mugkafb – all came back to her in a buoyant rush of fluid memory.

But what if those impressions weren't a side-effect, or a playful show of Diberkati's burgeoning power? Suddenly Amber worried that instead her friend might have summoned them deliberately as a compassionate distraction, for the serpent's outline seemed to shimmer as though about to dissolve and disappear entirely amidst the water. Amber felt at once overcome with awe for what Diberkati had done for the Realm, and yet bereft to know she must part from the serpent.

"I know you can't stay, but you're not dying, are you?" she managed anxiously, in a reverent whisper. "I need you to live, even if I never see you again."

"I am alive, and I am life," the serpent soothed, and her voice was as reassuring as ever even as it faded easefully, like a stream that has reached the sea after a lifetime of rushing, and has found its rest and recover within.

I was the Realm's core for thousands of years. And you have given me the strength to live a thousand more as its circulation. The hiss of the serpent seemed replaced now by the whisper of the water, and yet this echo of thought resonated in Amber's mind as intimately as an embrace.

I will always be part of the Realm, and we will always be part of each other. That purr of promise, which Amber gathered gratefully to her heart, rumbled like rapids over rocks as the serpent-stream gathering in strength and purpose, writhing and rippling rapturously with every powerful tail-like thrash of her tail as a coil of water as bright as starlight cleaved the parched lands and raced into the future.

This is no time for sadness, sparkled the dancing waters knowingly. *It will rain again. Be ready!*

Amber heard the hissing laugh amidst the roll and swell of the water, and she laughed as well, almost overwhelmed by the unburdening. Her pulse quickened as she realised how far Diberkati's reach stretched already: across the crust of the Realm, previously so imperilled, now rushed rapidly swelling streambeds in a life-supporting network: strengthening and connecting as far as the eye could see. Amber stared, caught in the wonder of it all.

And, at the centre, shifting and sheening like scaled muscle, coursed the arterial serpentine river, snaking through the arid, dust-clung stretches and reclaiming the Realm.

At last it slowed, and circled back. A snake-head formed amongst the froth and foam, and Diberkati, in full might and majesty, raised herself to stare in the direction of Amber's gaze, allowing herself to recognise the good she had wrought. Then, in a sudden soft cascade, she turned and rested her muzzle against the Fairy's shoulder, her snout nestling into her neck even as her outline sluiced into obscurity.

Amidst the few precious moments before her friend's form fell away, Amber embraced the serpent as wholly as she could. It felt like trying to hug the force at the centre of a waterfall, and it left her gasping.

But even as the water dropped back into the river, and stopped looking like a snake at all, it brimmed with Diberkati's power and vitality. Now that the serpent had fully transformed, an urgency like no other overtook the water. Amber stared, stunned, while, shimmering as though surfaced in scales, a muscular tide rippled through the river all the way to the edge of the still-smouldering Harpy settlement and a great wave washed out with snake-strike accuracy to douse the remaining flames.

With the quenching of the fire all remaining fear was quashed, and into the space left behind sprang quiet marvels of all kinds as life sought to re-establish and reaffirm itself. Amidst the unhurried murmurings of the newly-formed streams pouring across the plains in their plentitudes, the air, full of moisture and relief, grew mellifluous with birdsong, the long-hidden jewelled colours of tiny winged choristers revealing themselves suddenly enough to have been sprung by magic instead of summoned by the spectacular swirling clouds of insects which filled the air.

So much had been gained that Amber felt it poor remembrance to grieve now. But the water was just water again, although it held a serpent's memory. Shivering with the suddenness of it all, the Fairy couldn't help wanting to take a moment to honour Diberkati, for the serpent truly seemed gone: although gone where, and gone how, she couldn't fully comprehend.

But then something registered that tore all other considerations aside: all around her, the air erupted in the hooting and howling of a Goblin pack in full pursuit.

They had come after the serpent – who was nowhere to be seen.

And they would be on her in an instant.

Up Amber sprang and away she scrambled. She dared not spare a glance to the swollen sky, and in truth she scarcely spared a glance to either side of her, for the new rivers had carved up the Realm into unrecognition. Wherever she ran to she would find herself lost.

But the choice before her was lose her way or lose her life, so on she ran, on and on, the hideous caterwauling of the Goblins rendering everything around her unrecognisable, and what was worse, rendering anywhere inhabitable unreachable, for she could not risk leading this hateful horde towards anyone at all.

In despair she directed herself towards the furthest outreaches, the backlands such as even the hardiest survivors like the Harpies would avoid.

As the Goblins gave murderous tongue to realise she was running herself further and further into the wilderness, Amber began to hope even here. For an eerie army of trees arose ahead of her — and there was something about these forsaken groves she recognised: recognised with the full force of Nzizi's warning coming back to her. And so a great and terrible possibility sustained her, while she ran until she feared her heart would stop and her lungs would burst.

But the clouds burst before her lungs did. The gathering tattoo heralding the approaching rains sounded initially like a warning, she'd grown so unaccustomed to the noise, and the first drops hit with a violent urgency, spattering against a desiccated, pitiable landscape. Even despite the pursuit of the Goblins, Amber felt the touch of the rain with a wild ecstasy.

But as the deluge reached deafening pitch and swelled into an all-encompassing roar that drowned out everything past and future, Amber dared not slow. She unknotted her sash as she ran, and snatched it up hastily, binding it protectively around her face as she shut her eyes and held her breath and raced on blindly.

Through the torrent of rain and behind the haze of her makeshift mask the grove sluiced into a nightmarish blur. She had to get through the trees, beyond and away, before the toxic sap of their leaves was released. She had mere seconds.

Don't stand beneath these trees in rain, Nzizi had intoned to her, at a time when speaking of rain might as well have been speaking of stars falling from the sky.

Don't stand beneath these trees in rain
For there is nothing that will quench such pain
Don't breathe the air, don't touch the leaves
When fire apple blooms, the whole Realm grieves.

With the once track-hard ground now saturated to the point of sludge, Amber summoned the memory of Nzizi to lend her extra strength, for she hardly dared register the sinking slow of her steps, and she forced herself to power on regardless with the singlemindedness of a Sand Giant as the trees relinquished her to the clearing beyond and she finally escaped the reach of those doomladen branches.

Torek, behind her, was not so lucky. Nor were the rest of the slew of Goblins, who with singular arrogance had sneered at the warnings of Harpies. Now they shrieked and spat as their skin hissed, and Torek spewed empty curses and sprang away, taking his horde with him.

Bearing startled witness to their eviction Amber stood and stared in shock, until the downpour had drowned out every remnant of the Goblins' retreat.

With a shudder, she gathered herself and gave thanks to the most toxic tree in the Realm. She had passed through the grove unscathed. She had forged a way through fire; taken a route through the grove of trees none could stand. Now, soaked, sanctified, and still standing, she would find another way back.

As she set off to do so, the rain settled into steadiness, the air grew fat with moisture and relief, and Amber let the percussive beat of the first raindrops tattoo against her skin and into her soul.

She watched the lands around her with new eyes, now she had the luxury of safety, and she witnessed their transformation with the gratitude of one who had lived through their trials. And what a metamorphosis unfurled around her: for the Realm was growing so replete with rain it almost seemed obscene. Great swathes of it were falling in decadent curtains, great mists of it were lifting from the sudden pooling swells of lake-like puddles. Bird-song and frog-chorus almost brought her to tears with their melodies, so long had been their painful absence.

Life was restablishing itself by the second. The insects arrived with the next round of thunder: swirling clouds of them darkening the sky in an ecstatic floodscape, the air full of moisture and relief. As they skimmed across the surface, plumes of spray were flung up by the cavorting, and the resulting rainbows shimmered in an ever-changing vision. The air was abuzz with glorious displays of life after the enforced torpor of unending drought, and Amber felt her footsteps slow in reverent response. After the urgency and scarcity, all was leisurely and languid again, slick with dew and dreams alike. Rivers alone were running: eager streams splashed into brand new pools that overflowed into laughing silver waterfalls which cascaded into tumbling brooks which stretched into rivers which carved their broad strong strokes through the floodplains and flowed away to the sparkling sea beyond sight…

On she wandered, soaking in the wonder, and feeling caught in a rain-induced daze until finally she saw familiar figures shimmer through the haze towards her.

"The fires are all out, and it seems we no longer need worry about the rains returning," Jasper surmised shakily, as he approached with the others. "Would have been marvellous if we'd known she could do that before."

"I'm not sure she could, before," Amber admitted, relief flowing as she hugged each of her beloved companions. "Not until that moment."

"I am sure the Realm did not conjure itself serenely," Jasper admitted by way of acceptance. "We have the Way of Ice and Fire, we have Dread Mountain; we have the Song Weaver. Once, we had the Venom Spitters, for goodness sake. These are, arguably, not the creations of a peaceful Realm. But they are the creations of a Realm worth living in. And a Realm that keeps surviving. So perhaps, in all of its aeons-old evolution, it is not fated to continue itself serenely. I just wish it had not taken such trauma to trigger the final stage of Diberkati's transition."

"It wasn't the trauma, but your tending despite it, which enabled her transformation." Ruby burst into a fond flurry of excited claps for emphasis. "Don't you see, you four?" she thrilled. "She'd felt like this chance had been out of reach her whole life. And you helped her grasp it."

Jasper adjusted his cloak stiffly. "I'm not sure I can take any credit–"

Yenna shushed him with a quick kiss, her tawny eyes glowing. "It is offered freely: as you so quickly offered help on those scorched sands, even though you feared her."

"Feared *for* her, soon enough," Jasper sniffed in acquiescence. "Especially when Zaralathaar's gift finally reached its limit. But now Diberkati is safe, and it appears so are we." His voice trailed away in wonder.

Amber nodded quietly as she watched the sleek, unmistakeably snakelike river shift across slickening sands: Diberkati was not gone, just present in a different form.

Hearing her silence, Racxen enfolded Amber in his arms. Of course his tracker eyes, still streaming from the smoke he'd re-entered in his attempt to find her, picked up the signs the others did not. "Engo ro fash?"

Amber smiled, so softly it almost hid her sadness. "We might not have lost Diberkati, but there is another who is beyond our reach, now."

"And now there is finally time enough to mourn her." Racxen's searching eyes traced the strands of a deep longing tangled in Amber's unsure gaze. "Even a serpent-river must have a source," he suggested. "Diberkati will be there, in some form, and she will not be alone."

His smile gleamed then, moonshaft-bright. "But don't be too long. The rain, and the Realm, has had enough of waiting – and I don't want you to miss out on a second of it. Zaralathaar would understand this better than anyone."

Amber's eyes danced with the truth of his words, before urgency closed around her and she raced away with the river, her friends' understanding holding her for now instead of their embraces.

Despite her necessary haste, it felt shockingly indulgent to pass easefully through the land cloaked anew in verdure. The transformation she witnessed at every turn was so complete that Amber was glad of having the new river to follow, for fear that she would otherwise become disorientated enough amongst the unfamiliar splendours to get herself thoroughly lost. But surely enough the river was wending toward the Fountain Basin, and Amber drew from this realisation the hope that when Zaralathaar had been encircled by Diberkati before the end, the Water Nymph had indeed known she was being wrapped in the protective embrace of her most beloved element.

And so, on the power and peace of such thoughts, the serpent-sourced stream led Amber meditatively through meandering passages far from the chaotic jubilation outside, until she found herself finally amidst the ice-calm solace of the basin chamber. A chill far deeper than usual seemed to radiate, and Amber rushed forward, knowing suddenly what she would find and fearful of it.

But a Selkie's silence swelled also, instilling comfort. The uncanny thrall of the unknown could not hold sway here, with a friend in vigil.

"Hydd." Amber embraced him solemnly, his sorrow soaking through his skin. "I should have known you'd return here."

"I didnae expect her tae have returned also," the Selkie admitted shakily, gesturing with reverence towards Zaralathaar even as the scaled stream slipped its cleft-carven coils through the cavern to curl in protective embrace around the rod-straight form of the Water Nymph.

Amber swallowed, stilled. In the ice-touched chamber, beneath the watchful vigil of the Selkie, Zaralathaar looked serene, and herself.

"When I arrived, the waters, such as remained, were strange an' stagnating," Hydd explained softly. "They brought her back here, an' I didnae hae the heart tae leave her, nor the means tae move her." He paused, and Amber waited. "Ah wish she had seen this water. Ah wish she had seen this world."

A shiver seized the water-body, and it seemed to grow a more solid form in the ethereal gloaming of the basin. "Zaralathaar didn't need to see it to believe in it." A hiss slithered around the chamber, and for a moment snake eyes gleamed in piercing promise. "She told me, when I curled myself around her, that she could feel she had returned to her element. At the time, I thought it was the ramblings of a dying woman. But I know now it was the recognition of a clearsighted sage."

Hydd's eyes shone wonderingly, as wet as the water, while solemnity settled over Diberkati like ripples stilling atop a lake. "To some I can grant renewal, yet to one I can grant only rest," warned the serpent.

"Tha's all she'd wish," Hydd recognised, grateful.

"Then I will carry her where she wished to go," the watersnake promised softly. She rested her gaze on the Selkie and the Fairy in turn. "And perhaps we three shall meet again, under a darkening sky."

Amidst a swirling sigh of release and relief, the meltwater swell surged, and swept away the body of Zaralathaar with all the state and splendour she deserved, out to the ocean where her heart had always belonged.

The echoes of Diberkati's words lapped like water and sank, and water was once again all that curled and coiled through the basin.

Hydd's eyes were full of tears he let fall peaceably. Amber stood at his shoulder, heart overflowing, staying with him silently until he was ready to speak.

"My heart is full forever because she shared hers with mine. But I must leave this place, afair the chill claims me," the Selkie managed eventually.

"Zaralathaar would wish only the former, and we wouldn't allow the latter." Amber promised firmly. "But some warmth and light is a good choice now, to loosen the grip of sorrow and ease your heart a little." She affectionately adjusted Hydd's pelt around his shoulders more securely, and hr touch lingered over the thick, sleek fur. She could still remember, as though in a dream, when it had clothed her once. But it radiated a warmth and comfort entirely Hydd's own now. He had his soul back, safe and secure. The Nymph's passing would sadden him, surely — but it would not stain him.

In agreement, the Selkie closed the soft-bristled velvet of his webbed hands over hers, and his soulful eyes shone with the sea and with all he had shared — not just with the Water Nymph, which would of course remain sacred, but with her also, which would stay as special.

"We will take up the strands of the web Zaralathaar wove, and weave it into something that honours all our lives now," Hydd pledged, with a whiskery smile.

Amber returned his smile with her own, overflowing with pride and encouragement. "Against the shadow of Zaralathaar's death, there is such life out there tonight — which you played a momentous part in saving: from delivering water to the outskirts, through discovering the fissure whence Diberkati was disgorged, to helping evacuate the Harpy settlement to safety," the Fairy reminded, eager for the Selkie to reconnect with all he had sustained at a time when not everything or everyone could be saved. She let the solemnity of her words settle for a moment, and then she let the warmth of her smile spread. "You deserve to enjoy it, and Zaralathaar would delight in you doing so. And besides: your duty amidst the ice is done, and there is a flame-haired woman out there waiting for you."

"An' I return tae her as eagerly as ever." Hydd's response was as buoyant as the swell of the sea. "Though ye willnae stay tae lang here yerself, lass?" he checked gently.

"Only long enough to greet Diberkati when she returns, so that she does not feel alone after so solemn her task," Amber promised, hugging the Selkie a fond goodbye. "After that, I will be as ready for revelry as I am for the rain!"

An approving grin danced across Hydd's whiskery face, and he waved her good fortune with a webbed hand as he left.

The glow of friendship warmed Amber as she waited, while the chill darkness draped over her once more. The stillness aided her thoughts. The air felt not only cold, but also wet with relief. How familiar it felt, once again after so long. It made sense, and it was how it should be. And Amber allowed herself to realise that, while Zaralathaar's passing was a great sadness, it was also as it should be: the Nymph could not have lived forever, but she had lived fully.

As she contemplated this truth, Amber witnessed the meltwater flowing through the chamber suddenly surge and swell. The water grew clearer and clearer, until something other and unmistakeable shivered in the darkness, shimmering with scales, and relief shivered through Amber in return.

"It is done," the water whispered, and Amber felt a weight lifting away as though evaporating harmlessly from the surface.

Diberkati's features formed and floated, cresting the water like a wave. Her sinuous coils curled and curved as she flexed in luxurious experimentation and expansion alongside her waiting friend. "I shall love being a river," the serpent pronounced, rippling in quiet satisfaction. "I have my direction, now. A river never stays still, after all." A gentle smile flickered with her forked tongue. "And a river need not be mourned," she reminded sibilantly, into Amber's conflicted silence.

"My heart rejoices that you are safe, and not just alive — but eternal," Amber admitted with an over-awed grin. "And it would feel selfish to feel sad that we are parting ways, when I am blessed to know you will be even greater a part of the Realm than ever. I just wish I could give you something in return for everything you have done for us."

"Something more than you already have, you mean?" A subtle snake-form shimmered at the surface, as though just enough ice from the chamber had shorn away in just such a shape and was now floating before the Fairy, radiating a sense of soothing and satiation.

Amber wriggled an attempt at expressing what she meant, twisted her sash in her hands, and waited for the serpent to relent.

"Well, then." Amused contentment rumbled within the meltwater, and at first the Fairy thought Diberkati would ask her to pledge a trifle just to mark their friendship. But then those fluid reptilian features fiercened. "I know you here at our parting, enough to trust that you can prepare for the future without it staining the present," she murmured, fondly and firmly. "So, if you would give me something: give me another promise, on a moonless night."

A shiver, unsettling as a premonition, seized Amber as she leant in close. A chill rose from the surface like a breath as Diberkati lifted her head to within touching distance.

"This night I speak of will not come soon, and I do not wish this warning to poison or paralyse you," the serpent cautioned guardedly, but her words spilled with the same urgency as the water sluicing from her. "I cannot hold this form, but I can still help you forge your future before I fade. So if you will use these words for planning, and not fall prey to panicking, I will speak."

As soon as Amber agreed, a rush of words slipped from that flickering tongue and slithered into the Fairy's mind. Swirling and unable to settle, they felt to Amber as though they formed a phrase in a dream she wished she could hold onto forever but which she knew must drift away on waking, leaving only an impression until something in the far future were to reawaken it within her. But what she knew she could hold onto was how the words made her feel: held and healed, and whole.

"I give you my word. After all we have been through, there is not much I would not have agreed to," Amber confessed. "But how will I know—"

"There is no time, but that is pledge enough," Diberkati sibilanced. Membrane winked across one eye. "And, remember: promises made to a serpent, it is always best to keep."

Amber smiled back. That her friend was trying to keep her safe was undeniable. But from what? The starkest danger they had faced in seasons was over. She felt the transforming lightness of this truth in the overbrimming swell of the rainclouds, and she saw it reflected back to her just as surely in the serpent-swollen river brimming with peaceful potential.

And so she offered her own promise without fear. "We will prepare for the night you speak of, without worrying prematurely," she affirmed.

All remaining tension seemed to ease from the snake. "Then perhaps such preparation will prove preventative," she purred.

Amber grinned easefully. "Exactly. Meanwhile, the night of which you speak shall not shadow the one ahead. *This* night, once you go outside, you'll find the moon is fatter than a happy Selkie."

"I will," the serpent agreed gently, even as her voice sounded less spoken and more the spilling rush of a river gathering strength to surge.

Amber swallowed. "You're becoming the river entirely."

Diberkati nodded, and the rippling motion dissolved her form further.

Amber's smile was shaky now, but she was determined to stay and just as determined to not be scared. "How does it feel? How do *you* feel?"

"Powerful and at peace." Certainty filled the serpent, who smiled as only a snake could, every one of her scales shining mesmerizingly as her gaze lingered. And her gaze held Amber, when her embrace could not, and remembrance and reassurance flared in those serpentine eyes as Diberkati merged fully with the water.

"Thank you," Amber whispered to the wetness. She felt self-conscious speaking to a river, but she supposed people had always done it. And she pledged to continue to do so.

The Fairy stepped back respectfully, woven into the web of what had happened. The darkness seemed suddenly cavernous and empty.

But she wasn't alone. The water swirled and sparkled beside her, and it raced her into the wide open starlight, into a Realm that was reawakening, and rejuvenating, and relearning how to relax.

Returning Rain

The turmoil of recent moments washed away in elemental ecstasy as Amber stepped out just as the next torrent of rain began to fall. She stood gasping in relief and wonder as the sky opened itself above her and the tight-clenched clouds finally uncurled, laughing onto the land at last in an exultant, overwhelming downpour. After awaiting it so long she felt transfixed by the experience, let the phenomenon expand to fill her entire existence. All around her sprang signs of reinvigoration. Flowers unfurled, until the meadows were awash with riotous colour. There was so much moisture in the air that fog formed amidst the sheets of rain, hanging thick enough to rewrite a future and erase all trace of the hardships wrought by the drought they'd once feared would never end. And now, through this soft veil of renewing mist, half dazed by the sight of beauty she had feared consigned to memory, Amber watched the twisting muscle of a swollen river carving its course through the landscape, gathering all the hues of the Realm's many landscapes as it swept along and away, growing in might and majesty all the while.

Taking her cue from the river, Amber took the remainder of her return at a run, her pelting footsteps joyous and urgent. Soon enough she would join her friends, but right now there was one she sought above all others, and she reached Arraterr to find the marshlands erupting in a cacophony of life. The thrum of insects filled the air, and with them wetland birds whirled, sprung into the sky like so many stars. Frogs clamoured insistently, in a reverberating chorus of rejoicing.

Racxen ran to her, anointed with the soft wet earth, and Amber shrieked with laughter as he swept her up and the mud plastered her too. The clouds were crying with joy, and so was she. And so she danced with Racxen in the marshes to the rhythm of the rain, as the storm percussed the swamp's surface, and their tongues spoke as softly as the shower across each other's skin while the storm shielded them and sluiced everything else away into memory until there were only these glistening moments, anew and everlasting.

"I love you." The words spilled as eagerly as the water. It wasn't painful to say, now that she didn't have to add 'I'll miss you' and 'I'm so sorry I have to leave you'. Love filled her like the longed-for rainclouds filled the sky: all-encompassingly and intimately, without angst or unrequitedness.

"Engo ro fash," he promised, his clawed hands keeping her close, the sureness of his unhurried smile speaking secrets he only shared with her. "I love you too, Amber." Racxen's grin widened as he playfully added one more streak to the myriad mudlines adorning Amber's skin in emphasis of his next words, as he continued softly: "My love for you is like the mud of these marsh-pools: it will endure any drought, and in both hardship and happiness grow only ever the deeper."

Amber's grin mirrored his as she returned the gesture lingeringly, reaffirming a pledge that need not be spoken aloud but which would always sing in her heart, born of a bond immeasurable which had first grown roots that fateful moment long ago when she had been honoured by Racxen in a similar way in front of his whole tribe.

The present felt as indelible and precious as those beloved memories now, as they both tenderly locked hands and waded in wonder through the rapidly re-filling waterways of Arraterr it felt like they were exploring a new Realm together. And, with their feet sinking further into the silky sediment with each sloshing step, so too did it finally begin to sink in that they were safe. Intoxicated with the experience: light-hearted and light-headed enough that she felt as though her spirit were skimming with the raindrops that danced atop the surface, Amber drank in her surroundings as the waters regained their height. And once it was too deep to even laughingly continue, they clambered out into a land shimmering with verdance.

By unspoken agreement they steered their steps towards Fairymead. Later they would converge on the outskirts of Arkh Loban and walk back to the Harpy settlement, but Inqe and Nzizi must have built an intimate understanding of what had happened already, whereas the King and Queen would still be waiting on a definitive account.

The walk back felt long and luxurious. With how insidiously it had happened, she hadn't fully realised how much had leached from the Realm along with the water — but now the constant pressure, the pervasive anxiety that had intruded beneath closed doors and between sleeping eyelid, had all evaporated. Journeying was restored to being a pleasure, and Amber smiled unhurriedly. Jasper had probably availed his mother and father, the Queen and King, of as much as he could explain by now, so Amber and Racxen no longer needed concern themselves with duty, and all urgency had lifted like the steam now lifting from the marshes. The deluge eased across the sky like a lover sliding into bed, comforting and tantalising in equal measure, and the loose-tongued clouds whispered words of release late into the night.

So, they took their time together, restoratively slowly, and as they reached the solid land beyond the marshes, she knew they had time still. The knowledge buzzed through her, as intoxicating as the storm. And what a storm it was! It engulfed them utterly, overpowering all other sensations — or almost all: for Amber paused, seized by a suddenly reanimated awareness. Someone dear to her had remained at the periphery of her consciousness for the duration of the drought — and now she sensed his proximity in a strange, half-explainable way.

Racxen waited, and relinquished her hand, understanding. "Meet you at the Wolfren Camp?"

"Soon," she promised in agreement. She kissed him deeply, and lingeringly watched him leave, his silhouette flickering more enticingly than a lantern across the marshes.

Then she took a drier route, if any could be called that now, to the crags beneath the cliffs. The rain was easing, but the clouds were still gathered tightly, waiting with the expectant solemnity of proud elders watching over the land.

A chill wind lifted around the exposed escarpment as she arrived, and Amber shivered in her wet clothes. Amidst the rising steam, the air smelled of stalactites and stillness.

"Rraarl?" she whispered, the word holding as much hope as the rains had.

From the wind-warped hollows carved amidst the scree a stone-clean tang lifted through the rich, petrichorous scent of after-rain air, and from a darkness absolute and yearning the outline of the Gargoyle emerged, crouched and hulking.

He didn't move until her gaze had found its resting place in his own. *IT IS CELEBRATION ENOUGH TO SEE YOU AGAIN*, he promised, tracing the words onto her palm in an intimacy beyond language that made her shiver. *IT DIDN'T FEEL RIGHT TO JOIN THE REVELRY, WHEN I HAD NOT CONTRIBUTED TO ITS REALISATION.*

Amber raised her brows knowingly. "You got by on little, so that others had enough," she contradicted gently. "You stayed away, to not steal support from others. Your behaviour protected those around you, even though they didn't know it to thank you." She pressed herself in a hug against the coldness of him, and felt only warmer for it. His body was hard and angular, but it soothed the sharpnesses in her soul. The nights had felt emptier, knowing he had withdrawn to the deep chambers of the Realm, save for that infernal night when he had heroically assisted the refugees, before retreating again. But it was typical of his stalwart stoicism: in situations where he could not help, he had simply kept himself out of the way and not depleted diminishing resources: a quieter and equally heroic act.

"You contributed immeasurably, and I thank you for it, especially if no-one else has," she concluded fervently. Nothing more needed to be said, and relief and reassurance mingled in equal measure in the shared silence, as the companions let the bone-deep comfortableness of being in each other's presence envelop them both.

Rraarl's fierce stone features softened further the longer she settled beside him, but when he next spoke she could sense the care with which he chose his next words, and the tension controlled behind the gentleness of his touch.

THESE MONTHS I HAVE SPENT MORE TIME THAN USUAL ON THE MARGINS OF THE REALM, he began in explanation. *AND THERE I SEE FORMING A DARKNESS WHOSE MOTIVATION AND MEANING I CANNOT YET DECIPHER.*

Amber thought quickly. She wanted instinctively to tell him that it was impossible; that nothing could overcloud the Realm now. But they had each long ago learnt that neither could be overwhelmed by the other, nor should their quiet exchanges ever be overlooked. And so, she sat with his statement. "For now, let us wonder instead of worry about it," she offered.

The Gargoyle's grimace relaxed into a snarl-curled smile of acquiescence. *PERHAPS I HAVE SPENT TOO LONG ALONE, AND PERCEIVED AS DARKNESS A SHADOW I CAST MYSELF,* he admitted. *AFTER ALL: IN THESE MOMENTS, WE ARE MORE THAN SAFE. AND THE DARKNESS WE INHABIT NOW HOLDS NO FEAR.*

"Shadows fade in certain company. And flee from others," Amber agreed with a grin. She sighed appreciatively as she leant against his stone shoulder and stared up at the stars. "But I will ask the others about it tonight," she promised, hugging him farewell and feeling his eyes at her back keeping her safer than any torch as she left.

Descending the slopes, Amber stepped out into a wet, fresh darkness enlivened by a murmuring of rain as intoxicating as the earlier deluge .

Triumph was condensing amidst the clouds: every inch of the Realm was revelling in the rain even as Amber hurried back to her friends to celebrate it. It was a joy to have a destination to journey to, and she delighted in every moment of the way to the Wolfren camp. She picked her way lightfootedly between shallow pools sprung like glistening, oversized mushrooms. She let the reverberance of insects trilling and whirring fit to fill the night fill her soul too. She slowed her steps in astonishment to witness the gleaming-eyed, long-toed waterbirds first creep out of their refuges and then strut boldly to reclaim this space: their iridescent flutterings sprinkling rainbow droplets as they bathed and preened and called, and sang her cheerfully on her way as she headed beyond their territory towards Arkh Loban.

Even the plains were enjoying this new era of abundance: in the desert's great silence behind the softness of the settling rain, the reach of Diberkati's gift remained unmistakeable. Splashes of green spread with abandon across the sands: once-in-a-decade growth sprouting from dune and dessication alike. The proud waymarking trees which had been reduced to skeletal, pained figures now stood in salvaged splendour, berobed in the richest verdure.

Amidst such transformation, Amber thrilled to hear her friends' voices floating towards her, familiar amidst the freshness. She ran to join them, eager to share her joy, the exertion easy in the soaked and sultry air.

Everyone was chattering happily about their plans. Racxen was eagerly anticipating being reunited with his brother and then returning to the Harpy settlement with Amber to share plant-medicine knowledge and learn more tracking if the Harpies would have him. Hydd and Ruby were animatedly discussing creating an increasingly spectacular-sounding ice monument to Zaralathaar, as the focal point to a new school to teach any who wished to learn about the nuances of nurturing the Fountain of Bubbles, so that the responsibility did not fall solely on one Selkie's shoulders. And Han was gleefully reciting to himself the myriad species he would restore to the forests of the newly-irrigated Realm.

Even Jasper sounded lighthearted with relief. "With the rains returned, what have we left to fear?" he proclaimed, as the Harpies swept towards the company like a great life-giving shadow. Nzizi squealed and nearly knocked Amber over as she ran to her and jumped into a hug.

"Even light may be lost," Inqe murmured gently.

Amber's heart scudded, as Rraarl's prophecy began to take form.

"But not today," the matriarch conceded proudly, setting those keen eyes of hers on each of the friends in turn.

Amber felt better than flying as Racxen's clawed, kind hands closed warmly around hers. "If a day does come when we go without light," the Arraheng promised, eyes ashine, "we shall prove that the night, too, blooms as sweet."

"Whether we travel by wings or by feet," Amber added readily.

Inqe smiled at their certitude. "We will do well to remember it," the Harpy matriarch urged. "The vultures have foreseen a time of great darkness, some moons from now."

"But great does not have to be terrible," Nzizi reasoned, her dark eyes holding more strength and surety than the sun. "We shall make a plan."

A calm as extensive as the returning rains settled over Amber in response. "We can see anything through together. And Diberkati will be with us," she added, quietly confident.

Jasper nodded seriously. "Seems serpents have been in charge since day one, really. And her next thousand years will be her happiest."

The friends smiled their agreement, letting the knowledge swirl and settle in the balmy air.

"So, who knows," the Prince proposed dryly. "Mayhap we can actually enjoy the current season we have so unexpectedly been granted, instead of running off straight into the next problem."

"Well, I'm running back to the bush, as soon as possible," Amber declared proudly.

"We need you more than ever," Nzizi promised loyally. "The flames were doused quickly, not a soul was lost, and the bush is recovering already, she reminded the others, eyes shining. "The Wolfren have pledged their assistance for our rebuilding, so those in our care remain under the best protection. And we will rise from these ashes together."

"I'll be thrilled to help," Amber promised, beaming. "I still can't believe I'm lucky enough to have an apprenticeship with you!"

"Well, enjoy it while you can, because something is bound to put a stop to it," Jasper predicted cheerfully. "After all, we've probably awakened or annoyed some monster or other, what with all our galivanting around instead of dying. There'll be repercussions from this, you mark my words."

But not even those words could dampen the ardour with which joy sprang from the sky like the rain. So, Amber snorted amiably, listening more to the cloudburst's percussion than to the Prince.

The song of the rain soothed her, lulling her into a deep calm as she wandered entranced, witnessing the continuing metamorphosis of their beloved Realm unfurl around her and delighting in every detail. Everywhere they went, the dry red earth slicked into the deep brown of a sated soil, and the soft blue of the sky expanded above them, alleviating the squeeze-band pressure that had so long tightened itself around her brow.

She sighed contentedly, and dared to believe in the future she envisioned spooling out ahead of them, as boundless as the serpent now surging like a reawakened dream through a re-emerging Realm: a future containing the happiest possibilities shaken free amidst the mobilising of the river. After all: Diberkati had done it. In her riverform she had reanimated the land. Restrictions had been lifted and the future wound brightly ahead like the river they had been gifted with. A reprieve had been granted. Rain had returned, and with it, reason. The air smelled of life again. The land hissed its relief, snakelike, as the scorched earth welcomed the rain with the popping and crackling not dissimilar to the expansion of the tiniest, deepest parts of an airway reopening. For now, everything was blissful. Amber let the sensation wash through her, and permeate the parts of her which had feared she might never feel such things again. And her heart filled with hope.

She glanced instinctively to Nzizi. A film seemed to pass across the Harpy apprentice's eyes, and it felt to Amber as though a shadow crossed her mind also.

"You have seen something, in the distance?" She watched Nzizi closely, worried for her.

But her worry was dissipated, instead of mirrored, in those dark, determined, delighted eyes. Nzizi smiled dazzlingly, as steady and sure as the sun.

"It is far enough away," Amber's mentor promised. "And all our joys are so much closer."

About the Author

As a qualified Occupational Therapist with a Master of Arts in Psychoanalysis and experience working in a variety of psychiatric settings, Laura is especially passionate about using writing and other creative pursuits therapeutically to help children, teens, and adults cope with and recover from mental illness and trauma. A steadfast believer in the value of fantasy as a nurturing space and safe escape, she draws inspiration from everywhere wild and magical and seeks to both celebrate and inspire the indomitable nature of the human spirit through her writing.

www.ingramcontent.com/pod-product-compliance
Lightning Source LLC
Chambersburg PA
CBHW030121260626
47156CB00008B/2737